SECRET
OF THE
EGYPTIAN
CURSE

KIDS OF ANCIENT MYTHOLOGY

SCOTT PETERS

BEST DAY BOOKS
For Young Readers

Published by Best Day Books For Young Readers
Copyright © S. P. Wyshynski 2017

Secret of the Egyptian Curse/Scott Peters

Includes bibliographical references

ISBN-13: 978-1543278736
ISBN-10: 1543278736

For "HRH"

H.M. George Tupou V

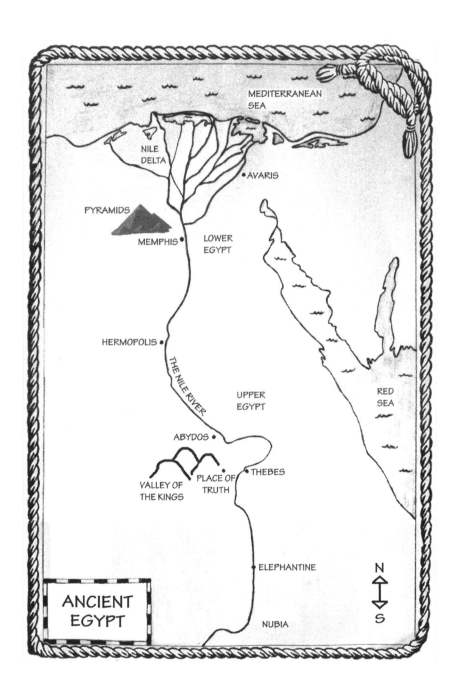

CHAPTER 1

The boy jerked back in shock.

What had he done?

Drawings surrounded him on all sides. They covered the Nile's soft, sloping riverbank, all grooved into the sand with his sharpened stick. A chariot fight. A pair of wrestlers. A panther chasing a fleeing gazelle.

But that's not what he was staring at.

He focused on his drawing of Osiris.

Was it an illusion? The wind?

No. It happened again! Osiris's eyes—eyes made of sand—were moving. They shifted to the acacia stick in the boy's hand. The god's gaze locked onto it. The eerie sand-eyes studied the simple tool that had drawn his huge form on the riverbank. After a moment, the sand-eyes shifted back to Ramses' terrified face.

Ramses sucked in a shallow breath. The air felt suffocating as a tomb.

What had he been thinking—drawing the God of the Underworld?

Why, when he'd never drawn a single god in his life, had he done so now?

Because he hadn't been thinking. That's why. He'd been drawing mindlessly, his worries elsewhere. He'd been thinking about his father and the strange priest, back at the farmhouse.

Standing in the dense heat, Ramses tried to tear his gaze from the god's painful radiance. The hot earth had grown almost blinding. It hurt to look at Osiris.

Ramses' throat went dry as the desert.

A strange, crackling tension spread around them, filling the clearing. On the ground, the God of the Underworld seemed to shift, first left and then right. Just a tiny amount, but enough to make the lines in the sand shudder.

Ramses couldn't move.

Osiris's image expanded a fraction. Then the shifting started again. Back and forth. Back and forth. Faster. Stronger.

Something whispered over Ramses. His skin turned cold. It was an ibis bird. The movement broke the spell. Ramses fell back a few feet, breathing hard. Meanwhile, the white winged creature came to rest on the Nile's dark surface. Opening its curved beak, it pecked at the floating reeds.

On the ground, Osiris went still.

I was seeing things, Ramses told himself. It was an illusion! Just the heat. A mirage.

He wanted to believe it—that he'd dreamed it all. But this wasn't the first time something like it had happened.

Once, when he was little, he told his mother his drawings made sounds—his lions roared, his arrows hissed and his warriors shouted. He told her they moved too, and that a chariot's wheels had kicked up so much dust he had to cover his face.

Her reaction stunned him. She cried.

She made him promise never to repeat it again. And he hadn't. And over time he convinced himself he'd imagined it all. That he'd never seen those things. The only thing that remained from those long-ago days was a niggling fear of drawing the gods. Because who knew what that would bring? And he hadn't.

Until now.

From the ground, the shush-shush noise of shifting sand started up again. Hairs prickled on Ramses' neck.

He looked down, slowly. It was starting again. In horror, he watched Osiris resume his terrifying motion. The god shifted back and forth. Expanded, and then shifted again. Osiris was growing before his eyes. Struggling. Working to burst free of his shell.

It seemed clear now that the sketched lines were the only things keeping the powerful God of the Underworld in place.

Stop, Ramses told himself. He's not real! He can't be real.

Sweat slicked his palms.

His mind flashed to his father. A great foreboding overtook him.

"No," he whispered. His limbs began to tremble. "No," he said, voice rising. Glaring at mighty Osiris, he shouted, "No! I won't let you take him!"

Ramses threw his stick at the god. Then he spun away. Frantic with worry, he ran for the bulrushes and forced his way through. On the other side, he sprinted across the fields of golden wheat.

Fear chased him like a towering sandstorm. It whipped him into a frenzy, urged him to run faster. Rocks and sharp roots tore his bare feet. He ignored them and ran headlong for home.

He could just make out the happy sight of his familiar farmhouse. His hearing was sharp, but he couldn't hear even the faintest sound of the chanting priest.

His stomach twisted.

If the words of the holy man's magic spell couldn't reach him here, they couldn't possibly reach the ears of the gods.

CHAPTER 2

When Ramses neared the house, he began to slow. The familiar sturdy walls looked exactly the same as he'd left them. Embarrassment crept over him. He felt childish, like he was running from a ghost.

He knew the kind of reaction he'd get if he explained why he'd come back. His father had no patience for such things.

Instead of bursting through the front door, he crept to his father's bedroom window and peered over the sill.

The two of them were still in there: his father and the priest.

The Wab Sekhmet stank of incense; his smell drifted outside, thick and cloying. He was tall with oiled skin and cold eyes like those of a serpent. A powerful hatred for the strange priest overtook Ramses. What right did he have to send him away? This was his house!

Worse, Ramses hated himself for obeying.

The priest turned suddenly, and Ramses sank out of view. He squished low against the thorny branches of the acacia bush. Burning with frustration, he pressed his face into his arms.

In the bedroom, a dish rattled.

"Drink this," the priest said.

"Forget your brew and listen to me," his father replied.

"Again?" The priest sounded weary. "Don't you think we've argued enough?" Still, the dish clanked down.

"Not until you agree. You have the authority to protect my son. To see that his talents aren't wasted. He's a good boy, you know that!"

"What your boy does is wrong," the priest said.

"What he does is a gift to us all. Only a blind man could deny it."

At this, Ramses' head came up. He'd never heard his father talk this way.

Inside, the priest began to pace. He burst out in an angry voice. "You think he's gifted? Look at you, lying there, your wife dead. And you call it a gift?"

Ramses' heart clenched. What was this? What was the priest saying?

"You think this illness is some godly punishment?" his father said. "The price of my son's talent?"

With a sickening feeling, Ramses' mind flashed to Osiris. Was it possible that he, Ramses, caused this . . . this horror? His head began to spin. It wasn't true!

"Listen to me, because it's the last time I'll say it," the priest said. "What that boy does is unholy. And I cannot—I will not—allow your son to meddle with things beyond his control."

"Beyond his control, or beyond his station, priest?" His father spat out the last word. "You're afraid because Ramses was born with a skill holier than anything you'll ever possess."

Ramses' breath caught in his throat.

Inside, there was a long, tense silence.

"You are ill," the priest said. "You don't know your own tongue. I warned you when you brought him to the temple on his naming day and he shocked us all with his workings. He was barely out of swaddling clothes. Yet there he was sketching his dark magic on the ground. No god meant him to have such power."

"An accidental gift, then," his father said, voice fading.

"Such accidents are always cursed."

The bedroom door scraped open. The click-clack of footsteps was followed by the sound of Aunt Zalika clearing her throat.

"Come now, dear brother-in-law," she said in a soothing voice. "Drink the potion so you might live to argue another day."

Ramses pictured his strange aunt with her painted face. She'd arrived at his house yesterday, dragging the priest and her invalid son in tow. Uncle Hay had stumbled in after them, sweating and bloated and loaded like a camel. His mound of filthy bags still lay in the cool front hall, where he'd ditched them to gape around. The look in his eyes had sent a chill snaking into Ramses' stomach.

His father's ragged gasps drew him back to the present. They sounded harsher, as if each breath were a struggle. The gods were crushing the life from him—stopping up his throat.

Ramses wanted to shout, Don't leave me! You can't!

But he stayed silent. The clay brick windowsill was rough and baking hot. Carefully, he raised the heavy drape, hoping to catch his father's eye. Instead, Aunt Zalika's back blocked his view. She was close enough to touch.

He froze.

"Your sister-in-law is right. Drink this," insisted the priest's voice.

Aunt Zalika shifted. Through a narrow gap, the bed became visible. His father lay amongst the rumpled sheets. The familiar, beloved face was pale and drenched with sweat, but set with its usual dogged strength. It was a strength that could frighten or comfort, depending on which end you were on. Ramses let out a silent breath of relief.

His father was too stubborn to die.

"The cup," his father said.

The priest reached into view. As he did, his sleeve fell back to reveal his forearm, sinewed and oily and painted with the image of a serpent. A cobra. Above the pincers of the priest's thumb and forefinger, the painted serpent ended in a staring turquoise eye. Like a creature of death, it snaked toward his father's lips.

"I don't need your ministering." His father snatched the cup away and drained the contents in one go. He wiped his mouth. "Now leave me. Zalika, you stay."

"You need rest, brother-in-law," Aunt Zalika said, after the priest left.

"I need to plan ahead for my son."

The words clutched at Ramses' chest. Plan ahead? He didn't need to plan ahead! He'd be here, and Aunt Zalika, Uncle Hay, and the Wab Sekhmet would leave with their disturbing chants and foul potions and never come back.

"Swear you'll protect him from this nonsense," his father said. "Swear it!"

"Don't worry yourself."

"His talent must be protected. Swear you'll do it. Swear you'll take care of him."

A drop of sweat trickled down Ramses' cheek. The acacia bush that hid him from view offered little shade from the blistering Egyptian sun. He made no move to brush it away.

"Of course I'll take care of him," his aunt finally said in a smooth, soothing voice. "Now sleep. We will talk later."

Whatever the priest had put in his potion began to take effect. His father sank backward, a shocked look on his face.

Ramses should have thrown himself over the windowsill. He should have ignored these strangers and their rules. Should have thrown his arms around his father. Said something. Anything.

Told him he loved him.

Instead, like a coward, like a fool, he sank lower against the wall. The setting sun bruised the sky purple. There would be time. His father would live. He had to.

Ramses dozed off.

Those last minutes were lost, never to be found again.

CHAPTER 3

The harvest came early. It mocked Ramses with its bounty—countless stalks, all shivering gold—more wheat than their fields had ever seen.

He hammered at it with his scythe, not caring that the blade needed sharpening, not caring to make it fall in neat rows, not caring to bind his palms with linen so they'd last the season. His parents were dead. There would be no harvest celebration this year, no festival of Min. Aunt Zalika and Uncle Hay knew nothing of the land beyond its worth in jewels and duck-fat.

A gong rang out.

Across the fields, workers set down their tools. They made their way to a cluster of shady palms to eat lunch. Ramses threw his blade down. Instead of heading for the trees, he made for the river.

Bulrushes waved gently, their soft brown heads pointing skyward. He slipped his way through them and onto the riverbank. The swampy Nile waters perfumed the humid air. He inhaled a deep breath. Underfoot, the sand felt damp and cool, a relief from the baking sun overhead. A swim in the slowly flowing river would've been inviting, if not for the brackish, thick coating that floated nearest to shore.

As always, his secret hideout was deserted. He knelt and rummaged amongst the papyrus rushes. Sure enough, a bundle of acacia-wood sticks lay hidden in their usual place between the tall foliage. He pulled one out.

The priest's words still haunted him, that his talent was something strange, something to be stopped. But he didn't see what it mattered now. The two people he loved most were dead.

Ducks played in the shallows, flapping their wings.

The sight made his shoulders relax just a little. Strong winds had blown all night, smoothing the sandy bank to a flat surface. With dirt-stained fingers, he grabbed a stick and began to draw. The horrible months since Aunt Zalika and Uncle Hay had arrived soon faded into nothing. The whole world just went away.

All that existed was the tip of the stick tracing lines in the sand.

The hot earth made him think of the desert. His stick moved quickly, swirling to form the wheel of a chariot.

As the drawing took shape, he could feel himself charging across the dunes in the horse drawn cart. The sound of rolling wheels and pounding hooves filled the air. Dust coated his tongue. Wind blasted his face. A second cart closed in from behind. A soldier shouted and whipped his horse into a gallop. Side-by-side they were racing, carts roaring in flashes of light.

Ramses came back to himself, letting the sensations fade.

He thought back to that terrible afternoon, when he'd drawn Osiris, God of the Underworld.

Slowly, he began to sketch. He started with a pair of sandals, then strong legs and a broad chest. His hand shook, but still he kept going. He told himself it was to prove his powers were false. But another part of him longed for a confrontation. When he came to forming the God of the Underworld's head, his resolve faltered.

He bit his lip.

With rapid strokes, instead of drawing Osiris, he drew Horus. The falcon-headed god of protection. The god of the sky, whose eyes were the sun and the moon. The son of Osiris. The keeper of secret wisdom.

Ramses didn't know what he'd do if Horus came to life. Demand answers? Ask him if Osiris killed his father as a punishment? Was it all Ramses' fault, like the priest said?

Staring down, he felt a faint flicker of hope mixed with

terror. But the lines remained silent. Still and empty of life.

The crunch of footsteps yanked him from his reverie. Too late, he caught a whiff of Aunt Zalika's perfume. He gulped, cursing himself for not being more careful, and spun around.

Like the fangs of a serpent, her fingers caught his ear. "What are you doing?"

"Nothing," he said quietly.

Her eyes cut to the ground. They widened as they swept over the scene of racing carts. They stopped at the sight of the life-size Horus. A shimmer radiated across the god's chest. It spread upward, into Horus's face. The god's falcon shaped head looked softer, almost feather-like.

A flicker of life shone up from the depths of those eyes made of sand.

Horus seemed to fix his gaze on Aunt Zalika.

For a moment, she looked more amazed than angry.

Stupidly, Ramses held on to the hope she'd forgotten the priest's words. Could she see what he was seeing? Would she accuse him of playing with dark magic? He never should have done this! He needed to shift her attention elsewhere, fast. He motioned to the racing carts.

"My father and I, we saw chariots like that once," he said.

Her cheeks flushed a deeper red.

"It was two years ago," he said quickly, trying to keep her attention. "Before the flood. We'd crossed the river from Thebes and—"

"Who do you think you are?"

He froze. "No one, I—"

"The priest said you were cursed. He was right. Cursed with stupidity! Hiding back here, pretending you're some god-given craftsman?"

"I never said I—"

She wrenched the stick away. "You're a flea-bitten farm boy, not Pharaoh's royal tomb-painter."

He almost laughed with relief. Did it mean she couldn't see Horus, who was staring at her even now? Become a tomb-painter? That's what she was thinking he was trying to? He'd never be stupid enough to imagine that.

She pushed him aside. "This nonsense ends now." Ignoring the worth of her beaded sandals, she kicked the image of the racing carts to pieces.

In a fury, she swirled across the sand and advanced on Horus. Yet as she approached, her footsteps slowed. She stopped before she reached the god's image, as if held back by some power she couldn't see. The God of the Sky shimmered and shifted, mirage-like in the heat. Maybe she didn't see the life blazing in Horus's eyes. Maybe she couldn't read the warning.

But Ramses knew, looking at her, that she felt something.

"It's just a drawing," she muttered.

A bead of sweat trickled between Ramses' shoulders. She wouldn't. Would she?

Her fingers tightened around the stick; her hand trembled. With sickening foreboding, Ramses knew it would be a bad idea to erase it. A really bad idea. She lunged, slashing the god's chest. Horus's eyes seemed to flick to Ramses' face.

He darted forward. "Stop!"

Aunt Zalika's arms shot out and sent him flying. The ground rose up, hard and unyielding. Ramses came at her again. He was strong for his age, but she was tall, wiry, and surprisingly powerful. She moved like a demon. The drawing stick cut left and right, deeper and deeper.

Unyielding, she hacked Horus to pieces.

Heavy silence fell over the riverbank. The hot air grew thick with a strange odor. It was the smell of rotting decay.

Aunt Zalika turned on him. She looked stricken and pale, and her hands were shuddering. For a moment, he thought she might throw up. Somehow, she wrestled control of herself.

"How dare you attack me?" she croaked.

CHAPTER 4

Ramses faced his aunt. All traces of the meek, concerned woman who'd stood by his father's bedside were gone. She forced her shoulders back until she stood tall and straight. Her new gold collar glittered with blinding flashes. Despite her pale cheeks, she towered over him like a queen.

Along the shoreline, flies buzzed amongst the moldering reeds.

Aunt Zalika raised his drawing stick overhead. Then she brought it down fast. The hissing movement broke the stillness of the air. When the stick slammed into his back, it tore away a layer of skin. He gasped. No one had beaten him. Ever.

The stick he'd sharpened so carefully, and had used to draw so many images, tore down a second time. He squeezed his nails into his fists, masking his fury behind a cold face. It took all his control to keep from shouting that she couldn't strike him. But she could.

Who would stop her?

Perversely, on the ground, Horus's eye—the legendary wadjet eye—remained whole.

It watched Aunt Zalika, steady and unblinking.

She threw the stick down, breathing hard. Sweat beaded on her oily temples; her kohl-lined eyes had begun to smear. Ramses knew he should keep his mouth shut. Instead, the two blazing welts on his back loosened his tongue.

"My father told you he wanted me to draw. I heard him."

Her fingers found his chin and tilted it up to hers. "A little spy, are you?"

The design of her features mocked him, for they reminded him of his mother. But they were all wrong—it was as if a sculptor had taken his mother's beautiful face and twisted it out of proportion.

"Your parents are dead." Her voice was flat.

His mouth opened, but nothing came out.

"I make the rules now. Are we clear?" she asked.

He glared, unable to believe she could talk about her sister that way. His fists balled against the gashes that were making his head spin.

"Answer me. Are we clear?"

"Very."

Yes, it was clear—that she didn't want him to draw. But he hadn't made any promises. Not to her. And why should he?

"Good." She pushed him up the Nile's bank. "Then wipe off that frown and march."

He felt Horus's wadjet eye blazing into the back of his head. They left the river and passed beneath palm trees heavy with dates and humming bees; they hurried across fields, and along paths still creased with his father's footsteps.

In the distance, the second gong rang out. Lunch was over.

Ahead, workers picked up their tools and moved to-and-fro, cutting wheat with curved scythes. Others gathered it into baskets. One sat on a stool, sharpening the men's blades as they grew dull.

"Where are you taking the boy?" called a deep voice.

Ramses glanced up to see Sobek, the farm manager, watching them. The man's blade rested over one ox-like shoulder. His eyes were bright blue, the irises ringed with a thin black line. They measured Ramses with a swift glance and then moved to Zalika's face.

"That's none of your business, Sobek," she said.

"It is, Madam, if you're robbing me of one of my workers."

"He'll be working. Just not with you."

Sobek's brow darkened. "I need my crew."

"You're out of line," she said.

"And you'll be out some riches, Madam, if the boy doesn't cut his share of wheat."

The shadow of an ibis flew across the ground between them.

Aunt Zalika studied the shimmering fields. After a moment, she said, "Tell me, do you know about this little flea's ridiculous drawings?"

"I do."

"How many others know?"

"No idea."

She smoothed her gold collar. "I find it interesting how intent you seem on guarding my nephew."

"My crew is my responsibility."

"Is it? Then why did I find him lazing on the riverbank? I don't want people thinking I'm spoiling him because he's my nephew."

Ramses said, "Lazing! It was break time!"

Sobek shot him a scowl. "The boy works as hard as any man."

"Well, if he didn't tire himself playing in the sand, he'd work harder." She laughed. "Ramses' has had his head filled with nonsense. But he's a worker. My worker. And do you know what your job is, Farm Manager?"

"Of course I know my job."

"Then know this. Your job, Sobek, depends on making sure Ramses does what he's supposed to. And that's work, not play."

"My job depends on it? That almost sounds like a threat."

"It is a threat. I want Ramses' drawing to stop. And if it doesn't, you'll feel the blame."

"Me?"

"Make him stop, or lose your job. Is that clear enough?"

"That's not fair," Ramses said. "It's not Sobek's fault if—"

"Silence!" Sobek roared.

Aunt Zalika smiled at Sobek. "We understand each other then." She paused. "One more thing, Farm Manager."

Sobek waited, mouth set.

"Keep Ramses away from my son."

"Why? The boys are cousins," Sobek said. "And why should

14

I be the enforcer?"

She raised her painted brows. "I have my reasons. Just do what I ask, and you'll be fine." Taking hold of her skirt, she turned and strode off.

"You can't treat Sobek like this!" Ramses shouted after her.

She didn't reply. Soon her thin shadow disappeared in the distance.

"Back to work. The day's wasting," Sobek said.

"I'm sorry," Ramses said.

"Don't be. No reason."

The next few words were a struggle. "I won't . . . I can't let you get in trouble. I promise, I'll—"

"You'll what? Stop drawing?"

"You heard what she said!"

Sobek clapped a strong hand on Ramses' arm. His nut-brown face creased into a smile. "Don't concern yourself with me."

Sobek was a powerful man.

But her words were no empty threat.

Ramses picked up his scythe and fingered its blade. Then he whacked the blade through a stalk of wheat. The golden head toppled to the ground. Broken, it lay shining in the dust. "I never asked to be born wanting to draw. What if the priest was right? What if I am cursed? What if it's my fault my parents—"

"Enough. I don't believe it. Neither did your father. No one does. No one who matters."

"What matters is I'm a farmer. And I should be happy about it. Because that's all I was ever meant to be."

"Is it?" Sobek demanded.

His tone snapped Ramses to attention.

"Is that all you were meant to be?" Sobek said.

"Of course. What do you mean?"

The farm manager shielded his face, staring intently. There was something strange in his expression. Something that made Ramses' skin prickle.

"Only the gods can answer that," Sobek finally said.

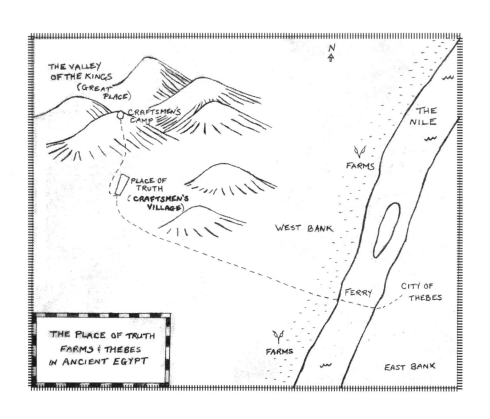

THE VALLEY
OF THE KINGS
(GREAT
PLACE)

CRAFTSMEN'S
CAMP

PLACE OF
TRUTH
(CRAFTSMEN'S
VILLAGE)

N

THE
NILE

FARMS

WEST BANK

FERRY

CITY OF
THEBES

FARMS

EAST BANK

THE PLACE OF TRUTH
FARMS & THEBES
IN ANCIENT EGYPT

CHAPTER 5

Less than an hour's walk from Ramses' farm, a girl hurtled across the desert. She was breathing hard. Long black hair flying, slim arms and legs pumping, She ran toward a towering wall. Her bare toes raked a sharp stone. She sucked in her breath, but kept going.

Avoiding the gates she skirted east, staying close to the perimeter.

The Place of Truth. That's what they called the tiny village hidden inside those dusty old walls. But they should've called it the Place of Mystery. People in Thebes spoke of it in curious whispers—they wondered about its guarded secrets, told stories of its ancient magic. No one knew the truth except its few lucky craftsmen; the village was forbidden to anyone who wasn't born there.

Blue shadows stretched across the rippled desert. At the sound of footsteps, the girl's heart skipped a beat. She pressed herself into a narrow crevice and held her breath.

A sentry rounded the corner. He paused, one hand on his dagger, and glanced into the distance. The sun capped the nearby mountain, sending rays slanting toward its base.

There, emerging from the Valley of the Kings, came a caravan of figures. Pharaoh's tomb-builders were on their way back home—back to her secluded village.

Neferet squinted, imagining she could see Tui and Paimu with their brushes and ink; imagined she could see the gilders, draftsmen, wood-carvers, and stone-workers with their hammers and chisels. And leading them all would be their chief, the Head Scribe of the Place of Truth. Her father.

She stifled a groan.

She had to get back inside, and quick. If only the sentry would leave!

She watched him, remembering the countless times spent waiting to climb back in. By now, she could clamber over with her eyes closed.

Today, the only thing missing was Paneb. They'd been friends for ages—even though people frowned on it. The first time she and the painter's apprentice met was when he found her trying to climb out over the village walls. She thought he'd be mad, and that he'd tell on her. Instead, he'd helped her out, and had followed her over. It became a habit. Their secret. Mostly they ran wild in the desert, daring each other to do crazy stuff like stir up scorpions' nests, or climb into lions' dens.

But two weeks ago, he'd been different.

"Let's go up to the east ridge," she'd said.

He scoffed at her.

"What?" she said.

"Are you ever going to grow up? I'm sick of climbing around these old dunes."

She felt like she'd been slapped. "Okay . . . "

"It's just . . . I want to do something new. Something exciting."

As she guessed his mind, she recovered quickly. She grinned "You want to find that pretty market-girl again. You want to sneak back across the river into Thebes! By the gods, I can still see her eyes when you said were from the Place of Truth." She giggled, picturing Paneb and the girl together. "I thought she was going to faint, she was so impressed. She acted like you were Pharaoh or something."

"I'm not talking about—"

"We could go back, and you could tell her you were just getting the gold collar to go with those crazy new cuffs. I bet she'd just die to see you again."

"Stop."

She looked up into his face.

"Forget the gold collar, Neferet. I'm talking about leaving."

"Leaving?"

"To Memphis."

"Memphis?" She stared at him, stunned. To Pharaoh's white-walled city in the north of Egypt? "Very funny." She punched his arm. "You wouldn't leave. Your father would keel over and die of shame."

"No, he wouldn't. Not him." He looked away.

Neferet was confused. She knew Paneb and his father didn't get along well, but she was sure Paneb was wrong. What was he thinking?

"Come with me," he said.

"You can't be serious."

"Can't I?" he said, sounding annoyed.

"It's not like the old days when there were piles of apprentices. Don't look at me like that. You know as well as I do. You're the only one."

"It's not my fault if half our women are barren."

His words shocked her. Even if they were the truth.

"What about money? You can't afford to go there."

"I have enough."

For some reason, she again remembered his gold cuffs. And the other trinkets he'd recently bought. A thought snuck into her mind, a horrible vision of Paneb stealing treasures from Pharaoh's tomb and bartering them secretly in Thebes. She pushed it away.

"What are you thinking, Neferet?" he asked, studying her face.

She thrust an arm toward the Valley of the Kings. "All you ever talk about is how badly you wanted to learn the magic they use in Pharaoh's tomb—all those spells to give your drawings power."

He took her hand roughly in his. "Come with me. You and me, on an adventure."

"Come with you?" She pulled away.

"Please?" he said softly.

"Paneb, you can't just leave! Everyone knows if Pharaoh has no tomb paintings to guide him to the afterlife, horrible things will happen to us. We need you. The village needs you."

"I'm not staying."

"How can you even say that? How can you even think that?"

"Things change."

"Things change?" Her voice rose a level. "Things change? By the gods, Paneb, the village needs you! Don't you see what danger you'd be putting us in? Me, my father, all of us." Then she remembered the pretty market girl in Thebes and said, "I get it. There's not enough attention for you here, is there? You want to go to Memphis so people will ooh and aah over you and pet your head and offer you gold and jewels!"

"You don't know anything about what I want."

"Well then find it and don't come back. You're not my friend. My friend disappeared when he pretended to grow up."

His face turned white, and he said nothing more.

She wished she could take her words back. But it was too late. Two nights later, while he and the other craftsmen were at their encampment in the Valley of the Kings, Paneb left.

She should have been able to convince him to stay.

Instead, she'd lost her temper and cut him off forever.

Now, alone, she watched the sentry finally leave his post. She shoved her fingers into the wall, jamming them so hard they bled. She clambered over the top and dropped inside, silent as a temple cat.

"Stop!" a man shouted. Metal rasped as he pulled his knife from its sheath.

CHAPTER 6

I t's just me!"

"Neferet?" The guard said in a low voice. "Again?"

"Please, Jabari. I just wanted to walk around. By myself . . . but don't tell my father, he'll be furious!"

"You need to quit this running around out there alone." He shoved his blade back in his belt. After a moment, he nodded. "Get going. He'll be back from Thebes any moment."

"Oh thank you!"

"Run."

She sprinted down the narrow alleys. Women leaned out of cool, shadowed doorways and shook their heads at her.

As she flew around a corner, a girl stepped out and blocked her way. Layla. She wore one of her smug smiles—the kind that made Neferet want to give Layla's hair a good, hard tug. Neferet tried to push past.

"Layla, move!" she said. "I'm late!"

The bigger girl spread her arms wide, touching the walls on either side of the alley. "Think you're too good for us, don't you? Always sneaking off outside? But I guess not with Paneb anymore, right? He showed you what he thought of you."

"Just move."

Layla smirked. "I guess your father couldn't keep your precious Paneb from leaving, either."

"He's not my precious Paneb. And no. He couldn't."

"So you agree, it is your father's fault? That's not very loyal of you," she sneered. "Then again, it's obvious to everyone he's incapable of governing our village. This is simply the last straw, isn't it? Hopefully for your sake, Pharaoh—may he reign long and prosper—will spare you from his wrath. After all, you're just the lowly daughter."

Neferet raised her chin. "My father can take care of himself."

"Oh, so he's found a new apprentice, out of thin air?"

"He will."

"Really." Layla flicked her beaded braids over her shoulder. "You know, I think my father will do your father's job much better, don't you? Not that his eminence, Pharaoh, will kill yours, but you understand. We can't keep your father as Chief Scribe—governor of our whole town—after something like this."

"Good. Fine. Now move."

"Especially since my father is trying to get results. Did you know last night he and the other sculptors carved ears on Ptah?"

"Wait. What?" Despite everything, Neferet started to giggle. "They carved ears on Ptah?" She pictured the ancient village statue with his new ears. How had no one ever noticed the craftsmen's own patron god—their protector—was earless?

"What's so funny?" Layla demanded.

"Ptah hasn't heard a word we've said for centuries!"

Layla clenched her fists. "It's not funny."

"No, it's not," Neferet said. "Paneb is gone. And all you care about is gossiping about my father. Well I'm sick of it. Now get out of my way."

She charged at Layla, who jumped aside with a yelp.

Layla shouted after her, "That's right, run! And keep running right out of town."

Neferet turned. "Why should I?" She laughed. "Our problems are over. Ptah will finally hear my father's prayers."

She took off, sprinting.

Shouting at Layla was easy. But the truth was, replacing Paneb was not. Even if Ptah could hear, he couldn't just create a boy out of sand. And searching for an apprentice outside the village was impossible, not to mention the idea broke centuries of rules and tradition.

The alley walls wrapped her in silence. Only her footfalls disturbed the dry air. She rounded the last corner and shot down the lane toward her door. Next to her front stairs, the clepsydra—the water clock that kept the hours—read half past five. Her heart skipped a beat.

Dinner wasn't ready. Her lessons weren't done. And her father would be home any minute.

Ignoring her dusty feet, she dashed into the kitchen. Ribbons of fading light gleamed through the slatted roof over the oven. She cracked a flint and lit the coals. Smoke curled up and escaped into the evening air. She shoved a half-cooked pot of vegetable stew inside.

Panting, she ran to her writing supplies.

She threw herself down and yanked open a chest to fetch her ink, brush and a shard of ostraca to write on. Using the chest as her table, she mixed the ink. In her hurry, black drops spattered her dress.

"Flea-dung!" she said.

She swiped at the spots. They smeared.

"Double flea-dung!"

The sun sank below the rooftop and a cold shadow fell. She had to get this done. She snatched up her brush and began to write hieratic script. Messy hieratic, but hieratic nonetheless.

Learning to write is a great privilege, her father always said.

Which is why she'd decided that privilege was just a polite way of saying huge chore. Take her father for example: Head Scribe, most important man in the Place of Truth, and therefore the most privileged. Privileged to have an irritable stomach, insomnia and a short temper. And now that privilege had landed him in big trouble.

Definitely privileged.

Footsteps sounded. Neferet toppled the ink. It spilled over everything. She groaned as the door opened.

"Neferet?" her father called, his voice gruff.

She ducked behind the chest to blot the ostraca shard. "Right here! Doing my lessons!"

23

"Ah. Good." He slammed the door on the day's heat, brushed the dust from his feet with his calloused hands, and headed for the kitchen. She could hear him banging around, filling a cup with water from a jug.

She went to the doorway and hovered there, clutching the shard and trying to cover her ink-stained dress. She shoved her fringe of black hair from her eyes.

"How was your day?"

He grunted. His face was grim.

"Oh father, what's going to happen?"

He wiped sweat from his forehead. "That's not your worry."

"It's not your fault Paneb left!"

"I said, it's not your worry."

She recalled the guard's words. "Is it true, you went to Thebes? Is someone there going to help us find a new apprentice?"

His cheeks flared. "Stop asking. You're being stubborn."

"Like you," she shot back.

For a moment, his rage looked ready to boil over. He glared skyward, as if willing the gods to grant him patience. "Ah. What did I expect, raising you without a mother?" He took a slug of water, and sank heavily onto a stool. "It's complicated."

"Meaning what?"

"Meaning we've been forced to take radical measures. Measures Tui suggested."

Old Tui? The painter? Neferet's breath quickened. She'd been desperate to help after Paneb left; yet, when she'd gone to Tui with her idea, he'd looked more than doubtful. He'd looked shocked.

"What is it?" she said. "What's this great plan?"

She listened, stunned, as her father outlined her idea—her idea—word for word. Softly she said, "Amazing."

He nodded. "It won't be easy. We need a boy who can learn quickly, who can keep our secrets alive. Tui has always had my respect. This plan might just save us."

She bit her lip to keep from shouting the truth. My plan!

"Now, show me your hieratic."

Reluctantly, she handed over the ostraca.

He took it and his face grew dark. "Neferet, you're smarter than this." He began to massage the bridge between his heavy brows.

She stared at the ground.

"Once," he said. "Just once, you could try to make me proud."

Suddenly, she smelled smoke. She ran to the oven. The odor of burnt vegetables filled her nostrils.

CHAPTER 7

Aunt Zalika couldn't tell him what to do! Ramses fumed. But the truth was, she could.

He swore at the blazing cuts on his back and straightened up, scythe in hand. Four hours had passed; the sun lay low on the horizon. Across the field, a worker bent to lift a basket of grain; his silhouette looked like a drawing, framed against the border of wheat and sky.

"Sound the gong. Day's over," Sobek shouted.

The blade sharpener stood and hammered the gong with the handle of a scythe. As it rang out, Sobek tromped across the wheat stubble to Ramses' side.

"Shame to stop," Sobek said. "We had a good rhythm going."

Ramses nodded, but for once, the thrill of harvesting the gold wheat was gone.

"It's a fine crop," Sobek said.

"It is."

"Best we've seen in years."

"You're right."

"Seems funny somehow, doesn't it." Sobek plucked a head of grain and rolled it in his palms. The man's hands were like Ramses' father's hands: strong enough, Ramses had thought, to hold up the world. To make the sun rise and fall. To be there for him always, season after season until eternity.

Ramses took the grain and crushed it.

It was just wheat. And there was a lot of it. Almost a whole field of it still to cut. And for what? So Aunt Zalika and Uncle Hay could buy jeweled collars and sleep in his parents' bed?

Aunt Zalika had promised to protect him as if he were her son. But she had a son, and he didn't sleep in a windowless storage cell. He slept in Ramses' old room.

A farm worker, loaded down with baskets, stopped in front of Ramses and Sobek. "Your cousin sent for you," he told Ramses.

"What does he want?"

"How would I know? You're to go to his room. He said it's urgent."

Urgent? What could Sepi want that was urgent? Ramses glanced at Sobek. He remembered Aunt Zalika's words—that Sobek was supposed to keep them apart.

"I better not go," Ramses said.

The farm manager shrugged. "If it's urgent . . . See what he wants. Just don't get caught."

"I won't."

Ramses ran across the fields, past the fishpond, and into the sunny courtyard. Keeping an eye out for his aunt and uncle, he entered the large, clay brick house. Its familiar coolness settled on his skin.

Aunt Zalika's screech drew him up short. It echoed from the kitchen where she was scolding someone—about what, Ramses didn't wait to hear. He darted down the hall and stopped at the third door. The handle was stuck, like always. He gave it its usual wiggle and the door opened.

Inside, the dry heat felt stifling. A trickle of sweat slid down his neck.

On the far side, where his bed once lay, stood a polished desk. Ramses' cousin sat there with his tutor. Despite the heat, Sepi wore a linen blanket around his shoulders. He turned.

"What took so long?" Sepi demanded, his eyes bright in contrast to his pale cheeks.

"I work, that's what took so long. What's so urgent?"

"Hold on." Sepi waved a trembling hand at his tutor. "We're finished here."

Ramses waited while the tutor packed his things. Outside an

ox lowed; a cat appeared at the window and quickly disappeared. Finally, the man bowed his way out.

"And close the door!" Sepi shouted after him.

The man's footsteps died away down the hall and Sepi shot him a grin.

"Got any food around here?" Ramses said.

"You won't care about eating when you hear what I have to tell you."

"Want to bet?" He headed for the chest at the foot of the bed.

Sure enough, inside lay a plate piled high with spiced beef, dates, and a chunk of bread. His cousin's lunch, untouched as usual. Ramses dug in, closing his eyes with relief as he chewed a greasy mouthful of roasted meat.

Sepi watched, his thin legs tucked up to his chest. It was funny how Sepi liked to watch him eat. His cousin sat on the only chair Ramses had ever seen. The rest of the household used low stools or simply sat on the floor to dine, work, or relax.

"The best part," Sepi said, "is mother's face when she finds my plate empty again. Complete confusion. I swear it almost kills me not to laugh. Poor thing."

Ramses didn't share the poor thing sentiment, but he couldn't help grinning. "You should eat. Although I sure don't mind covering for you."

Red hues of dusk streamed through the openings in the vaulted ceiling. It radiated in bands across the bed, which consisted of a luxurious woven mat stretched over a wooden frame with panther shaped legs.

Ramses sank to the floor and leaned against the bed's footboard, still holding the empty plate in his dusty arms. Feeling pleasantly human again, he said, "So what's this urgent thing?"

"You have to guess." Sepi pulled his blanket tighter around his shoulders. "Since you cut me off so rudely."

Ramses' grin widened. "Okay, did you hear it from your tutor?"

"I did."

"Which tutor is he again?"

"Mathematics. But that's not important."

"Mathematics, huh. Sounds hard."

"It is." Sepi frowned. "But forget that."

"So do you like him? Your tutor?"

"Ramses! You're not playing the game!"

"But I am," Ramses replied, laughing. "And looks like I'm winning."

Sepi stood on his frail legs and inched to Ramses' side. He grabbed Ramses' nut-brown wrist and shook it. "You'll never believe it." He looked more excited than Ramses had ever seen. "There was an announcement in Thebes this morning, the Chief Scribe himself—"

"Wait." Ramses cut him off. "You had me running here because of what some scribe said?"

"Just listen."

"I'm dying to. I bet it's really interesting."

"Stop being so hard-headed for once. I'm not talking about a scribe who writes letters for hire. I'm talking about something different. Who's the only scribe you care about?"

Ramses yawned, sleepy after all that food. "None. Don't know any."

"Maybe not in person . . . But you've heard of this one." His cold fingers tightened around Ramses' wrist. "Come on, what's the only scribe you're interested in?"

A scribe he cared about? A thought flickered on the edge of his mind; a thought he couldn't quite catch. A draft brushed like fingers across his neck.

The room was nearly dark. The air felt static, as if a storm were about to break. Soon Ra, the sun god, would drop below the horizon and begin his nightly voyage through the underworld. Ramses glanced to the window. The fiery disk hung on the horizon.

"I told you, none."

As he said it, a bolt of crimson shot across the sky. Straight and narrow, the beam surrounded him with blazing light. Ramses looked down to see his whole body glowing bright gold. When he looked at Sepi, his cousin's mouth was agape.

And then the light was gone.

CHAPTER 8

"Did you see that?" Sepi gasped. "What was that? That light?"

"What scribe?" Ramses demanded.

In a low voice, Sepi said, "The Chief Scribe—the governor—of the Place of Truth."

"The Place of Truth!" Just whispering its mysterious name sent what felt like a rush of spider-feet down his spine. But maybe Sepi was wrong. The governor of the craftsmen's village never appeared in public. "You're sure?"

Sepi nodded.

Ramses' heart skipped a beat. The annual Nile inundation wasn't expected for weeks. So why did it feel like the gods were about to unleash a flood this moment—a flood so huge it would wash away the foundations of this house?

"Hurry up!" Ramses said. "What did he say?"

"According to my tutor—you're really not going to believe this—they're looking for an apprentice."

"An apprentice? He said that? Are you sure?"

"Positive."

"Why? From the outside? Why would they?"

"I guess they need to. Apparently their numbers have been dropping for years. Their women are having fewer and fewer children. There's only half a dozen boys, all of whom have positions as sculptors and gilders and the like. And there's a handful of girls, who of course can't be craftsmen."

"Well, what kind of apprentice?" Please don't let it be a woodcarver, or a stone-mason, Ramses thought.

"You don't need to worry," Sepi said. "So wipe that horrible look off your face. They need a painter. Someone who can draw."

A breathless silence filled the room.

Then Ramses grinned and stood up. "Place of Truth, huh?" He started to laugh. "You seriously had me!" He lit the oil lamp on Sepi's desk.

Sepi didn't answer.

Ramses glanced at him over the flame. "It is a joke, right?"

Silence.

"Are you . . . for real?" The lamp slid from Ramses' hands. He caught it just before it crashed and brought Aunt Zalika running. "By the gods, do you realize what this means? I could apply!"

Sepi rolled his eyes. "Yes. That's the whole point."

Ramses' thoughts came to a halt. Apply? And if by some miracle he won the position, leave his parents' farm to Aunt Zalika? Abandon it to her like his parents and his past meant nothing?

"My tutor tells me they're holding an examination in three weeks. At the Place of Truth," Sepi said. "Outside their gate."

"And anyone can enter?"

"Any young man. All you have to do is bring a sample drawing on a sheet of papyrus."

"Hold on—hold on," Ramses said. "On papyrus?" He groaned.

The expensive sheets, made of reed fibers woven in a crisscross pattern, then dampened and pounded flat until dry, were hard to come by. Nearly impossible to come by on a farm. Even Sepi, who had tutors, never used it.

"How am I going to find papyrus?" Ramses said.

Sepi shrugged. "I'll order my tutor to bring some."

"Your mother can't find out," Ramses said suddenly. "About any of it."

"Too late. She heard this morning."

Ramses turned to the dark window. "Then forget getting me papyrus. Nothing gets past her." The lamp guttered; his reflection shrank and bobbed against the walls. "She'd kill me if I applied. But she'll want you to. Bet my life on it."

"Number one, I can't draw. Number two, I'm dying. No one wants a dying apprentice."

"Don't be morbid."

"But you're right," Sepi said. "Mother sent a courier to the capitol, to Memphis, to fetch some famous drawing tutor. Two weeks to get him. That leaves a week to mold me into an artist." His face twisted into an ironic grin. "Typical mother."

Ramses let the news sink in.

Aunt Zalika was bringing a famous tutor all the way from Memphis? He was going to train Sepi to draw? Sepi was supposed to learn a skill like that in just two short weeks? What kind of man would take on a job like that? Either the tutor was a good salesman to convince Zalika it was possible. Or he had some magic technique that was worth all the gold in the world.

Something else flared in Ramses' chest. Fury. Aunt Zalika had beaten him to make him stop drawing. The priest had called him cursed. And now they wanted Sepi to do it? Horrible jealousy rose in him and he tried to shove it away. It wasn't Sepi's fault.

"Mother's sure this apprenticeship is my calling," Sepi said. "She kept telling me how prestigious it would be for me to get in. How the villagers are honored as Pharaoh's own royal men. How they have every luxury, and are pampered with the best of everything." He laughed. "That's all she talked about all afternoon." He sank back in his chair, looking suddenly exhausted.

Ramses thought about his aunt's words this morning. Now it made sense. Of course she hated his drawings. Of course she wanted to keep the news of the exam from him. He was competition, a threat to her own son.

A cough contorted Sepi's narrow frame. He bent double and crammed his fist to his mouth. Red flecks spattered his skin.

Stricken, Ramses ran to the bedside for a linen cloth.

"Here," he gasped.

33

Sepi fumbled to take it from him, his fingers cold as death. Ramses' heart clenched at the sight of his cousin. Don't you dare take him, too! he wanted to scream. Instead, he stayed silent, willing strength into Sepi's weak form. Another cough racked Sepi's body. Ramses barely caught him from falling as he lurched forward.

The door flew open.

Dark and towering, Aunt Zalika stood rooted to a spot in the doorway. Ramses held Sepi by the shoulders, the bloody rag clamped to his cousin's mouth.

"Murderer!" she screamed. "Let him go!"

Ramses backed away.

She flew at her son. "Are you hurt?" she cried. "Did he hurt you?"

Sepi started to speak, but whatever he wanted to say was lost to a coughing fit.

"Take this," Ramses told him, pouring a cup of water from the jug.

Aunt Zalika snatched it away before Sepi could take it. Her face was ashen. "How dare you? After what I just saw?"

"I was trying to help him."

"You were trying to kill him."

"I don't care what you think," Ramses said.

"Get out."

"I won't."

She stepped forward and backhanded him, hard. Her rings drew blood.

"This is my house," Ramses said. "I won't get out. Ever."

"You'll regret that." She grabbed Sepi's walking stick. Ramses ducked as she brought it down on his head; it slammed his shoulder. He stumbled sideways as she hit him again.

"Stop it," Sepi managed between racking coughs. "Stop!"

"Stay away from my son. You come in here because he's weak? Trying to get him on your side? Filling his head with lies?"

"Sepi is my friend."

Her face turned crimson. He ducked as she raised the cane again. It landed with a thud on the wooden chest. A second blow cracked across his forearm. Ramses rolled away, trying to protect his hands.

"Stop it," Sepi shouted. "Stop this instant. Stop or I'll die. I'll make myself die."

Aunt Zalika hesitated.

Ramses didn't. He forced himself off the floor and bolted.

He ran, stumbling down the hall.

In a tiny alcove, he paused and sank down against the wall. He put his bruised head between his knees to stop its spinning. How could she have promised—to his father's face, while he lay on his deathbed—to care for him as her own child? Ramses' cheek felt slippery with blood. His heart boiled over with rage.

But beneath his rage, he felt shame. Shame at what life had become in his own house. His parents' house.

He remembered Aunt Zalika's fury when she found him drawing this morning.

She was scared. She should be.

He was going to do it.

By every god, he would win that position.

He just had to.

CHAPTER 9

Still sitting in the tiny alcove, Ramses heard Sepi's door open and close. Aunt Zalika's voice echoed down the dark passageway. It was answered by Uncle Hay. His aunt and uncle were headed straight for Ramses' hiding spot.

He pressed deeper into the shadows, wishing he could disappear. They stopped in front of the household shrine. He heard the crack of a flame. Then the cloying smell of incense filled the air.

"I want to kill that boy," Aunt Zalika said.

"He's not worth worrying about, is he? He wouldn't really hurt our son, would he? Let it go, dear wife, that's what I say."

"Let it go?" There was a long pause. "Is that what you just said to me?" Aunt Zalika's voice was a mix of disbelief and rage.

"I just meant, well, we want him to work, don't we?"

"You think I don't know what I'm doing?"

"Not at all, my sweet! It's just, well he is your . . ." Uncle Hay paused.

Was Uncle Hay defending him?

"He is my what?"

"Of course, I wouldn't presume to tell you—"

"Then don't," she snapped. "I'm done being ordered around. I'm done being anyone's lackey. I had enough of it living with your mother. I certainly won't be yours."

"I understand, my darling."

"I have a headache. I'm going to lie down before dinner."

As their footsteps receded, Ramses let out a huge breath. Uncle Hay had defended him. What else could his words have meant? Ramses should talk to him. Maybe his uncle would help him try for the apprenticeship. Buoyed at the thought, went in search of Sobek and Hebony.

The kitchen door stood ajar. Warm cooking smells wafted out, along with the sound of laughter.

Wait until they heard the Chief Scribe's news.

He peered inside; here was something that never changed. Water jugs stood in a row; bowls overflowed with dates and juicy pomegranates; onion bulbs and bundles of herbs hung from the ceiling; two oil lamps flickered on the big sycamore table.

Sobek sat on a low stool, leaning back against the wall, and watched his wife, Hebony, as she worked. She had her left arm wrapped around a giant bowl of dough; the other struggled with a spoon. Clouds rose as she stirred. Flour covered the floor, her apron, her hair, everything.

With a grunt, she gave it one last turn and plopped the bowl on the table. "Will the gods please bring this harvest to an end? Eight months of my ghastly cooking, I can barely stand to eat it myself. I'm surprised anyone does!"

"We wouldn't, if we didn't mind starving." Sobek's eyes twinkled.

"Hey!" Hebony tossed a lump of dough at him. "The correct answer is, wife, how wrong you are, we love your cooking."

Sobek took a bite of raw dough before she could stop him. "Delicious!"

She smoothed her hair. "Oh, you're such a flatterer."

Ramses grinned. His father used to say that Hebony might lack cooking skills, but she more than made it up in secretarial expertise: calculating taxes, keeping tabs on work supplies, all the clerical duties that went along with running a farm.

He pushed the door open. It scraped against the beaten-earth floor. Hebony and Sobek turned at the sound, still laughing. But seeing him, their laughter died. The lump where the cane had hit Ramses' cheek seemed to swell under their scrutiny.

Sobek's face darkened; Hebony's jaw dropped.

"What . . . by the gods . . . what happened?" she said.

He pressed his fingers to it. "Nothing, I'm fine—"

"That's what you call fine?" Hebony hurried over and closed the door. Her floury hands examined his face and skull.

"I'm fine. You're not going to believe what I just—"

"Who did this to you?"

"It's not important. Just listen."

"You have a lump the size of a goose egg on your head!"

He wiggled away and turned to Sobek. "The Place of Truth is having an examination. They're looking for an apprentice!"

"Impossible. Where did you hear that?" Sobek said.

"Sepi's tutor told him. He heard it from the Chief Scribe himself."

Sobek looked amazed. "Well this changes everything."

Hebony said, "That's all very exciting and I wish Pharaoh's craftsmen the best of luck—now come and let me fix you. Look at your beautiful cheek, and your shoulders! Oh dear!"

"So Zalika knows about it?" Sobek said.

Ramses nodded.

Sobek sighed. "Let me guess. She wants Sepi to try for the apprenticeship." He took a wet cloth from a bucket and draped it over his shaved head. Water trickled past his ears and down his broad shoulders.

"She's bringing a tutor from Memphis to train him," Ramses said.

"When's the exam?"

"In three weeks."

Sobek flung the dripping rag into the pail. "No one can make an artist in three weeks. Only a thief makes promises like that."

The clouds of flour had settled. Ramses dragged his toe through the white dust to make a circle. "Maybe not. Maybe he has skills we can only dream about."

Sobek snorted. "Not likely. At least now we know what this morning was about."

"I don't like the sound of that," Hebony said, looking up from her box of medical supplies. "What happened this morning?"

There was a long pause.

"Zalika found him drawing during lunch and went mad."

"During his break?" She spun to Ramses. "That's why she beat you? It's none of her business what you do on your break!" She yanked the lid off a pot of salve, crossed to him and dabbed a glob on his cheek.

"Actually," Ramses glanced at Sobek as a horrible realization hit. "She beat me in Sepi's room because—I'm sorry Sobek! She warned you not to let me visit him. Now I know why! She knew Sepi would tell me about the apprenticeship. But I was stupid to go there. By the gods, I'm so sorry. I can't believe I let her catch me in there."

How could he have been so stupid? How could he have been so selfish?

What he'd done had just cost Sobek his job.

CHAPTER 10

In the kitchen, Ramses' head spun in horror at what he'd done. Forehead in his hands, he leaned his elbows against the big table and tried to think. Sobek was like a father to him now. Would Aunt Zalika really fire Sobek and Hebony and send them away?

"I'll swear to her you didn't know," Ramses said.

"Swear you didn't know what?" Hebony demanded. "What's going on?"

"Nothing," Sobek interjected.

"Nothing?" Hebony said. "Will someone please explain what happened?"

"Zalika makes threats," Sobek said, "but they're meaningless. She can't do anything. She needs us too much."

Ramses wasn't so sure. He wiped his slick palms on his kilt. If only he'd gotten out of there before Aunt Zalika came! He never should've stayed so long. How could he have been so stupid?

"Stop worrying," Sobek said. "We'll deal with her anger when the time comes. Now tell me what Sepi's tutor said. About the apprenticeship. How does one enter?"

With effort, Ramses pried his mind away from the black hole of fear. He tried to focus on Sobek's question. "Sepi said, people who want to enter have to submit a drawing."

"Good. That can be done."

"No. There's a problem. To qualify, it has to be on papyrus."

"I'm confused." Hebony wrinkled her flour-smudged forehead. "Are you talking about trying it yourself?"

"Yes."

She started to laugh. "Why? Why would you do that?"

"Why?" Sobek said. "You've seen his drawings. That's why."

"Because this is my chance, Hebony!"

She looked beyond shocked. She looked offended. "You don't need a chance. You're heir to this estate. Your duty is here. Not off indulging in some wild dream."

Wild dream? Was that all she thought it was? Her words hurt.

"Your parents worked their whole lives to build this farm. They did it for you, and for your children. Do you have any respect at all for what an accomplishment that was? This house? Those fields? People would die for what you have. You promised them you'd take care of everything, of your home—"

"You think this is still my home?" Ramses said. "Look at me. I'm a servant!"

A lamp sputtered and died. Half the room was thrown into shadow.

"I know things aren't easy right now—"

"You think I want to leave? You think I don't look at my parents' room and want to scream when I see Aunt Zalika in there, wearing my mother's clothes?"

"Things will get better," she said. "I promise."

He straightened. On the table, a dish of dates glittered in the half-light. He plucked one, but instead of eating it, he crushed it between his thumb and forefinger. Sticky pulp oozed out. "I thought you'd be excited for me."

"Don't do this," Hebony said. "Please. Just try to go along with things."

"Go along with things? I've been going along with things for months! And for what? To fill my aunt and uncle's pockets?"

"Shhh! Keep your voice down . . . To go along with things until you come of age and can take what's yours."

Sobek cut in. "Ramses will make up his own mind."

Hebony looked taken aback by her husband's words.

"Uncle Hay might help me get papyrus," Ramses said. "I

41

heard him talking and—"

Sobek's brow darkened. "I wouldn't be so quick to trust Hay."

"Why not?"

From outside the door came a soft rustle; it sounded as if someone was listening. Ramses looked from Hebony to Sobek; then he darted over and pushed it open. Shadows mottled the walls blue and purple. The air felt still as a tomb.

The hall was empty.

He glanced down. Bastet, the cat, greeted him with her golden eyes.

"Thank the gods," Hebony said, sagging against the table. "Just our little friend, come to say hello."

As if in agreement, Bastet leaped into Ramses' waiting arms.

From the sitting room, Aunt Zalika shouted, "Sobek!"

Bastet shot for the dark window. With a twitch of her tail, she disappeared.

"Sobek," Aunt Zalika shouted again, "Get out here. We need to talk. Now!"

"I'll talk to her," Ramses said.

"No." Sobek pushed past and strode down the hall.

Hebony watched her husband go.

Ramses wanted to tell her he was sorry he'd been so stupid, that he never meant to get Sobek in trouble. Instead, he said nothing. Those happy moments in Sepi's room seemed ridiculous now. It felt like he had a hole in his stomach. A hole to the underworld, into which every good thing was falling.

"We need onions," she murmured.

Mouth dry, he headed for the garden behind the house.

In the twilight, the purple spikes of larkspur looked gray. Bastet dozed in the shadows with her back to a large cabbage. The dark mass of trailing peas had grown thick and tangled. Instead of climbing around the vines, he wrenched them apart and forced his way through, sending leaves tearing and tumbling to the ground.

On the other side, he knelt where onion tops sprouted in a row. He tore one up; as he did, a rotting odor burst from the dirt.

Squinting, he saw the onion crawled with maggots. Growling, he flung it away, hard. To his shock, nearly all the rest were the same. He returned with one small one just as Sobek entered from the hall.

Hebony ran to her husband. "What happened? What did Zalika say?"

Sobek closed the door. "She fired a farm hand."

Ramses swore.

"That's what she wanted?" Hebony pressed her hand to her chest. "I'm ashamed to admit it, but that's a relief. Still, now? At the height of the harvest? What did he do?"

"Nothing. It's to punish Ramses."

"I don't understand."

"I do," Ramses said.

Sobek gave a grim nod. "In her words, if you have so much free time, you can do the work of two people."

Ramses stared out the window. He'd never have time to find papyrus now, or to figure out how to draw with brush and ink, let alone design an entry piece worthy of the exam. He'd be slaving long before dawn and long after dark. It was stupid to think he could've won. To think he could've beat her.

"But that's crazy!" Hebony said. "He's a boy! That's impossible. Ramses doesn't have to do this."

"No. But I do," Sobek said. "If our output falls short, Zalika's going to deny us our annual share. We won't be able to pay our living dues."

"She wouldn't."

Sobek didn't answer.

"She'd leave us homeless? Without a coin to our names?"

"I swear," Ramses said. "That won't happen. We'll get your annual share. I'll do the man's work. I swear it Hebony, I can do this."

But it felt like an impossible promise.

CHAPTER 11

There was only one way Ramses knew to finish the work on time. He did it in secret, glad beyond relief that Sobek and Hebony hadn't been sent away. The thought of losing them was too much to bear.

Under cover of darkness, the whack of his blade was followed by the swish of falling wheat. He moved swiftly, guided by the jab of cut stalks underfoot. His arms were numb.

It was the third time he'd worked through the night.

The extra work was taking its toll. His blade caught his shin. He clamped his hand over the gash. Exhaustion was making him clumsy. He needed to lie down. Just for a few hours.

Moonlight splashed cold across the paving stones of the courtyard. The smooth stone felt cool under his blistered feet. He reached the door to his cell, which had once been used to keep the goats penned up and safe from predators at night. He pushed the door open.

Air, hot as an oven and rank with the smell of sour bed rushes, closed over him. The smell of goat urine and manure had never faded. He grimaced, threw himself down and took a thick, stuffy breath. Sweat trickled down his gritty forehead; he scrubbed at it and rolled over.

The filth and stench were unbearable. He slammed outside into the cool night and headed for a bend in the river where the water ran clear. Wading in to his waist, he bent forward and plunged his head under.

Still dripping, Ramses made for a stand of rushes. He started to cut a fresh bundle for his bedding when he heard a cry. It sounded like a child. He pushed deeper into the foliage, squinting in the silver moonlight. He would've tripped over the trap if not for the creature's whimper.

Crouching low, Ramses peered inside.

A tiny duck, more fluffy than feathered, huddled in the claws of a wood and metal contraption. It came alive at the sight of him, flapping its wings, frantic. Even though Ramses had hunted himself with his father, the sight of this poor creature tore at his heart.

"I'm not going to hurt you," Ramses said, examining the trap's workings.

His fingers found a clamp. He struggled with it, trying to get the creature free. It thrashed against him. A slick substance was turning Ramses' hands slippery and he pulled away to wipe them on his shins. They left smears of blood.

Quickly, he reached again for the clamp. "I'm not going to hurt you!"

This time the bird stopped struggling, went limp and let him work.

But there was too much blood; it would be dead in minutes. Still, he kept working. His fingers slipped against the bird's slick body. It shifted its head and looked up at him. Ramses knew what it felt like to be trapped, with no way to escape. A frightening foreboding overtook him, and he began to feel that his own freedom was dependent on freeing this poor, lost creature.

"Almost there," Ramses whispered to it. He could hear the desperation in his voice.

The bird's glistening eyes met his.

Then the bird's ka slipped from this world and disappeared.

With a growl, Ramses smashed the trap to pieces. He dug a hole and buried the bird deep. Deep enough that the hyenas would never find it. Then he prayed to Osiris to care for the bird's everlasting soul.

Back in his cell, he threw himself down, only then realizing he'd left the fresh bedding abandoned on the bank.

45

It seemed like only minutes before the chatter of bleating goats announced the start of a new day. Early light stabbed the cell door's rotted gaps. Shaking off his black mood, he yanked the door open on its rotting hinges and stepped into the courtyard.

On the far side, Sobek unlashed two enormous water jars from a sledge. His neck shone with sweat as he lifted them single-handed to the ground. Seeing Ramses, the farm manager's grey eyes sparkled. He tossed Ramses a small loaf of bread studded with dates and almonds and said, "Follow me."

Ramses swallowed the loaf in three bites, only tasting its sweet, nutty flavor after it was gone.

"What's up?" he said, wiping the crumbs from his mouth.

"Not here." Sobek strode deep into the barn's shadowed interior. He stopped and said in a low voice, "I'm giving you the morning off."

Ramses couldn't help it. He started to laugh. "Are you crazy?"

"Probably. But you need to work on your design."

"I have no papyrus."

"For now, practice in the sand, like always. Decide what you're going to draw. It's important to plan carefully. No doubt, there will be hundreds of submissions. Your drawing must stand out from the crowd. Drawing well is one thing, but winning will be more than that. You have to do something memorable. Something that makes them know you're the one. Something they can't deny."

Ramses hadn't thought of that. Sobek's words were wise. And daunting.

"As for the papyrus," Sobek said, "It will come."

Now Ramses was itching to go. Sobek was right, he needed to get to work. Still, he said, "But I can't just leave! The harvest—"

"The harvest is doing fine. Actually," Sobek added, studying Ramses with a look of suspicion, "Somehow, we're ahead of schedule."

"Really?" Ramses kept his face blank, but inside he was thrilled, glad his secret night forays were paying off. "Huh.

That's great."

"Yes. But we have a new problem. Nothing to do with your drawings, or the harvest."

"I don't like that look."

"Come in here," Sobek said. He walked deep into the barn, back to where no one went except to toss a broken tool on the pile Ramses' father had been planning to repair. He stopped and spoke in a low mutter. "I haven't said anything because I was hoping I was wrong—"

"About what?"

"It's not good. Hay's been bribing people . . ."

"Uncle Hay?"

Sobek glanced toward the door. "He's been paying off government officials. His visits to Thebes weren't to improve our irrigation rights. He wants to make sure you have no legal claim to your parents' estate."

"But that's . . . that's impossible, he defended me. He wouldn't . . ."

"He would. He has."

Light filtered through the roof where it had begun to cave in overhead. Flies buzzed in and out of the shadows, nesting in a rotting pillar.

"He had your birth wiped off the records." Sobek said.

The air suddenly felt thick, hard to breathe. Ramses reached for the pillar; splinters jabbed his palm. "So if I'm not my parents' son, then who am I?"

"Right now, you're a worker of unknown origin."

Unknown origin?

In one stroke, Uncle Hay had made him no one. Not only in the eyes of humans, but worse, in the eyes of the gods. Without a birth record, when he died he'd be lost to wander in darkness forever. Unable to rest. Stuck in limbo. The ultimate horror.

He'd believed Uncle Hay cared about him, that they were on the same side. Ramses' cheeks burned. Of course they weren't. But beyond his fear, what hurt most was that his parents' long years of work—all their sweat and love—had been used to pay for Uncle Hay's bribes.

Blackness crept into his stomach.

"We could try to put your case before a judge," Sobek said. "But it doesn't look good."

All Ramses could do was nod mutely at his friend.

"That's why we have to act." Sobek pulled up the cellar door.

Ramses followed him down into the cool darkness to where they stored the vegetables from the back garden. The farm manager hefted a sack of garlic onto his left shoulder, a smaller one of dried chickpeas onto his right, and hurried back upstairs.

"This is our chance. Right now."

"So what are we doing?" Ramses asked.

Sobek glanced outside. "There's your uncle. No time for questions. Play along."

"But—"

Sobek shoved Ramses so hard he flew from the barn. The farm manager emerged a second later, his face livid, his back to Uncle Hay.

"I'm warning you," Sobek growled.

"But Sobek—"

The slap of Uncle Hay's sandals came to a stop. He leered at Ramses, clearly thrilled at stumbling on a juicy fight.

CHAPTER 12

I'm the manager," Sobek shouted, his back to Uncle Hay. He thrust the bag of garlic at Ramses and sent him sprawling on the dirt. "You'll do what I tell you!"

The sack split open. Garlic rolled everywhere. Ramses scrambled around, gathering it up.

"Think I like taking up your slack?" Sobek said.

Ramses swallowed. "I work hard."

Sobek's shoulders swelled, panther-like, ready to strike. "Don't talk back!"

"What's all this, then?" Uncle Hay said.

Sobek spun around in apparent surprise.

As if pleased to have snuck up on them, Uncle Hay grinned. His eyes looked like two eggs being squeezed from their sockets. "That's my nephew you're talking to."

After a moment, Sobek said, "I was out of line."

Hay glanced at Ramses. "You're becoming a real pest."

Ramses scowled.

"What did the runt do now?" Hay asked Sobek.

"It's not worth your time."

"Let me be the judge of that," Uncle Hay said, voice curious. "I'd like to know."

"It's nothing. It's about the sacks we need for the harvested grain."

"And?" Uncle Hay rested one chubby hand on the hip of his pleated kilt. His belly bulged from under his tunic like a sackfull of water.

"And nothing. I'm manager here, not some fool delivery boy.

It's not my job to stand in line for three stinking hours, broiling like a slave behind a herdsman with goats that smell of rotting fish. But your nephew says deliveries aren't his job."

"Oho, he does?"

Sobek's ruse seemed to work. Maybe too well.

Ramses ducked as his uncle aimed a smack at his head.

"It's late," Sobek said. "Someone has to go. The line'll be a mile long."

"You heard him, you grubby little rat, get a move on. We need those sacks."

"These will cover the barter." Sobek heaved the bags of chickpeas and garlic onto the sledge. "So don't let them tell you otherwise."

"Yes, sir," Ramses muttered.

"And stop scowling. It'll serve you right if you have to wait all day," Sobek said.

All day? Ramses coughed to hide his grin. He knew the errand would be quick, and Sobek had just bought him precious time. He started to leave, but Uncle Hay caught him by the wrist.

"You're not going like that." Uncle Hay wrinkled his nose. "Not in those rags. And wash your face. People will see you. You'll give my house a bad name."

And so, shortly after, Ramses stood scrubbed and dressed in one of Sepi's finest tunics. The day was growing hot and Uncle Hay was sweating. He grimaced at Ramses with satisfaction, his kohl-lined eyes dripping onto his bloated cheeks.

"Now. There we are," he said. "Off you go. And no meddling about. Hear?"

Ramses nodded.

Yes, he heard. But he'd promised nothing.

It was exhilarating to escape, even for a few hours. First, he'd do the errand. Then, with the sacks safely stowed away, he'd stop to draw.

The sledge bumped along behind him. How funny he must look, hurrying down-river in a gold embroidered tunic as if dressed for a royal Theban festival.

Lush palms arched overhead. The scent of date blossoms filled the air. Red earth sloped gently upward from each bank. In the river, a crocodile swam in lazy arcs, snapped at a passing bird and sank beneath the surface.

As he walked, he mulled over Sobek's words—that a simple drawing wouldn't do. He'd have to draw something that would stand out. But what?

A particularly smooth patch of ground came into view and he slowed. What was the rush? The boat wouldn't leave until noon. And noon was hours away. The air by the water still felt cool; he could fetch the sacks later.

There was plenty of time.

He parked the sledge.

After finding a stick, he knelt down and grew completely lost in his work.

It seemed like only moments had passed when Ramses realized he was no longer casting a shadow. Hot sunlight radiated up from the sand. He squinted in the glare, studying the ground that was busy with images. Then he glanced up at the sun.

It climbed high in the sky.

Flea-dung! It was getting late.

He blew out a breath. All these drawings, and none were right. Out of nowhere, an image flashed into his mind. A statue of Ptah. He tried to bring the mental picture into focus. Had he seen that statue somewhere before?

Excitement flowed through him, like currents in a stream. Ptah was patron god of craftsmen. What better way to appeal to the examiners than to draw their own guardian?

Still, did he dare draw another god? Sweat dampened his palms.

He struggled with his thoughts. He only wanted to do what was right. Why was life so difficult? Nervously, he pulled a handful of long, dry reeds and swept the ground clean. He dropped the reeds and wiped his hands on his tunic.

A lizard scurried across the sand.

The lizard reminded Ramses of the crocodile-like monster that waited with Osiris at the gates to the Underworld. The monster that consumed the souls of sinners.

The lizard loped across his clearing. It made dry, rustling noise as it slid into the tall reeds.

Suddenly angry, Ramses kicked sand over the reptilian claw marks. He'd had enough of death. He was here, and he was alive. And he would draw his image of Ptah. Right here, right now. And Ptah would be a drawing, nothing less, and nothing more.

It wouldn't come to life.

Ramses had no magic.

He refused to believe he did. Whatever he thought he'd seen before, he'd been wrong. He was an artist. He needed to get into the Place of Truth. And if he was afraid to draw, he might as well give up now. Because to continue would be pointless.

Carefully, he set to work. First, he drew the god's feet, and then his legs. His kilt and broad chest. Arms and hands. A noble face, with keen eyes and brows. Then Ramses gave Ptah his magical staff, with three powerful symbols: the Was Scepter—symbol of power, the Ankh—symbol of life, and the Djed Pillar, symbol of stability.

They were the three creative symbols that allowed Ptah to perform his miracles.

"Are you what they want?" Ramses whispered.

He stared down at Ptah's face.

A rustling noise sounded up the riverbank. Ramses jerked upright.

What time was it? The rustling sounded again. Someone was headed this way. Was it Aunt Zalika? Had she come after him? If she found him drawing, she'd kill him.

Carefully, staying low, he went to the edge of his clearing and peered through the tall grass, back the way he'd come. There was no one there.

The strange impression that someone, or something,

was staring at his back made him turn. His gaze flicked to his drawing of Ptah. It was happening again. His stomach clenched. This was not his imagination. The god's eyes had shifted, so that the pupils no longer faced straight ahead. They were looking at Ramses.

Even more frightening, the eyes seemed alive. Intelligent. There was life behind them. An entity looked through them just as surely as Ramses looked back from his own.

Why was this happening? He didn't want Ptah to come to life!

His breath came faster. He wanted to run, or to wipe the drawing out.

The priest's warning came to him: What the boy does is unholy! No god meant him to have that power.

No. Calm down. He was seeing things.

He blinked hard, hoping the illusion would disappear, hoping he could force that steady, godlike gaze to turn to sand once more. This couldn't be happening, couldn't be real. Those lines were sand! He'd drawn them himself. He was a nobody! Why would the great god Ptah come to threaten him? What had he done so wrong?

Trembling, Ramses stepped away further, tripped and fell on his back.

On the sand, the bearded god's chest began to rise and fall.

Ramses' heart stuttered.

Ptah—the god who'd dreamed this very world into existence—grinned at him. Yet, Ramses hadn't drawn a grin.

He scuttled backwards on all fours. That's when he heard the rustling footsteps coming closer. He'd forgotten about the approaching person.

Trembling at the fear of turning his back on Ptah, he forced himself to turn away. He crouched in the tall grass and searched for the source of the sound.

A reed of a girl with shoulder-length hair and a fringe of black bangs marched along, a woven basket over one arm. She wore a short white dress, made of the finest linen. Her arms and legs had a catlike grace that held him mesmerized.

In his surprise at seeing a girl walking alone in the middle of nowhere, he forgot all about Ptah and simply stared.

The girl's gaze was focused on the ground, so he kept watching.

There was something almost regal about her. Closer now, he saw a carved turquoise amulet hanging from her slender neck. Judging by its quality and craftsmanship, it must have cost a small fortune.

What could she be doing here—completely unprotected? How in the name of the gods had she wandered out, alone? Did she not know there were hyenas and snakes, and men who might attack her here on the edge of the desert?

He suddenly realized if he didn't stand or say something quick, she'd think he was stalking her.

"Hey!" he cried.

The girl glanced up. And then, with a tiny gasp, she disappeared.

CHAPTER 13

Baffled, Ramses stared at the grassy bank where the girl had stood just seconds before. He recalled stories of unhappy spirits, wandering the earth for all eternity. Is that what he'd just seen?

A muffled shout of fiery curses changed his mind. The girl was human. Very human. He ran to where he'd seen her last and stopped short. An open pit gaped at his feet. He'd barely missed falling into the hunter's trap.

Reeds that once camouflaged the hole had caved in on all sides. He leaned over the edge, careful not to slip. She crouched at the bottom in a fighting stance.

"How dare you?" she shouted.

"Are you okay?"

"Stay away from me, jackal-breath!"

"Let me help you."

"I'm not falling for that. Get away!"

He groaned. "Don't be silly. It's an animal trap, not a girl trap."

"Yes, and that's why you startled me. So I'd fall in?" She scrabbled at the sides.

"No. I was trying to not surprise you."

"To not surprise me?" She rolled her eyes, dug in her fingers and inched upward. He couldn't help being impressed. Even when she scowled up at him.

"It'd be a lot quicker if you just let me help. Come on, do I look like a criminal?"

Every one of her muscles was tensed, and she was breathing

hard. "How do I know what a criminal looks like?" As she spoke, her hold came loose. She hit bottom with a growl.

"You're being ridiculous," he said.

"Ridiculous?" The beautiful girl glowered at him.

Wrong word, he decided—really wrong word. On the far side, she managed to scale partway up. The section of wall caved in and sent her sliding to the bottom. She landed on her back with a thud. A layer of sand showered her arms and legs.

Water began to trickle from the cave-in, seeping through from the river. Her eyes flicked up to Ramses.

"The wall's going to give!" he said. "Just take my hand."

Frowning, she stumbled upright and attacked the wall. Again, she started to climb. Again, the dirt slid from under her hands and feet. This time, the whole section bulged inward and collapsed. She gasped as liquid mud trapped her to her knees.

He lay on his belly and reached down toward her. "Grab on!"

"I can't reach!"

He glanced around for a stick. Nothing, only thin reeds.

"Hurry!" she shouted.

Water gurgled around her now, up to her waist. Ramses did the only thing he could think of. He stripped off Sepi's grand tunic. Lying as close to the edge as he could, he held it down to her like a rope.

"Grab on!"

She caught hold. "Pull," she gasped, water rising to her armpits. "Quick!"

"I'm trying, but you're really heavy!"

This earned him a scowl. She thrashed at the end of the line.

"Try wiggling your legs!" he said.

"What do you think I'm doing?"

The water surged higher. It rushed over her face. He saw her black hair disappear. By the gods, this couldn't be happening! He pulled harder, praying she still held on. The tunic suddenly felt lighter. She'd let go!

Choking with horror, he kept pulling. Faster and faster.

The end of the tunic emerged from the swirling mud.

And her pale fingers still gripped a small piece. He shouted with joy and yanked harder. She broke the surface, her face alive with terror.

"Don't let me—"

"I've got you. I've got you!" He fastened on to her hands, and then her arms. She flailed, desperately grabbing him. Reaching for her waist, he lifted her from the swirling deluge with a strength he didn't know he had.

They both fell backward, collapsing on solid ground. A moment later, she rolled on her side and coughed up water, her fingers still gripping the tunic. Her coughing subsided and she rolled onto her back.

Except for the slowly calming pool, and the sound of their breathing, the bank was silent. A breeze brought Ramses to life. He clutched the reeds around him, pulling them over himself. He tried to tug his tunic from her clenched fist. She still clutched it in a death grip. He pulled more reeds over his middle, and tugged again. The girl rolled over and blinked a few times as if clearing her head.

Then, as if seeing him for the first time, her mouth opened.

"Oops." She clapped her hand over her eyes.

"Um, could you maybe let go now?" he said.

She smothered a nervous giggle.

Ramses struggled into the muddy garment. After a moment, he said, "Thanks. You can look."

She sat up and wiped her forehead. "Sorry about that. And about your trap."

"The trap's not mine."

"Actually, I don't think it's anyone's now," she said with a shudder. "I'm glad I'm not still in there. Look at it."

The sides had caved in; the pit was only half as wide, and shrinking. Brown water flowed over the edge in a steady stream toward the river.

She scanned his face. "You saved my life."

Her irises were flecked with gold. They felt familiar and foreign all at the same time. Like he could talk to her about anything, if only he could think of something interesting to say. And that was the problem. He couldn't think of anything.

The air pressed close, all hot and humid; on the river, an ibis sang out and another replied.

To his surprise, the girl dropped her gaze to the ground. Her cheeks colored.

Ramses felt his do the same. Feeling incredibly awkward, he tried to break the tension by saying, "What were you doing here by yourself?"

"I was . . . wait, what's that supposed to mean?"

"Well, I was just—"

She smiled. "Oh, it doesn't matter. If you want to know, I was gathering herbs. And I feel pretty dumb right now. I walked right into that hole."

"If I hadn't been so slow . . ."

"My basket!" she said. "By the gods, it took me all day to gather those herbs—please don't tell me it drowned." She slicked dirt-smeared hair from her face and leaped up. She ran, searching. "It has to be here!"

Ramses stood and pushed through the rushes. "Is this it?" He held up the woven reed container, and then started to gather the spilled cuttings.

"That's twice," she said when he gave it to her.

"Twice what?"

"Twice you know what. Twice that you saved me. Thanks."

Although she was coated with half-dried muck, he couldn't tear his eyes away.

She laughed. "We look like mud-rats. My father's going to kill me."

Ramses remembered Uncle Hay's warning to keep Sepi's best tunic clean.

"Yeah, I'm pretty much dead, too."

"Really? Your father will be mad?"

"No . . ." He let the words hang, not wanting to say more.

CHAPTER 14

S o what are you doing out here?" the girl asked.

Ramses had a sudden impulse to show her his drawing of Ptah—to tell her he was practicing for the exam at the famous Place of Truth. Then just as quickly he pushed it away. The drawing might frighten her, the way it had frightened him.

And if it didn't, she'd probably think he was a show-off.

He shrugged.

At this, she said, "Well, who are you?"

"A farmer. My name's Ramses."

"A farmer?" She eyed his fancy tunic. "Your farm must be pretty impressive to go around dressed like that."

He glanced down at Sepi's ruined outfit. Uncle Hay was going to kill him. But for some reason, he couldn't stop himself from laughing. "I don't usually dress like this. I'm running an errand."

And he was late, he reminded himself. Very late. Still, he didn't want to leave.

"I better let you go." She paused. When he made no move to depart, she said, "I always wondered what that's like. Living on a farm. I bet yours is nice."

"It's good . . . it's—" Wait, she didn't live on a farm? Then what was she doing out here in the middle of nowhere? Again, he noted the regal tilt of her head, the rich cut of her muddied linen dress.

"Where are you from?" he said.

"Not far."

"Well if it's not a farm, what is it?"

She laughed. "Right now it's a place in a lot of trouble." He watched her wring out her dress. Muddy droplets sparkled with sunlight as they fell.

"I guess if you wanted to tell me about it, you would," he said.

"It's not that I don't want to, it's just . . . can we talk about something else? How about you. Do you have a big family?"

"No. It's just me. My parents are gone."

"I'm sorry." Her cheeks colored. "I didn't mean to pry."

"It's okay. It's not like it's a secret."

After a moment she said, "How old are you? You look like you're the same age as me. And you're in charge of a whole farm?"

"Well I'm not exactly . . ." He thought of Aunt Zalika and felt his face growing hot. "I mean, yes, it's my farm, but . . ." He swallowed, searching for words.

"No wonder you wear such fancy tunics to run errands along the river," she said, admiration in her voice.

"It's not like that." He had to correct her. Quick. Before it was too late.

"Neferet!" a man shouted in the distance.

The girl leapt to her feet. On a rise to the west, a crowd of men appeared. Ramses eyed them in surprise. There had to be at least a dozen of them. At first, he saw only a mob. But then he realized the men wore uniforms. Kilts with thick leather belts at their waists. Weapons dangling from straps. Several carried fiber shields. They were soldiers of some kind. And they were no mob—they were walking in formation, with a single man at the head.

He turned to Neferet, but she was staring at the men, pale-faced. "Jabari?"

"Thank the gods," the man cried, "We've searched everywhere!"

Neferet gulped. "I'm in big trouble," she told Ramses. "I have to go."

"Why? Who are they?"

"My father must have sent them."

Her father? Who was her father to command such men?

Looking worried, Neferet hurried away a few steps, but then turned back. Reaching her hands up around her neck, she removed the turquoise amulet. "I want to give you this."

It was a carved figure of Maat, goddess of justice and truth. The goddess held a tiny feather: the feather she used to weigh the truths of men.

"I can't take it," he said, awed by the valuable piece.

"Please." She pressed it into his fist. "As my thank you?"

Being this close to her made his stomach go all fluttery and strange. She bit her lip, and he wondered if she felt it too. For a moment, they held the amulet between their palms. When she gazed up at him from under her dark lashes, she looked like a drawing come to life.

"Will I see you again?" he said.

She nodded, swallowing. "I'll try to come back here sometime—"

"Step away from her!" the man she'd called Jabari barked.

Ramses jumped, and she pulled away quickly.

"I said, step away!" The man's hand went to his sword. It rasped free of it's sheath.

"Stop!" Neferet said. "He's a friend!"

Still, Ramses did as he was told. Friend or not, the other men were advancing on him.

"Are you all right?" Jabari demanded.

"Of course I'm all right," she said. "Everything's fine."

"Everything's not fine. We must go," Jabari said, shooting a dark look at Ramses.

She nodded and called, "Goodbye then."

"Goodbye," Ramses said. "Thank you." Awkwardly, he stood there, holding her amulet.

The men closed around her in a protective circle. He watched in amazement as they led her away. Again, he thought of how he'd found her wandering alone. It seemed even stranger, given she was clearly someone important. A merchant's daughter, perhaps?

The group marched south twenty paces or so. He realized they were about to trample the drawing. He opened his mouth to warn them, when Neferet cried out.

"Stop!" she said.

The group staggered to a halt, nearly tripping over one another. He saw them all stare downward, following her gaze. They were staring down at Ptah. Were they afraid of the sight, the way the priest had been? The way Ramses himself had been just a short while ago?

He saw Neferet between them, speaking quickly to the guard named Jabari. She pointed back at Ramses. The man shook his head. Firmly, he guided her away. The others fanned out to walk on either side of the image.

The last guard glanced back, and his expression shocked Ramses.

It wasn't fear. Instead, it was an unmistakable look of respect.

The group made for the rise. Four uniformed men lifted a curtained litter onto their shoulders. The fabric blew back to reveal a glimpse of Neferet. He couldn't just let her go. He had to see her again!

His fingers closed around her turquoise amulet.

He ran after them.

Jabari turned and barked, "Step back. Now!"

"Who is she?"

Legs planted, sword glinting, the guard measured him from head to toe. Never had Ramses felt so small and insignificant. "She's daughter to the Chief Scribe of the Place of Truth."

The Chief Scribe's daughter?

Daughter to the man who'd announced the apprenticeship? Daughter to the man who—to Ramses—was the most important person in all Egypt, except for Pharaoh Tutankhamen himself? This was unbelievable.

"That's right," Jabari said. "You should look awed. Now step back, or I'll be forced to arrest you."

Ramses did as he was told. Jabari turned and joined the

procession, his belt and sword jangling from his waist. The guards marched in rhythm, disappearing into the shimmering distance.

"Neferet," Ramses said. The beautiful one.

Still, he thought, even if she were a simple peasant, he'd feel the same. Neferet was unlike any girl he'd met. She was courageous. She was smart. And she was funny.

He stood for a long time and stared after them, her still warm amulet clutched in his fingers.

CHAPTER 15

In the curtained litter, Neferet's stomach fluttered. She wiped her sweaty hands on her legs and tried to fix her dress. It had dried stiff and muddy as a board. She gave up and knotted her fingers together.

The sun god, Ra, shone through a gap in the curtains. Ra had long since crossed his zenith in the sky as her procession neared the front gates to the Place of Truth.

She couldn't believe her father had sent a search party to find her.

She was in huge trouble.

She thought of Ramses. No matter what happened, meeting him was worth it.

The men slowed and the curtains grew still. Hot sunlight burned through the linen hangings. She heard the village gates creak open. Footsteps echoed off the thick, mud-brick walls as cool shadows enveloped her.

"We're here," Jabari announced.

"I know." She pushed the curtains aside and slid from her seat, her eyes cast down. "Thank you."

"You had us worried. I was worried."

"I'm sorry you had to search for me like that," she mumbled.

"Humph."

The sight of vegetable sacks and water jugs waiting by the gate gave her a jolt. It was later than she thought. Much later. She hadn't been gone that long, had she?

"Today's supply caravan came already?" she gasped.

"Hours ago."

It was that late? She was in serious trouble.

Behind her, wood thudded against metal as two guards secured the gates.

"Locking them won't stop her," Jabari said. "She'll just climb right out!"

"I said I'm sorry."

"It's not me you need to worry about."

Neferet thought of her father. She could already see his furious face. "I know."

She ran down the narrow, shaded alleys. Her feet stirred up dust and her stomach twisted into knots.

She had good reason to be out in the desert, she told herself. Very good reason. She was getting Merit's herbs! So what if she'd gone further than she was supposed to? The physician would back her up, wouldn't she?

She groaned.

Nothing could excuse her for staying out so long, or for going so far. It would be back to Layla's house. Back to being Layla's mother's prisoner.

"She's a good girl," Layla's mother would tell her father. "All she needs is a woman's care." And then she'd force Neferet to sew curtains for the whole village.

She'd never see Ramses again.

As she neared the last turn to her house, the babble of women's voices carried down the street. She slowed, edging up to the corner. Carefully, she peeked around it at her front door. Girls with their mothers swarmed around her doorstep.

She pulled back into the shadows.

Flea-dung!

"Just wait until she gets here. I'll give her a piece of my mind," a woman said. "Shaming her father like this. Where has she been? She wants attention, that's what this is. She's spoiled rotten."

"She'll ruin our village," said another, "Running wild like she does."

"She already has!" said a third. "She made Paneb run away."

Neferet gasped. She hadn't made him run away! She'd tried to stop him!

"The girl is evil."

Evil? Neferet felt as if she'd been stabbed.

"It's so sad," came Layla's voice. "Who does she think she is? That she can just take off, whenever she likes?"

A woman said, "Well—she does work for the physician gathering herbs."

"Gathering herbs?" Layla cried. "That's just an excuse. She likes to cause drama. She's desperate for attention. Always was. And now she has guards out looking for her? What's next? It's embarrassing to have a girl like that in our village. I told you, she's a troublemaker. All we had to do was wait."

Well, Neferet had waited long enough.

Every head turned as she strode out of the shadows. Layla flicked invisible dust from a crisp new skirt. Feeling suddenly self-conscious, Neferet tried to look as lady-like as possible, but her gritty dress made walking difficult. It rubbed against her legs with a rasping sound that made her blush. She pushed matted hair from her dirt-baked forehead.

All around her, jaws slackened.

Layla broke the silence with a snort of laughter. "Did you get lost digging for grubs or something?"

Beside her, Layla's mother's painted brows were high with shock. "Neferet!" she sputtered. "What in the name of the gods?"

"I was picking herbs for Merit and I fell."

"You fell? And then what—did you roll all the way home?"

At this, Neferet bit back a laugh. She couldn't help it. That was funny!

"Oh, you think it's funny to mock us, do you?" demanded Layla's mother. "You and your father, he's no better for letting you do it! Our whole village is in trouble, and here you are rolling in the dirt, and he's done nothing to help us! Nothing, do you hear? He—" Layla's mother's mouth snapped shut.

Everyone glanced up as the door to Neferet's house opened.

Her father emerged on the top step. He stood beneath the inscription of his name, his eyes dark and his shoulders dusty with work. In silence, he surveyed the scene.

"Good evening, ladies," he finally said. His gaze stopped on Layla's mother. He stared at her steadily, the way he sometimes stared at Neferet when she did something wrong.

Layla's mother grew flustered. "Oh! Yes, good evening!"

Neferet felt a surge of pride. He'd be furious with her later, but for now she ran to him.

He dropped a protective arm around her shoulders. His stern eyes swept over the gathering, moving from one face to the other until they all looked embarrassed. "Why are you here, at my house, instead of at home cooking dinner?"

"Have you seen Neferet?" Layla's mother said.

"I see her now."

"Well, where has she been?" She gestured at Neferet. "We were worried!"

"Your worry is appreciated," he said in a voice that made it clear he knew their motives had more to do with gossip than actual concern. "Ladies, good night. Please go home. Now." He led Neferet inside and shut the door.

"Hello Father!" she said, forcing a bright tone.

"Where have you been?" he demanded.

"Just, well, you know . . ."

"No, I don't."

CHAPTER 16

Standing just inside the door, her father stared down at her, unsmiling.

When Neferet felt nervous, she talked quickly. She stumbled through an explanation at breakneck speed. "Well I didn't mean to take so long, but this morning, Merit, the village physician, said she needed more of those plants she uses for Tui's salve. It's that lotion for his arthritis? It's the only thing that helps, he can't paint without it. So I thought you wouldn't mind, and then, I had to get a new reed basket, because mine has a hole in it . . ."

Neferet eyed her father. He hated long-winded explanations. She was in enough trouble already; did she have to tell him about Ramses?

"Go on."

"Right. So anyway, I was barely outside the village, that's where I usually look for the herbs, but couldn't find any! I guess everyone in Thebes must have arthritis too. I had to walk and walk and still only found a couple of tiny shoots. It's hard work you know. I didn't notice how far I'd gone, because I was very focused on doing a good job. Tui . . ."

"Who's the boy?"

She felt her cheeks turn red. So, he already knew. Of course he knew. When the sentries found her, they must've sent a runner to tell him.

"The boy, yes, I was just getting to that," she said.

"Then get to it."

"Well I didn't see him, and then I tripped into this trap. But it's not like he did it on purpose. Tripped me, I mean—"

"See why I don't want you going out alone?" he shouted.

From beyond the door came the shuffle of feet and the muffled murmurs of women and girls.

"You could've been killed," he growled.

Neferet knotted her fingers in the folds of her filthy dress. "He wasn't dangerous."

"Yes, because the guards came."

"No! They came later. We were there for a long . . ." she stopped.

"For a long time?" His wooly brows arched.

"He saved me! But father, listen, he's an artist! An incredible artist!"

"An artist?" He laughed.

"Don't laugh. Yes! He'd drawn this amazing . . ."

"Stop right there. I see what happened. It was all planned! He watched you come out of the Place of Truth. He saved you to win your favor! For the apprenticeship."

"But . . ." Neferet's words trailed away. No. It couldn't be. Could it? Ramses planned it? All of it, just an act, to get her favor?

"We'll find this lout," her father said, patting her dirty hair. "Don't you worry. Bar him from the exam."

No. She couldn't believe it. It didn't make sense! "No. He couldn't have planned it! It's not like he handed me a sheet of papyrus to give you. Nothing like that! He was just drawing in the sand. He didn't tell me about it, I was the one who found it. He never tried to show me his drawing. He never even mentioned he'd been drawing. And on top of that, how would he know I'd go that way? I didn't even know it myself."

Her father stared at her. "He was drawing in the sand?"

She nodded.

He closed his eyes and shook his head. "He's not an artist. Artists don't doodle in the sand."

"He is!" She wrung her fingers.

"We need a craftsman's son. I'm surprised at you. Not a

69

simple-minded farm boy who's caught your fancy! We need someone from Thebes, the son of a jeweler, or a furniture-maker, a house-builder even. Someone who has at least a basic grasp of line and form!"

A basic grasp? Ramses had more then a basic grasp! Her mind ran back to the clearing, and the amazing vision that stretched across the sand. "If you only saw what I saw. His drawing looked real."

"Then he got lucky."

"That was not luck," she said. "Not even close."

He pressed his temples and groaned.

"If you don't believe me," she cried, "then think about this! What god have you been praying to? It was Ptah. He'd drawn Ptah!"

Her father grew very still.

"And when I looked down at the god's face, the god looked right back up at me. Like he'd been waiting. This strange bolt shot down my spine. It was as if Ptah was saying he'd heard your prayers. That he'd led me there. To find him."

Emotions crossed her father's face. Finally he made a frustrated noise. "You infuriate me. I'll admit, there's something intriguing about this. But calm down. There's no hurry. We'll see him when he comes to the exam."

"The thing is—" She fiddled with her dirty dress. "I don't know that he'll apply. I don't think he will. I don't think he'd even want to. He runs a farm."

Now her father threw up his arms. "For the love of the gods!"

"But he's the one. I just know it. We have to convince him. I have to go back there."

"Enough!" he roared. "If Ptah wants the boy, he'll find a way. There will be no more leaving the village."

She stared at the door in the fading light, and tried to muster a new argument.

"I could go with someone. With Jabari."

"The only place you're going is to Layla's," her father said.

"Layla's," she gasped. "That's not fair. You saw them out

there! You know what they'll do. Her and her mother are completely—"

"Yes," he said. "And they'll watch you like a jackal."

"But we need to find Ramses!"

He sighed. Deep worry lines cut into his face. The weight of the village, and worse, of Pharaoh, seemed to loom over him. She had to convince him. She knew Ptah had led her to Ramses for a reason.

"Just once, with the guards . . ."

"I've made my decision," he growled. "I won't hear of it again."

CHAPTER 17

Ramses stood for a long time on the riverbank, holding Neferet's amulet, watching the dust from her procession slowly disappear.

Soon, the grassy bank felt immense and empty.

Slipping the amulet's leather cord over his head, he tucked the slender piece of turquoise into Sepi's muddy tunic. He'd find her again. He had to. Kneeling, he marked the spot with stones, but then caught himself.

What was he thinking? That he could just take off when he wanted?

And what about when she learned the truth—that he wasn't who she thought? He was no longer the son of a prosperous farm owner. He lived like a servant. A servant who couldn't even afford the papyrus to enter her father's examination.

He'd led her on. But he hadn't meant to.

The hiss of a cobra brought him to life. He jumped back, searching for it amongst the stalks. The hiss came again. Heart slamming, he rotated around.

Two feet away, the cobra's hood rose from the ground like a muscled triangle of death.

Ramses took a slow step back, raising his hands in submission. The snake darted toward him. Its powerful body snapped side-to-side. Primal terror rooted Ramses to the spot.

Don't look, he thought, don't meet its eyes!

But the creature's gaze drew him in.

What he saw turned his sweat cold. This was no ordinary cobra. Its eyes were blue. As blue as if they'd been carved from the turquoise in Neferet's amulet.

All strength drained from Ramses' legs. There was no point in running. It was as if the old priest's tattoo had come to life; as if it had uncoiled and slithered here to deliver its message once again. This time with deadly consequences.

What he does is unholy! No god meant him to have that power.

Ramses knew for certain that he was in the presence of Meretseger—the snake goddess who protected the craftsmen of the Valley of the Kings.

Her pale throat flexed, and her forked tongue shot forward. But she made no move, only drilled into him with her eerie, turquoise eyes.

"Then kill me," Ramses said.

She snapped her tail.

"If I'm cursed, kill me."

Her tongue darted from her mouth. Her head nodded. Then she flicked away. Coiling back on herself, she turned and cut a path across the dry earth. She headed the way Neferet had gone. Back to the craftsmen's village.

Meretseger was following her people home.

Ramses sagged with relief. But it was relief mixed with despair. Was this some kind of warning? Why did his drawings always bring him trouble? The midday heat seared his nostrils. He jolted from his reverie and glanced skyward.

"I'm late!"

Snatching his sledge, he ran along the Nile.

He rounded a bend and spotted the barge. In a panic, he saw it move away from its moorings. The sledge bumped and jostled behind him. He sprinted harder. But he was too late. The barge was leaving. He'd never get the sacks.

Terror drove him flying across the sands. How would he explain being away all morning if he came home empty handed?

"Wait," Ramses shouted. "Wait!"

The big captain hauling in the ropes glanced his way.

"Stop! Stop, I need sacks!"

The big man ignored him. He swung himself on board and barked out an order. Rowers on both sides dipped their oars into the current. The barge surged away from shore.

"No!" Ramses let go of the sledge and threw himself into the water.

River birds rose, startled and squawking.

Something large brushed against his bare foot. Something enormous and rough skinned. Something that felt dangerously like a crocodile. He thrashed his arms and legs, desperate to get clear, struggling to propel himself across the swirling, murky surface to the safety of the boat.

"Rowers, halt!" the man ordered.

The rowers ceased rowing.

"Can't let this little water-rat drown." The captain reached over the side, got hold of Ramses and fished him out onto the deck.

Ramses coughed up water. "Saved my neck," he gasped.

"Next time, learn to swim."

"I can swim." Ramses pointed overboard as the croc surfaced. "I was talking about that."

The man threw back his head and laughed. "Serves you right for holding up my boat."

"I'd rather be crocodile-lunch than go home without some sacks."

"And I'd rather make you crocodile-lunch than turn my boat around."

"I'll pay you well!"

"Ha! I should throw you back in," he joked. "Men, row us ashore!"

The bow slid up on the sand. Ramses avoided the crew's angry stares and leapt down to grab his chickpeas and garlic to pay for the exchange. The captain took a few sacks from the stern. He tossed them down.

"You know I can't go back to my master with so few."

Shaking his head he said, "What was all that about paying me well?" He grabbed a second armful and threw them over the stern. "Tell your master he was lucky."

"Really lucky," Ramses said, grinning ear-to-ear.

The captain pushed off. "Never seen a boy so happy to buy wheat sacks," he growled, and hauled the ropes in. "All clear!"

The oars dug in and the boat moved off into the current.

Ramses checked to make sure Neferet's amulet was still safe. Then he tucked it back into Sepi's tunic.

He'd have to make sure never to let Aunt Zalika set her jealous eyes on it.

CHAPTER 18

During the drowsy hour after lunch, Ramses arrived back at the farm. In the fields, the workers rested in what shade they could find. The house was silent. His aunt and uncle were most likely snoring in his parents' room. He pulled the sledge across the courtyard and dragged it into the barn.

Ignoring the warning in his head, he stole to his old bedroom window. Raising the heavy curtain, he climbed inside. His eyes took a moment to adjust.

"Sepi?" he hissed, squinting in the dark room.

"Thank the gods. I was dying of boredom," Sepi called from the bed.

Ramses laughed, and then slapped a hand over his mouth.

"Open the window," Sepi whispered. "I can't breathe in here."

"Yeah, and I can't see." Ramses pulled back the curtain. Hot sunlight poured in. Flies, bright green in the light, buzzed through the opening. He struggled to keep his voice down. "You're not going to believe what happened!"

Sepi sat up. His heavy, elaborate neckpiece—as wide as Ramses' hand and sewn with hundreds, maybe thousands, of tiny jewels and gold beads—made him look even thinner and paler than usual. "Shh," he warned. "I think someone's in the hall."

Ramses grasped his cousin's narrow shoulders and whispered, "I met the daughter to the Scribe of the Place of Truth!"

"Great, very funny," Sepi hissed. "Now get out, someone's coming!"

"No one's coming. Everyone's asleep. And I'm not joking. She gave me this. Look!" Quickly he removed the amulet from around his neck and flashed it at his cousin.

Sepi's eyes widened. "What in the name of the . . ." He struggled upright. Two feverish spots colored his cheeks. "She gave you that?"

"So you believe me?"

"Let me see it." Before Ramses could protest, Sepi had it in his pale fingers. "A girl gave you this?"

"Yes. From the Place of Truth! Now give it back. I better go."

"She just handed it over? What did you say to her?"

"I saved her life," Ramses said.

Sepi rolled his eyes. "I'm sure you thought so, anyway. A girl really gave you this? Or are you pulling my leg because I'm bored and can't ever go out and meet girls?" He slipped it over his head and let it drop around his neck.

"Give it back."

Aunt Zalika's voice pierced the hallway. "Sepi, my little artist-to-be, have you taken your tonic?"

Sepi jolted at the sound. He grabbed the amulet's cord and tried to pull it off.

"Hurry up," Ramses said.

"I'm trying, it's stuck!"

"Sepi?" Aunt Zalika called.

"Yes!"

"I said, did you take your tonic?"

Ramses realized the amulet's cord was stuck on something behind Sepi's neck. He pushed his cousin forward. The cord was caught in the beadwork of Sepi's elaborate neckpiece.

"Why are you even wearing this ridiculous shirt?" Ramses whispered.

"Mother gave it to me, I like it," Sepi hissed. Then shouted, "Yes I took it!" He scowled at Ramses' filthy, mud-stained outfit. "Anyway, I see you've ruined my favorite tunic."

Ramses yanked harder. The amulet wouldn't come free.

Aunt Zalika's footsteps sounded outside the door. "What's going on in there?"

Sepi yanked the covers up to his chin. "Get out the window!"

The doorknob rattled.

"Get out!" Sepi mouthed.

Cursing, Ramses made for the window. He turned to see the amulet's thick leather cord peeking out above the covers. He flew to his cousin's side as Aunt Zalika struggled with the door. After stuffing the cord under, he launched himself at the windowsill, and tumbled over the edge.

From overhead, the acacia tree cast a tiny noonday shadow. He sensed a pair of watching eyes and looked up. Bastet crouched on a branch. The cat's yellow eyes met his.

In Sepi's room, Aunt Zalika sad, "It's too hot for all those covers, isn't it sweetness?"

Please no. Don't let her pull them off. Say something, Sepi! Stop her!

"Mother, when I need you I'll call you. Can't you see I'm resting?"

"You're so flushed! Be a pet and let me turn them down."

It's over now, he thought. She's going to find it. And what could Sepi say?

The slap of sandals on paving stones sounded from outside the barn. Someone let out a huge belch. Bastet shot up the branch. Ramses launched away from the wall, right into Uncle Hay.

"What are you doing, loitering around?" Uncle Hay asked in a sour voice.

"Uh . . . looking for you. I'm back. With your sacks."

"You just got back?" Uncle Hay said, suspicious.

"I was last in line."

"Well, you're lucky you missed lunch." He belched again, then rubbed his belly as if it pained him.

Lunch? Suddenly he was starving.

From Sepi's room, Aunt Zalika cried, "What's this?"

His hunger vanished as he pictured her holding his amulet like a prize. She'd probably think it belonged to Ramses' mother, and that Sepi somehow found it. The next time he'd see Neferet's gift would be around his aunt's ugly neck.

"Husband, where are you? Get in here, quickly!" she shouted.

"Coming, dear!" Uncle Hay turned his bloodshot eyes on Ramses. "Don't just stand there. Get to the fields!" Wiping the sweat from his greasy forehead, he trotted toward the house.

Ramses shot one last glance at his old window. He wanted to leap through. He imagined ripping his amulet from Aunt Zalika's fingers, and leaving this farm forever.

Instead, he turned and headed for the waiting stands of wheat.

CHAPTER 19

Ramses, furious, tried to focus on his work. He slashed at the wheat; how could he have been so stupid? Worse than stupid, a coward! Why hadn't he done something? Blood pulsed at his temples.

He should do something now. Go take what was his.

In the far distance, he could see Uncle Hay's plump silhouette. Perched high on the mound where the plough shed stood, Uncle Hay gestured at half a dozen field workers. It looked like he was giving them incredibly important instructions, from the way he postured around. What could he be doing over there?

Then Ramses saw a man paint a white streak down the plough shed's wall.

Unbelievable. The men were whitewashing the building's walls? Now? Could his uncle have chosen a more pointless exercise? He was a complete idiot!

They needed to be cutting wheat!

Shaking his head, Ramses got back to work. He didn't care about the shed. All he cared about was the amulet. The end of day gong rang out. Finally.

Consumed by thoughts of Neferet's gift, Ramses flung his scythe down, turned and ran for the house.

"Wait," Sobek called.

Against every fiber in his being, Ramses forced himself to slow down.

"How did it go?" Sobek said.

Ramses glanced at the farm manager, frowning.

"This morning?" Sobek said. "You did go draw, didn't you?"

"Oh, right." Ramses let out a huge breath. "Yes. Yes I did. Thank you."

"Is everything all right?"

"Fine. Sorry, I just . . . everything's great." He forced a big smile. "Thank you for getting me the morning off. It was great."

"Excellent." Sobek slapped him on the back.

They reached the sprawling courtyard. Next to the kitchen door, a pile of vegetable peelings showed where Hebony had been sitting. Flies buzzed around. A bundle of wilted herbs reminded him of Neferet's crushed reed basket. He cursed silently, thinking of her amulet around Aunt Zalika's neck.

A melody drifted from the kitchen; it was Hebony, humming a tune in time with the chopping of vegetables.

In a low voice, Sobek said, "I'm glad it went well. All we need now is papyrus."

Ramses nodded. But all he could think of was the priceless turquoise amulet of Maat. He couldn't go to the examination without it. It would be an insult, the worst he could imagine— to Neferet and to her father.

"This goose is like crocodile skin!" came the shriek of Aunt Zalika's voice, echoing down the hall from the dining room. "Inedible!"

In the kitchen, Ramses sat on the floor eating dinner with Hebony and Sobek. He gnawed on his own serving of goose, pretending to enjoy his dinner as Hebony looked up from her plate. He'd been chewing the same tough piece for several minutes and his jaw ached. He forced his bite down.

"Leave it," she said. "I'll fix you something else."

"No, no!" he and Sobek cried at once. It might be something worse.

A plate slammed in the dining room. "Ramses!" Aunt Zalika screamed.

Ramses' heart flip-flopped, Hebony jolted, and Sobek swore.

"Bread! Now!" she screamed. "Get your spoiled hide out here, your Uncle's fainting with hunger."

Hebony leapt up. She filled a basket to the brim with thick

pieces and passed them over. He was glad for the excuse to go in there. He'd been waiting all evening. Gritting his teeth, he made for the dining room.

This was it. She'd be wearing his amulet; he'd have to take it from her. He'd have to. He couldn't just stand there and watch her wearing it. He wouldn't.

His knuckles turned white as he clenched the basket and entered.

The family lounged on plush cushions around a low table with carved legs. A vase of blue cornflowers and yellow chrysanthemums from the garden brightened the room. As usual, Sepi colored at the sight of Ramses playing servant. He struggled up from his seat, slamming his knees and spilling a cup of wine.

"Sweetness, how many times do I have to tell you? Sit down!" Aunt Zalika said. "Now hurry up Ramses, we're trying to have a nice family dinner."

He turned slowly to face her, afraid of what he'd do when he saw the amulet around her wiry neck.

But it wasn't there.

So where was it?

Ramses shot Sepi a questioning look, but his cousin turned away.

"Don't just stand there," Uncle Hay said. "Bring the bread over!"

Ramses, stone-faced, stuck out his arm. Uncle Hay's pudgy fists raided the basket. He grabbed six hunks—three in each hand.

"Enough, Hay," Aunt Zalika said. "Your teeth are wearing away into ugly little stumps."

Ramses stifled a snort of laughter. For once, he felt glad it was impossible to sift sand out of ground wheat. It would serve Uncle Hay right if he got a toothache from all that gritty bread.

"Don't give me that grumpy face, boy," Uncle Hay said. "You act as if you're the only one doing any work around here. I'd like a little respect. I spent the whole day slaving to keep this place in shape." He glanced at Aunt Zalika. "It's hard work, this farm business," he said and tried to flex his flabby arms.

"You look ridiculous," Aunt Zalika said.

Uncle Hay's arms plopped against his sides.

Suddenly Sepi spoke in a harsh tone. "You haven't offered me bread, cousin." Everyone turned to stare. "Bring it. Now."

A smile curled the corners of Aunt Zalika's thin mouth. "Well then."

Ramses walked stiffly to Sepi's side.

"Lower," Sepi said. "Do you want me to stand? Don't you know I'm a cripple?"

"Of course I know," Ramses muttered.

"My darling is hungry?" Aunt Zalika asked with delight.

"I need to get strong for when my drawing tutor arrives, don't I?" Sepi took a slice. "Wait." He wiped his mouth with his napkin. "This is filthy," he said. "Bring me a new one." He shoved the napkin at Ramses.

"Don't stare at me. Go!"

CHAPTER 20

Seated on her cushion across the dining room table, Aunt Zalika laughed.

Ramses' arm shook with growing fury. His fingers tightened around the napkin. Then he felt something hard inside the folds of fabric. Something hard and small. He met his cousin's eyes, and for an instant Sepi's flickered with delight.

A warm feeling flooded Ramses chest. He should've known he could depend on Sepi to keep the amulet safe.

"Did you hear me?" Sepi asked.

"Well, well, listen to you!" Aunt Zalika said. "Looking so strong."

"Why are you waiting?" Sepi cried. "I want a clean one, now!"

Aunt Zalika smiled at Ramses in triumph.

Ramses bowed low. "Cousin," he said, watching his aunt's smile begin to fade. "I am so grateful for the opportunity to bring you a fresh one. More bread, Uncle?"

Aunt Zalika snatched the basket. "No, now get out!"

"As you wish."

He darted into the hall and pumped his fist in triumph.

Happiness surged through him as he unfolded the napkin and touched Neferet's amulet. At the sight of the goddess's face, he remembered Neferet grinning with her mud-stained cheeks. He could still hear her laugh, could still see her bright eyes.

He just had to get to that exam.

He just had to win.

Suddenly he knew practicing in the sand wasn't good

enough. He'd have to find a better way. His thoughts drifted to the freshly whitewashed shed. Maybe Uncle Hay's undertaking wasn't completely useless after all. He had a great idea.

Until he tried it, he wasn't sure it would work. For now, he decided to keep it to himself. He tucked the amulet into his tunic and started down the passage. He could still hardly believe it was safe! When Hebony and Sobek asked what he was grinning about, Ramses opened his mouth, unsure what to say.

"He's happy because we're ahead in the harvest," Sobek said.

"Yes, I'm definitely glad about that," Ramses said, relieved he could speak true.

Hebony seemed contented Ramses didn't say it was because of the apprenticeship.

Darkness had long since fallen when he was finally able to leave the kitchen. He made his way across the courtyard and shoved open the door to the old animal stall that was his windowless cell. As usual, the smell of manure lingered like a curse. That, combined with the still sour smell of his rushes, made him groan.

He hurried inside, tripped over something, and landed in a sprawl.

"Ow!" came a voice. "That was my leg."

"Sepi?" Ramses whispered. "What are you doing in here?"

"That's how you greet your best friend?" Sepi said. "Some host you are."

Ramses grinned. "Shh, you'll get us both in trouble."

"Don't be such a scaredy-cat." Sepi flopped back on the straw. "You might think about changing this stuff once in awhile. Or does it always smell like this?"

Ramses gave up and reached for his lamp. "Look, you can't stay here!" He lit it, using the oil he'd managed to save up—which wasn't much. The walls flickered and bobbed to life.

On the straw, Sepi crossed his thin arms behind his head. "So let me get this straight," he said. "The girl who gave you that amulet—what's her name?"

"Neferet."

"Yes, Neferet. Her father's the most important man in the Place of Truth, right?"

"So?"

"So, problem solved. Get the papyrus from her. She must have piles of it."

"I can't."

"Why not?"

"Just—" Ramses rubbed his forehead. "Forget it. It's too hard to explain."

"Why?"

He grabbed a fistful of straw and groaned. "Only because I let her think I'm some rich farmer who goes around in gilt-edged kilts. That's all. Nothing major."

"Oh. I see. Not good."

Ramses rolled his eyes. "Great. That makes me feel a lot better." He let the straw drift to the floor. "You know what? What if I'm wrong? I bet I'm wrong. I bet she's not like that. I bet she wouldn't care. I'm going to find her. I'm going to find her and tell her the truth!"

"Whoa! Whoa, whoa," Sepi said. "Stop! Are you crazy?"

"What?"

"You can't tell her that!"

"Do you think?"

"Of course I think. Come on, she's daughter to the Scribe of the Place of Truth. You can't tell her. Ever!"

"Ever? What if I get in?"

"Deal with that later. Right now, don't even think about it."

"Well then how am I supposed to—"

"Hold on." Sepi straightened up, staring at the muddy object draped across a battered wooden chest. "Is that my tunic?"

"Um . . . yeah?"

"Please say you're lying. That isn't really my favorite tunic? Is it?"

"Yes . . . yeah. Sorry."

Sepi looked skyward. "Tell me you had good reason for this abuse."

"It made a great rope?"

"It what?"

"Listen." Ramses yanked open the lid of his trunk, "I can't talk now! I have to go." He pulled out his secret collection of lamp wicks. There were five: at an hour each, they'd give him five hours of lamplight.

"Where? It's the middle of the night."

Ramses bundled up the wicks and jar of lamp oil, blew out the lamp and wrapped that up too. "To work on my design. Out on the plough shed."

"On some shed? How do you draw on a shed?"

"Charcoal from the stove. The building is freshly whitewashed. I have to go."

"I get the picture, I'm leaving. But don't be an idiot." Sepi grabbed Ramses arm. "Don't forget to be back before the farm wakes up."

"Do you think I'm crazy?"

"Definitely."

CHAPTER 21

Ramses waited until Sepi had safely returned to the house. Then, carrying his bundled lamp and oil jar, he headed for the outdoor stove.

The night seemed strangely silent.

All he needed were a few pieces of charcoal and he'd be gone. He crept past the window to his aunt and uncle's room. It was dark. They were asleep.

Almost there.

His big toe slammed into a rock. His foot exploded with pain as Hebony's grain-grinding stone clattered across the paving tiles, loud enough to wake the underworld. Strangling a curse, he pressed his bundle to his chest and froze.

Aunt Zalika must have heard!

Overhead, heavy palm leaves shushed together, moved by a sudden gust. It died away. The hum of insects rose in one long note and then fell silent.

Several minutes passed. No lights came on in the house.

He exhaled and tiptoed the last few steps. Easing open the oven door, he winced at its low whine. Reaching inside, he flicked some charcoal pieces forward, avoiding the still glowing coals.

Almost there, he just had to wrap them in his bundle and—

A light flared in Aunt Zalika's room.

Ramses' breath caught. He scooped up everything and slouched in the stove's shadow.

The kitchen door opened. Aunt Zalika stepped outside.

"Sobek!" she barked. "Get this monster out of my house."

Bastet shot out the door.

Aunt Zalika raised her fist at its retreating tail. "Next time, I'll kill it!"

Kill a sacred pet of the gods? She wouldn't dare!

The bundle shifted in his arms and the clay lamp threatened to topple free. He clutched it against his thighs. Her light pooled at her feet. One glance to her right and she'd see him.

"Sobek!" she said.

A door slammed.

"On my way," Sobek said in a weary tone.

A beetle tickled Ramses' foot. He clenched his jaw as it crawled up his ankle.

Sobek crossed from his sleeping quarters, sandals slapping. His face grew visible as Aunt Zalika raised her lamp; as she did, the farm manager's eyes strayed to Ramses' hiding place. For a heartbeat, his stride slowed. Sobek coughed and quickly turned to Aunt Zalika.

"Where's the cat?" he asked her.

"You're too late. But look what it did to my arm." Three long red scratches glistened from elbow to wrist.

"Go inside. I'll find honey for those wounds."

"Humph," she said, but let him turn her around.

To Ramses' relief, the two disappeared into the house.

A red moon brushed the horizon and began its slow climb. Ramses tore across the fields. In the distance, the plow shed looked like a small, shadowy cube. Its walls glowed faint crimson in the moonlight.

The dirt felt hot and soft against his bare feet. Behind him, the inky cluster of buildings dozed in silence, while he alone was awake and free.

He slowed and began to whistle a tune.

Something rustled in the rows of wheat. The tune died on his lips.

Was someone following him?

A spitting hiss sounded low against the earth. Barely two paces away lay the terrifyingly familiar sight.

The blue-eyed cobra had tracked him down. It was as if she were watching him. As if she knew what he planned to do. As if she were furious that her last warning hadn't stopped him. This time, she was livid. She rose, hissing and flaring her hood. She bared her teeth and shot toward him.

He shouted, stumbled on the rutted ground, and fell.

Charcoal scattered everywhere.

Nerves on fire, he braced for the strike. Scrambling to his elbows, he prepared to make a crazed sprint.

The snake was inches from his face.

Blood pulsed into his head, constricting his vision.

Do not even swallow.

The snake began to sway. Her forked tongue flickered between her fangs.

Mesmerized, he stared into her blue gaze.

"Meretseger," he whispered, calling the cobra-goddess by her name.

At the sound, the cobra grew larger, swelling as if the goddess herself had come to earth and slid into the creature's jeweled scales.

Ramses' hair prickled in terror. His damp limbs shook and his teeth chattered. Sweat stood out in beads on his face. He knew now he'd never make it back to the house alive.

He truly was cursed. The gods had given him his talent, but by using it, he'd earned their disapproval.

And now, deciding to take this exam, he'd gone too far.

CHAPTER 22

The cobra held Ramses' gaze.

He set his jaw in defiance. "Kill me or let me pass."

She swayed, her eyes challenging his, locked on as if it were a deadly game.

He wouldn't back down. Not now. He'd never asked for the talent to draw! If the gods wanted him to stop, she'd have to kill him.

She continued to sway and her hiss grew louder, swelling like the buzz of a thousand bees. The wheat stalks shook. His jaw and bones began to vibrate. He balled his fists against the shaking.

He would not turn away. She couldn't make him.

Grinding his jaw, he shut his eyes.

He still saw the goddess; her image burned through his lids.

A smoky light shot from her. It swirled into him, streaming downward, moving and twisting into his chest. It coiled around his heart. Tighter and tighter it squeezed until he could barely breath, until his head spun.

"Stop!" he shouted.

He opened his eyes, but saw only swirling light.

Like an intruder, it felt as if she'd crawled right inside his soul—was seeing the images of his life past, was seeing Neferet's face through his eyes and laughing at him, was searching for the source of his talent, searching for treasures worth stealing.

"Stop!" Ramses shouted again.

The light crystallized into a million points, and fell in a shower of blinding sparks.

He found himself face-to-face with the cobra. Huge now, her jeweled scales glistened with a glow of their own.

It was over. He waited for her to rear back and strike.

Instead, she sank to the ground.

Her halo-like light disappeared. For a moment, he wondered if fear had made him imagine the whole thing.

The snake, back to normal size, shot him a mocking glance. With a flick of her tail that reminded him of Bastet, she slithered over his foot, into the wheat stalks and was gone.

Shaken, Ramses waited for his heart to stop pounding.

What did Meretseger want with him? Had that been a test—or a warning?

Again his frustration rose. He felt the familiar, awful confusion. He was a farmer, but he loved drawing. His parents were dead, but he owed it to them to try and get the farm back, to take control of his inheritance. That much he knew. So what was he doing out here? There were no easy answers. He wished the gods would simply come right out and tell him what to do, but it didn't work like that.

Swallowing his frustration and unease, he gathered his charcoal, his lamp and his jar of oil. He resumed his trek, but as he walked, the moonlight made the world look strangely different. The stalks seemed taller and, instead of cut wheat, the earth smelled of exotic, fragrant flowers. His stomach clenched as he passed a boulder he didn't recognize. Where was he?

He wandered, lost, before finally spotting the building. Baffled, he corrected his course.

Finally, he reached the mound. The air lay silent and dead as a tomb.

Above him, instead of the simple building his father had built to keep the plows dry during the Nile inundation, the shed rose like a great monument. It was the moonlight, he told himself, that's all.

Still, something had changed. He sensed that the boy who'd stood before the cobra was no longer. He was different now. He shrugged off the frightening thought.

"Don't be an idiot," he said out loud. Shouldering his bundle, he climbed to the top and unpacked his lamp. He was here to work, and that's what he'd do.

Quickly, he cracked his flint. A moment later, a circle of yellow light sprang up. The strange night fell away, forgotten. All that existed in front of him was the wall.

It was time to focus.

The moon rose higher. Ramses was still staring at the wall. It was completely blank.

He was stumped. For the first time in his life, he had no idea what to draw.

It wasn't just a matter of drawing. Like Sobek said, it was drawing the right thing—the thing the examiners wanted. And how could he know what they wanted? A scene or a simple figure? Human or a god? Maybe a specific figure? Was it too simple to present an image of one god, of Ptah, for example, the way he'd drawn him on the riverbank?

Maybe he should draw a big battle, showing Pharaoh conquering his enemies. Ramses was good at carts and horses. He ground his flint against his charcoal, sharpening it to a smaller and smaller point.

What would the other boys draw? Maybe they'd all be ten times better. Maybe he was fooling himself, thinking he was better than he was. How could he know? The only people who said he could draw well were farmers like his parents and Sobek. And one priest. But what did they know of drawing?

He had a horrible flash of arriving at the Place of Truth and being laughed at. What if they told him his drawings were amateurish? What if they told him he was a stupid fool, a farmer who didn't belong and never would? Maybe that's why Meretseger warned him off, to save him from himself.

His flint nicked his finger. He looked down to see he'd sharpened the charcoal away to nothing. He threw it down and picked up another piece. He wouldn't spend all night going in circles. He wouldn't spend all night agonizing over things he didn't know.

He just needed to draw something. Now, on this wall.

He stuck the charcoal to the surface. Pressing hard, he drew a firm line. His eyes widened at the sight. He'd been afraid, unsure of how the charcoal would react on the whitewash.

It worked. It really worked.

The line stood out a deep black against the smooth plaster. It was nothing like drawing in the dirt. When he did that, the earth bulged up as he pressed down. That was the nature of dirt. When you grooved down into it with a stick, the displaced material had to go somewhere.

But this—this was beauty itself! He stared, mesmerized by his one single mark.

He drew a second line, then another; why had he ever bothered with sand? Why hadn't he thought of this years ago? It was so clean. So crisp. So vivid! A new world was opening up before him, right here on his father's shed.

A magnificent image almost leapt from his fingers. It was of Pharaoh Tutankhamen, charging into battle against his enemies. Pharaoh rode in his wheeled chariot; Ramses felt as if he stood shoulder to shoulder beside him. He felt the wind in his hair, heard the groan of chariot wheels; tasted the salty sweat of fear in his mouth as the battle lines closed in, the two fronts preparing to clash.

Pharaoh held a great bow in his outstretched arm, an arrow ready to fly; he leaned forward, eyes narrowing at the approaching foe. Egypt's great king urged his horses onward; the animals pounded ahead, fearless, their royal plumed headdresses fanning out.

Eyes on the forward flank, Pharaoh shouted, threaten Egypt at your peril!

Behind him, Egypt's forces followed swiftly at his back.

Overhead, the sky darkened with gods. They came one-by-one, flying above the king. Whether to protect him or simply witness the battle, Ramses didn't know.

CHAPTER 23

Neferet sat on a stone in front of the Place of Truth. The vaulting sky was strangely dark, although she was fairly certain it was midday.

Beside her stood fourteen grim-faced craftsmen, shoulder to shoulder, all in a row. Silent as soldiers, the group guarded the village gates behind them. She glanced back and saw that the entrance was barred shut.

To her left, something moved. She squinted to see. A body, long and sinuous, crawled along the edge of the village wall. She recoiled in horror—inching closer, jaws dripping, came a monstrous crocodile.

A servant of the Underworld, here?

Shaken, she shook the man next to her, but he brushed her fingers off. She tore her eyes away from his face to see what held his attention. Directly ahead, boys were marching toward them. An endless line of them had sprung up out of nothing. The boys stretched out across the desert, winding away over the dunes, each carrying a sheet of papyrus.

The closest one approached.

Neferet's father stepped forward. He reached for the boy's scroll. When his fingers wrapped around it, the boy's papyrus turned to dust.

He frowned.

A second boy arrived, and then a third. Yet, each time was the same. The scroll dissolved, rained to the ground in a shudder of sand.

Finally, only one applicant remained. The boy stepped

forward. He lifted his head to look at her father, and Neferet gasped. He was not a boy, he was a jackal. The jackal began to howl. From the distance came the roar of chariots.

Her father turned and spoke to her. "It's Pharaoh. He's coming."

Neferet jerked awake in a cold sweat, blood pounding in her ears. It was a dream. It was just a dream.

She pulled her covers to her chin and tried to push the images away. Her thoughts strayed to Ramses. Was it possible he'd gone back there to look for her?

What if he'd gone there and waited? Or, what if—what if he'd gone there and left a note? Her heart fluttered. That's what he'd probably done. Left a note to tell her when he'd be there!

Well, she could do the same. Even if she couldn't meet him. Not with the way Layla's mother watched her all day. But right now? Right now the whole world was asleep. And she could bring a note to the river and leave it for him to find.

Neferet pressed her ear to the wall and listened for her father's snores. Sure enough, the plaster vibrated in a slow, steady hum. Pulling on her kilt, she hurried downstairs to her father's writing supplies. Quietly, she slid a piece of hard ostraca from a basket. Her father had mountains of the white, limestone shards—more than he'd ever use for his record-keeping. He'd never miss this one.

And anyway, never—in his wildest dreams—would he think she took it. He knew she hated writing.

She did hate it, until this minute. Suddenly it seemed like a useful skill. Nearly a form of magic, in fact. How else could one speak to another person without actually being there?

She found a brush and chewed thoughtfully on the end.

Maybe Ramses had forgotten her already. He probably knew lots of girls.

She raised her chin—well, it's not like she was obsessed with him either. She just had to explain why she hadn't come, for her own sake. It was the right thing to do.

The overstuffed floor cushions were thick and comfortable.

She hugged the ostraca to her chest and sank back against the wall, remembering how he'd pulled her out of that trap. With his tunic! Who would think of using their tunic? A giggle escaped her—she could still see his face when he asked her for it back.

He'd been so calm and collected about it all. That's what she liked best.

What was he doing right now? Sleeping in his comfortable bed?

Outside, beyond the narrow window of her father's writing room, the moon hovered over the village rooftops. If he looked up wherever he was, they'd see it together.

She rolled her eyes, feeling silly. Time to write. But what?

The low howl of a jackal came from somewhere outside. Neferet's skin prickled. It sounded like the jackal from her dream. Her giddiness drained away. She'd never crossed the desert at night before, let alone by herself. Did she really have the courage to do it?

For some reason, the drawing of Ptah flashed in her mind. She remembered the god's mischievous eyes, the way he'd looked at her. This was about more than just seeing Ramses again. She had to do it for her father's sake. For the sake of the village.

The risk of Ramses not coming to the examination was too high. As a rich farmer, he had no reason to apply as an apprentice. Drawing was probably just a personal hobby. They'd sat together on the riverbank, and he hadn't even mentioned it. Clearly, he had no idea the level of his skill. They needed him in the Place of Truth. That's why Ptah brought them together. How much clearer could it be? If only she could get Ramses here, the craftsmen could make him understand.

She dipped the brush in the ink.

Ramses,

I hoped to see you again, but I am unable to leave my village. Please look for me at the gates to the Place of Truth on examination day. I will wait for you.

Neferet

That had to be enough, for it was getting late. Writing it had taken too much time already. She had to go.

Silent as a cat, she slipped outside. Darkness, thick and black, enveloped the alley. A shiver slid down her spine. She'd be all right. She could find her way. She'd get there, leave the note, and sprint home before anyone noticed her missing.

On tiptoe, she ran down the steps.

A huge figure lunged at her, growling. He caught hold of her thin shoulders.

She stifled a scream.

CHAPTER 24

A gain?" Jabari said in a low whisper. "You're the most stubborn thing I've ever met. And where to this time?"

"Nowhere!"

Deftly, the sentry swiped the ostraca from her hand. "What's this, a note?"

She scowled in the dark. "Give it back!"

"For your young noble, I presume?"

"Don't be mean, Jabari."

"Mean?"

"Oh, please, let me go."

"Where?" Jabari gestured down the eerie alley toward the village's outer walls. "To fight the lions alone?"

She took a chance. "Not if you'll go with me."

He chuckled. "I see all reason has flown out the window?"

"It's not like that," she whispered hotly. "Will you help me or not?"

"Help you do what, my little friend? What are you trying to do?"

She tried to swipe back her ostraca. "I'm trying to get him to come here! To take the exam."

"Indeed?"

"You saw his drawing. Oh, I can't explain it right now—I have to go. Will you help me? Just say yes!"

"You could never keep up," he said.

She caught her breath. "So you'll do it? Go with me?"

"No. I'll go alone. And don't try to follow me, little one, or I swear, I'll—"

A crash exploded next to them. Jabari pulled Neferet sideways. A second roof tile slammed into the paving stones. She looked up and caught the silhouette of a girl on the roof above. Layla's roof.

The silhouette quickly vanished, but not before Neferet heard Layla's low, tinkling laugh.

Windows of homes on either side of the narrow street flickered to life. A moment later, Layla's mother opened her front door. At the same time, Neferet's father opened his.

"What's going on?" they demanded at once.

Neferet slid the ostraca from Jabari's palm.

"Good morning, sir," Jabari said, addressing Neferet's father.

"By the gods, is Neferet running out at night?" Layla's mother said. Her tone was all too familiar, and it made Neferet's stomach churn.

"I'll handle this," Neferet's father said.

Layla's mother hitched up her robe and bustled over to Neferet. "Have you no modesty, child? What's the hour?"

"I said, I'll handle this," Neferet's father said.

She raised her lamp and shone it on Neferet. "What's that you're holding?" She stepped closer, grabbing her wrist from behind her back. "Is that a message?"

"Of course not."

"Is that what you're doing? Delivering love notes in the middle of the night?"

Jabari stepped forward. "Sir? I believe the ostraca belongs to you. We found it on the street a moment ago."

Neferet's father hesitated, but only for a moment. "Yes. You're right. I must've dropped it earlier. Thank you."

"Don't be silly!" Layla's mother said. "I know it's not yours, Nakht!"

Neferet's father glowered at her. "Are you calling me a liar?"

They faced each other down.

"Well?" her father demanded.

Layla's mother waved like a chicken fluttering its wings. "Then what was she doing out here in the dark? Layla doesn't go out at night! She sleeps in her room like a well brought up young lady."

"If my daughter wishes to stand on our front steps for air, she'll do so."

Layla's mother's mouth worked, but no words came out.

"Now good night," he said. "And thank you, Jabari."

Neferet followed him inside.

He walked silently to the room where he kept his writing tools. There, he sat heavily on a cushion, held Neferet's note up to the lamplight, and scanned its contents.

Standing in the doorway, Neferet's cheeks colored.

"Where were you planning to leave this?" he demanded. "Were you going to the river? Alone?"

She gulped. "Father, we have to find him."

His face reddened. He spoke, barely controlling his anger. "We discussed this already. I gave you my answer."

"But—"

"The exam is not your business." Cords stood out on his neck. "Stop meddling!" He crushed the ostraca in his fist. "Leave me. Now."

He bent his head and began sorting through the towering stacks of papyrus and official documents on his table.

She bit her lip. "I'm sorry," she said softly.

He suddenly looked so tired. She felt a tiny hum of fear. He never looked tired—not like this. She noticed gray hair spreading at his temples. When had that started? And his shoulders, had they always been so rounded?

He couldn't grow old! Not yet!

Why did the village have to hang every problem around his neck? It wasn't his fault Paneb left. Or that they had no boys to take his place.

Even if her father was Chief Scribe, it wasn't fair. She couldn't remember the last time he took a day to relax. Like the other craftsmen, he was supposed to partake in the weekly three-day rest. But here he was, like always, under a pile of official business: letters and records of work completed in the tomb;

making accounts of all the stuff everyone spent so much time ordering—fabric, wigs, and perfumed oils, ink, brushes, gold, jewels, chisels and mallets. It all had to be reported; royal favor was to be enjoyed, not abused.

And tomorrow, when the three rest days were over, he'd be right alongside the others—trekking up to the Great Place to continue work on Pharaoh's tomb.

A small part of her would be happy to have him give up his post to Layla's father, and to become a simple craftsman. But he would never stand for it. And Layla's father frightened Neferet. He drank too much beer, and dealt with his problems by shouting. Under his rule, the village would be a dark, unhappy place.

"I'll bring you something to eat," she said, and went to the kitchen.

Lighting the stove, she raised her chin.

It didn't matter she had to go to Layla's today. It didn't matter Layla's mother would make things worse than ever. She wouldn't beg to be allowed to stay home. She wouldn't complain.

They would get through this frightening time.

They just had to.

CHAPTER 25

There is a moment between darkness and dawn when the temperature drops to its lowest. The sky turns from black to gray. Stars wink and disappear. Birds stir in their nests and crickets hum. Ra, the sun god, peeks over the edge of the earth and burns through the foggy mysteries, sending mist swirling upward to disappear like wraiths.

Ramses blinked at his drawings as if rousing himself from a strange dream. A vast mural covered the white wall. His fingers ached. He frowned and glanced eastward.

A pale line across the horizon announced the arrival of morning.

Morning!

Cursing, he snatched up his things and ran. The whole house would be awake and buzzing by now. Aunt Zalika would be demanding to know where he went. What would he say? How could he have left it so late? He could almost hear Sepi saying I warned you to get back on time.

Sprinting faster, his heart slammed in his chest. He flew headlong through towering stalks, over wastelands of harvested crop. The sharply cut stubble jabbed the soles of his feet. A rock slammed his big toe, tripping him. His lamp and charcoal flew from his arms. He scooped them up and kept going.

Fresh horror struck.

His drawings. He'd planned to wash his drawings off the wall! Idiot! How could he have forgotten? He nearly turned back. His stomach churned with indecision.

No. There wasn't time. He made for the kitchen.

"Ramses," Hebony whispered as he reached the door. She yanked him inside, took his bundle and threw it into an empty jar. "You've been out all night?"

He nodded, gasping, bent forward with his hands on his knees. "Do they know I wasn't here?"

"I told Zalika you were cleaning the new tutor's bedroom."

"Thank you," he gasped, relief flooding over him. "I better get in there and start doing it."

"I did it already," she said. "When I saw the cold stove, I realized you hadn't stoked it this morning. I went looking for you. Your room was empty."

He couldn't meet her eye. "I had something to do."

To his surprise, her voice caught in her throat and she sounded tearful. She said, "I thought . . . I thought you'd gone for good."

Glancing up, he saw such fondness in her face that his own heart clenched.

"You can't get rid of me that easy," he said.

"Come here," she said and wrapped him in a hug. When she let go, she dashed a tear from her cheek. "I'm on your side. I want you to know that."

"Then you know I have to take the exam."

Her face stiffened.

Morning light flooded the kitchen in warm orange hues. The air smelled of cinnamon and flour. Even with Hebony looking angrily at him, it felt safe here, as if he stayed in this room, nothing bad could happen. But he knew that wasn't possible.

Hebony said, "Do you remember the old priest who came here? The Wab Sekhmet?"

He nodded.

"It wasn't his first visit. He came after your naming day ceremony. You were four. Your mother told me to hide you. While you played in here, I snuck out to listen."

"What did he say?"

" He was outraged. Furious about the drawings you made at the temple. Of course, we all knew your skill was no ordinary thing for a child, but for him to come here? I think he was frightened. He warned your parents to put a stop to it."

"Why didn't they tell me?" Ramses said.

"Because they disagreed. Your mother—"

"Hebony!" Aunt Zalika yelled. "Where's breakfast? We're starving out here."

"My mother what? What did my mother think? She never stopped me from doing it!"

"Later, or we'll both be in trouble." Hebony quickly filled a dish with dried figs. This she set on a tray alongside a pot of wheat porridge and a bowl of honey.

"Please, Hebony!" But the moment had disappeared, and he knew he'd get nothing more out of her. He reached for the tray. "I'll take that out there."

"I don't think so. Unless you want to tell your aunt you slept in the stove?"

He frowned at her, confused. She grabbed his elbow and lifted it. His fingers, his hand, his forearm, all were smeared black with charcoal. He thought of his habit of rubbing his face. Despite everything, he grinned. "I bet she'd like it."

Hebony rolled her eyes. "Don't give her any ideas. Anyway, you'd better get to work. Sobek and the others are in the west field. Take some bread, that'll have to do you until lunch." She headed for the door.

"Wait," he said quickly, "What did my mother say? Please, I have to know."

"I've forgotten. And I'm frightened. Something terrible is unraveling. A curse. I feel it."

The door shut behind her. He stood there, alone, unable to remember how this house had ever felt like home.

Leaving the bread untouched on the table, he headed for the west field.

The farm workers moved in the steady rhythm that came from generations of training. For them, it was just another year in a long line of years. Nothing had changed and nothing ever would. The harvest would end. A new season would begin.

Not for Ramses. That comfortable world no longer held a place for him. No matter how hard he wished, he couldn't find a way back in.

Sobek greeted him with a broad smile. "Don't tell the men— but we're making good headway. We've cut a lot."

"We're going to be able to make your share?"

"Long as we keep going like this, we're safe," Sobek replied.

Ramses nodded. They just had to keep up, and Aunt Zalika wouldn't kick Sobek and Hebony out. "Thank the gods."

Ramses headed for the section indicated by the farm manager and began to work at a steady pace. Despite staying awake all night, he felt wound up. The morning sun seared his back. It promised to be a scorcher.

"Sobek!" Uncle Hay called from the house. "Come here. Bring Ramses. Now."

Uh oh. Fear prickled over Ramses. Hay must have seen the shed.

A short distance away, Sobek shot Ramses a puzzled look.

Ramses swallowed, but said nothing.

Sobek headed over. "I wonder what your uncle wants?" Cupping his hands, he shouted to the other workers. "Keep moving. We clear this section by midday."

All the exhaustion of the sleepless night dropped on Ramses like a weight.

Uncle Hay tapped his sandaled foot as he and Sobek approached. He didn't look angry. He looked triumphant.

"Sobek, you're in the kitchen today," Uncle Hay said, fists resting on his bulging hips.

Sobek bristled. "You want me to cook?"

Everyone knew about Sobek's skills in the kitchen. His father had been a cook in a wealthy household. Sobek had learned to bake light, airy cakes and rich fig puddings. He could roast a duck to perfection, with crisp golden skin and tender meat that made your stomach rumble.

"Zalika's orders." Hay smiled, as if he'd won some longed for prize. "She's paying Sepi's new tutor to teach, not to die from

Hebony's cooking."

Sobek winced.

Hebony tried hard, Ramses thought, glaring at Hay. Maybe she wasn't the greatest cook, but she kept the farm prosperous through her skilled account keeping.

Sobek said, "Do you want to lose the harvest? I'm not your personal chef."

"Oho! Getting a bit big for your tunic there, aren't you? I don't think my workmen out there will notice one less person."

Sobek wasn't 'one person', he was the farm manager. Ramses' mouth gaped. Was Uncle Hay a complete idiot? He wasn't just the manager, either; Sobek was built like an ox. Everyone knew he cut more wheat in an hour than the rest cut in a day. And what about Sobek's share, and Zalika's threat? How could he meet her demands unless he worked in the field?

"Your workers are good men," Sobek told Hay. "But with no master and what little you pay them, they'll be snoring in the shade by noon."

"Your self-importance is getting on my nerves," Hay said.

"The harvest needs all hands. Walk the fields and see."

"Looks to me like the men are doing fine."

"Right now. Yes. But when they're finished that section, then what?"

"Anyone with eyes knows what to do."

"It's not that simple!" Sobek said.

"I know what you're thinking, you don't want to come inside and do real work. Where you have to answer for your time."

Clearly there was no way to make Uncle Hay understand.

Sobek's hands tightened, and his rough cheeks colored. He looked ready to explode. The two men faced each other. Ramses could almost hear the scarab beetle scuttling across the earth at his feet.

If Uncle Hay was unaware of the power behind Sobek's fists, he was dangerously close to finding out.

CHAPTER 26

A hot breeze stirred. Ramses watched Uncle Hay and Sobek face off.

Finally, Sobek let out a disgusted snort.

Without a word, he turned and strode for the kitchen.

Uncle Hay grinned. "As for you, scrunge-brains, your aunt wants you to clean the tutor's bedroom."

"It was cleaned this morning!"

"She found dust on the windowsill."

Then tell her to dust it off! Ramses wanted to shout.

But like Sobek, he could say nothing; only do as he was told.

The morning wore on. The sound of scrubbing and the smell of Sobek's cooking made a mockery of the farm. It hadn't been enough to wipe the non-existent dust off the sill. Aunt Zalika had ordered the walls washed. She'd come in to oversee Ramses' work, and now stood at the window.

"It's about time he brought that bed," she said.

Bed? What bed? What was she talking about?

Ramses craned to glance past her narrow shoulders. Outside on the drive came a ragged boy dragging a carved-frame bed on a sledge. As if sensing them watching, the boy glanced up. To Ramses' surprise, the delivery boy's eyes were wild with excitement.

Aunt Zalika shouted, "You're late. I paid for morning delivery."

The boy ignored her scolding. He dropped the sledge and waved his arms. "Lady! Come quick!"

"How rude," she muttered, then, shouting, "What is it?"

"You have to come!"

Clearly Aunt Zalika didn't enjoy being ordered around, especially by a furniture maker's servant. But her curiosity must have gotten the better of her. "Stay here," she told Ramses, and hurried outside.

When Aunt Zalika reached the boy, he started babbling and gesturing with his arms. Ramses strained to hear, but was only able to catch snatches of words. Then the boy pointed across the fields—straight in the direction of the painted shed.

Ramses felt dizzy.

His aunt's cheeks turned crimson.

He had to hear what the boy was saying! Tearing through the house, he reached the dining room window and hid behind the curtain.

"I'm telling you," the boy said, "it's a huge crowd. They're gathered around that old building in the field."

Ramses broke out in a sweat.

"On my property?"

Flea-dung! How could he have been so stupid? Why hadn't he washed the drawings off?

"What are they doing there?" she demanded.

"Like I said, I saw them from the road. It was pretty obvious something terrible happened. I bet I know what it is." The boy lowered his voice. "I bet it's a dead body!"

"A dead body? Someone left a dead body here? How dare they?"

He heard her run off, heels clacking.

"But where do you want this bed?" the boy called.

Ramses clenched his fists. Should he go after her? He had to stop her. But how? Horrified, he sped outside.

"Hey!" the delivery-boy said, cutting in front. He latched onto Ramses' arm.

"Let go. What do you want?"

"Don't go talking all high and mighty at me!" the boy said, eyeing Ramses' grimy fingernails and tattered kilt. "Help me move this bed."

"Move it yourself. Third door on the left." He started after Aunt Zalika.

"I can't do it myself. It'll bang up the walls. And I'll blame you for it."

Ramses let out an angry breath. He ran to the sledge and started unlashing it.

Sepi stuck his head out of his window. Dark circles ringed his eyes. Grinning, he said, "What's the big excitement?"

"By the gods, Sepi." Ramses threw down the ropes and pressed his hands into his eye sockets. Again, he remembered his cousin's warning when they'd sat together in Ramses' cell. "She found out."

"My mother?" Sepi's smile faded. "About last night, you mean? How?"

"I'm so dead."

The two friends stared at each other.

"Don't tell me you actually left it all covered with . . ."

Ramses nodded.

"Covered with what?" the delivery boy cried. "What are you talking about?"

"Well don't just stand there," Sepi said. "Stop her!"

Ramses bolted. He tore across the fields.

Ahead, a huge crowd had gathered. Men from the neighboring fields stood in clumps, all talking at once. He recognized Kontar, a gruff man who owned the next farm over. Ramses crept up and hid behind his back.

The members of his own crew posed up on top of the mound next to the building, looking important. And beside them, staring at the wall and gritting her teeth, stood Aunt Zalika.

The paintings looked larger than he'd remembered. Many times larger. In fact, they were huge.

Kontar whispered, "It's amazing."

"Who do you think made it?" the farmer beside him asked.

A third said, "I never did see something so real. Makes my hair stand on end, it does."

Kontar said, "I saw Pharaoh on the river once. That looks just like him."

"Maybe one of Pharaoh's artists made the thing, you know, just passing through like. And he needed to keep his skills in order?"

"Are you gogglers deaf?" shouted Aunt Zalika. Her face was purple. "I said leave!"

Kontar sighed. He called out. "I don't understand, my lady. What's the harm?"

A man who'd been chewing straw pulled it from his mouth and shouted, "Bet you didn't even know this old shed was here."

This got a laugh from the others.

"Enough. It's my land!"

"It may be your land, Zalika," a second man said, "But this is a miracle. I'm a simple man, I lead a simple life. And I never seen something so beautiful. I want my wife to see it. And my children. This is a gift of the gods."

"Gift of the gods?" Her eyes flashed. "This is vandalism!"

The straw-chewing man said, "It's drawn in charcoal. Don't like it? Wash it off."

"I don't like you talking to me. I don't like your face. I don't like you trespassing!" She snatched up a scythe and advanced on him, the blade singing.

The man shoved backward. Others did the same.

Ramses found himself suddenly exposed.

Aunt Zalika froze. "You," she hissed, tightening her fingers around the blade handle.

Everyone turned to stare at Ramses.

"You mean—" Kontar shot him a look. "You drew this, boy?"

Here was his only chance. He stepped forward and started to speak.

CHAPTER 27

Aunt Zalika plunged downhill toward Ramses. He backed away and quickly appealed to the crowd.

"It's true, they're mine," Ramses told them. "I'm practicing for the—"

She seized his neck. "Him, draw this? Don't be fools!"

"For the exam," he managed. "At the Place of—"

She clamped her fingers over his mouth and smiled. "What a joker he is."

Ramses' own field crew frowned. Over the years, they'd seen his drawings in the sand, and they looked doubtful at her words. For a moment, he felt sure they'd defend him.

A man opened his mouth. He glanced at Zalika. All that came out was, "Better get back to my work."

One by one, the others began to leave. Meanwhile, the men from the surrounding fields started to laugh, Kontar along with them.

"Very funny!" one shouted. "He really had me!"

"Yeah," shouted another, "Him? Draw this? And I'm a prince of Egypt."

Zalika smiled.

Ramses struggled. "Please," he begged Kontar. "You have to help me!"

"Boy, this is between you and your mistress."

The crowd dispersed, shaking heads, smirking.

"You there," Aunt Zalika shouted at one of their last departing crew-members.

The man—Kepi was his name—tensed.

"Fetch me a bucket of water. And be quick about it."

"Yes, ma'am," Kepi said, relief clear in his voice.

When he returned, Aunt Zalika said, "Don't look so sullen, I don't bite. Now splash it on the wall!"

Kepi sent out a drenching spray. Pharaoh Tutankhamen and the legion of gods slid into confusion.

"At least one person knows their duty. You may go back to work."

Kepi hurried off, leaving Ramses to face Aunt Zalika alone.

A vein bulged at her temple. "No one makes a fool of me on my farm."

He dodged as she kicked the heavy bucket at him. To his surprise, she doubled over in pain and grabbed her sandaled foot. Her face was white and her lips were peeled back. She sucked her breath in and out and clutched her toes. She appeared to be seeing stars.

Finally, she let out a yowl. "I've broken it! Ow, my foot! This is your fault! You'll pay for this, river scum," she gasped. "Help me back to the house."

Ramses was surprised at the weight of her sagging body. Aunt Zalika's perfume couldn't mask the rank sweat that dribbled from her armpit onto his shoulder and down his chest.

She recovered as soon as they reached the barn.

Shaking him off, she loped inside. She reappeared, holding a whip, and wearing a jackal's grin.

"Hands on that rock," she ordered. "This time, I'll fix you for good."

He glared at her.

Aunt Zalika cracked the whip across his neck. "Hands on the rock!"

The lash caught him across the neck a second time. Ramses staggered forward. Aunt Zalika forced him to kneel and open his hands.

For an instant, Ramses stared down at them. Then the lash came down and tore away a layer of flesh. He couldn't breathe; his chest froze in a gasp. Down the lash came again, and a third time, flaying the skin from his palms. With a shout, he pulled his hands away. The lash tore into his knuckles. He saw blood, and saw the lash rise again.

Huge fingers closed around Aunt Zalika's forearm.

"Enough!" Sobek said. "You'll make the boy useless. There's work to be done."

Aunt Zalika's face twisted into a sneer. "Of course. Anyway, I think he's learned his lesson, right Ramses?"

In answer, Ramses retched at her feet.

Sobek led him the roundabout way to the kitchen.

"We'll fix you up good as new," Sobek said.

Ramses nodded, staggering along, his limbs damp and shaky.

"I'm sorry, my friend," Sobek said.

"I was stupid," Ramses managed. He opened his fingers. The sight was shocking. "But I'll live."

Sobek grunted. To Ramses' surprise, a tear shone on Sobek's rough cheek. A moment later, the scorching air shriveled it away.

In the kitchen, Hebony was busy cleaning flour from a table. Half a dozen neat loaves of bread stood ready for baking. When she saw Ramses, her face paled. She rushed to his side.

"What have they done?" She pulled him close and let out a smothered sob. "By the gods, your precious hands!"

Ramses didn't dare look at the mess of torn flesh. Somehow he thought that if he didn't see it, he could imagine it wasn't as bad. She quickly went to work, her face a stony mask. Cleaning supplies came out. Towels were dipped in warm water. Soon the horrible sight was hidden under pure white bandages.

"Better get going," Sobek told Ramses. "Zalika will be looking for you."

"To the field?" Hebony said. "He can't work like that."

"Sure I can." Ramses held up his throbbing hands. "Good as new."

CHAPTER 28

Ramses was proud of his scythe. It was shaped like a donkey's lower jaw. Instead of teeth, it had serrated flint glued tightly into the grooves. The scythe cut wheat with ease. Workers eyed it with jealousy, claiming it was too heavy for him.

He ignored them. He wouldn't part with it for all of Pharaoh's gold. It had belonged to his father, and besides, the weight made his back strong.

Today however, its weight bit into his bandages. He grunted, trying different handholds. Each seemed more useless than the last. The linen wrappings sprouted red, wet stains. As the hours passed, the swelling grew unbearable.

Sobek appeared, holding a dripping cup. "Drink this."

The liquid tasted bitter. He drained it and handed back the cup, now blood smeared.

Sobek took Ramses scythe. He gestured with it at a shady spot. "Take a rest. Cooking's done. I'll take over."

"What about Aunt Zalika?"

"She went to the harbor with Hay to meet the boat from Memphis. Sepi's drawing tutor comes today."

Ramses brightened at the news, but his head pounded too hard to do it real justice. Under any other situation, he'd argue with Sobek. He didn't want anyone doing his work. Now, he was thankful for a moment of rest. He headed for the shade, sank down and closed his eyes.

The end-of-day gong woke him. He pushed to his knees and winced at a splitting sensation in his palms. Fresh blood surged through the dried bandages. His tongue felt thick and dry. He needed water. Desperately.

A neatly cut section showed where Sobek had been, but the big man must have returned to the house. Ramses decided it was time he did the same. He licked his lips and stumbled back.

Beneath the roof's eaves, four fat water jars sweated in the shadows. He shook as he poured himself a cup and brought it to his lips. Before the cool drink wet his throat, Uncle Hay appeared and dashed it to the ground.

"No resting until you're finished. And you're not finished."

Ramses stared at the water, soaking into the dirt.

From somewhere down the drive came the crunch of footsteps, accompanied by soft laughter. Aunt Zalika rounded the corner, talking. Beside her walked a dark-haired man, impeccably dressed and smiling.

Ramses forgot his thirst.

The famous drawing tutor was here. Right in his courtyard! Until now, he'd been an imaginary thing. But seeing him made it suddenly real. A professional all the way from Pharaoh's white-walled city of Memphis. His formal kilt had an amazing number of pleats. He carried a satchel made of leopard-skin, along with a matching tube-shaped container that must contain drawing scrolls. They lent him a worldly air unlike anything Ramses had seen.

Aunt Zalika swept her hand wide. "Welcome to our humble home."

Ramses followed the man's gaze, trying to imagine it through a stranger's eyes—the large house with its promise of private, shady rooms; the precious front door made of wood, which his parents' had been so proud of; in front of it, the tiled courtyard, edged with green cultivated herbs. Overhead, date trees heavy with fruit swayed slowly. Then there was the lily-strewn pond he'd loved to splash in when he was small. And still, there was more. The servant's sleeping quarters. And beyond that, the barn.

"I am impressed, my lady." The tutor pointed out a cluster of clay pots. Rings shone on every finger. "I see you enjoy flowers."

"Flowers?" Her eyes found Hebony's colorful blooms. "Oh yes, I love to putter around out here."

At this, Ramses snorted.

"Come inside," she said. "Let me show you your room."

Uncle Hay gave Ramses a shake. "Stop gawking." He held up a mallet. "For you."

When Ramses didn't move, Uncle Hay swung it at his shins. Ramses jumped back and caught it.

Furious, he wrenched it from his uncle's fingers. "You want me to do what with this?"

"Get out there and get rid of the shed!"

"You want me to tear down a building. By myself?"

From inside, Aunt Zalika and the tutor's laughter rang out.

"Please," Ramses said, suddenly too exhausted to fight. "Tell me you're joking."

Uncle Hay picked at a spot on his tunic of what appeared to be spilled stew. The smell of roasting meat drifted from the kitchen. Angrily he said, "It's your fault, and you know it! So don't stare at me with your big round eyes. Get going."

Ramses tried to think. "What about the ploughs? That's where they're kept when the harvest is over." He knew he was grasping at straws. "Where are you going to store them?"

"Ask Sobek. That's his job, not mine."

"But—"

"Beat it," Hay said, not looking at him.

Ramses reached for the cup. "Okay. I'll go. Just let me have a drink."

Uncle Hay snatched it first. "When you're done." He took the cup with him into the house.

A window shade rustled.

He caught sight of Sepi's pale face. Ramses turned away. But not before he registered the rage in his cousin's eyes.

Night had long since fallen over the farm. Plaster and dust exploded as the building grudgingly surrendered to Ramses' assault. Each mallet stroke tore at his hands. He'd managed to pull down a small section, but that had taken hours.

He'd never finish by morning.

Something touched Ramses shoulder. He spun around, hefting the mallet high.

"Whoa, it's me!" Sepi shouted.

"By the gods, I almost cracked your skull in two!"

"Well that wouldn't have been much of a hello."

"What are you doing out here?" He'd never seen his cousin so far from his sickbed. How had he made it here, by himself, in the dark?

CHAPTER 29

Insects hummed in the night fields, their harmonies both soft and sharp.

Sepi wore a grin from ear-to-ear. He wheezed as he set a large basket on the ground. Then he wiped his brow and stared up at the sky. "Would you look at that? The stars are mind-boggling, there are so many of them."

Ramses shoved the basket's linen cover aside and rummaged through its contents. He grabbed a sweating jar of water, tore off the lid and gulped it down.

"Sepi, you're a champion." The scent of roast duck wafted up and he unwrapped the meat and took a huge mouthful. He groaned. It was delicious. The fact Sepi had carried all this seriously impressed him. There was a ton of food. It couldn't have been easy. He stuffed his mouth so fast he had to gasp for air between bites.

"Wow, remind me not to get my fingers in the way," Sepi said.

Ramses swallowed the last bite, sank back, and drew a long, slow breath. "That deserves a reward. If I had one, I'd give it to you."

"Oh, before I forget." Sepi pulled a small container from his pocket. "Hebony sent this. You're supposed to rub it on your cuts."

Ramses opened the lid. There it is. Hebony's cure all. This stuff stinks."

"Phew," Sepi said, covering his nose. "That stuff stinks."

Ramses grinned. "Yep. Hebony's cure all. Stinks, but works."

He unwound the bandages and gooped the paste on without looking too closely. He was glad of the dark. The paste felt cool and slimy. The coolness eased the pain; he sighed with relief. Sepi leaned against the wall while Ramses rewound everything.

"So how's that new tutor?" Ramses said.

"Ha! I wondered how long you'd take to ask."

"And?"

"Well, he's . . . different."

"What does that mean?"

"Apparently I'm his first 'un-famous' student." Sepi rolled his eyes.

"Well, he is from Memphis. What's his name?"

"Weris—anyway," Sepi said with a frown, "this drawing business is ridiculous, embarrassing. Like I want to be an artist? My mother knows I want to be a scribe."

They sat together in silence, staring up at the stars.

"It's too bad you couldn't take my place," Sepi said. "At least you'd appreciate it."

"Maybe I can't be there but—"

"What are thinking?"

"If you took notes, you could give me some tips?" Ramses said in a hopeful voice.

"Groan!" Sepi grinned. "Not a bad idea. But then I'll actually have to pay attention!"

Ramses nodded. "For just two weeks."

"I might die of boredom in two weeks. But I'll do it."

Energized by the promise, Ramses whooped.

Sepi stuck a piece of grass between his teeth. "Speaking of boredom, this place will be a lot different when you take off to be the big apprentice at the Place of Truth."

It was the first time Ramses actually considered going away for real. His cousin was looking at him and Ramses tried to lighten the mood. "Like it would ever happen. What chance do I have, honestly?"

Sepi ignored the question. "You better visit me at least once a year."

"I really doubt I'm going to get in. So don't even talk like that."

"You'll be too important to visit a lowly person like me." Sepi laughed. His voice was joking, but his eyes looked serious.

"No, I won't. You're my best friend. Whether I get in or not, I'll be here all the time."

But he realized it was a lie. His life would change. Everything would change. And Sepi would become part of his past.

"Listen to me," Ramses said. "No matter what, even if I do win this crazy position, you and I will always be best friends."

Sepi shoved the empty water jar back in the basket.

"We'll swear on it. Right now," Ramses said.

Sepi straightened, then nodded.

"Best friends forever. Agreed?" Ramses said.

They took hold of one another's forearm.

"Agreed," Sepi said.

Hours later, after Sepi left, Ramses had managed to reduce most of the building's west wall to rubble. Half of the roof had caved in some time ago. Exhausted he hammered at it, his swings haphazard, his arms numb.

His eyes drooped. He snapped them open and rubbed his face on his forearm.

A faint scent of jasmine floated on the air. He blinked. Night blooming jasmine, his mother's favorite. In the far corner of the shed, the moon revealed a large bush that had somehow grown up inside. He picked a bloom, sat down, and closed his eyes.

He needed to rest.

Just for a moment.

His head nodded back. The bloom fell from his fingers. He drifted off, dreaming he lay in his mother's arms.

A large hand grabbed Ramses' ankle and shook it.

"Hey-ho! Morning sleepyhead," came the voice of Sobek.

Ramses opened one eye, squinting in the sunlight. "What time is it?"

"Late."

"Flea-dung," Ramses muttered, clambering to his feet. He glanced around. "What the . . ." The mound was empty. All that remained of the shed was a neat pile of dirt and bricks. "Where's the building?"

Sobek held up his dusty palms.

"You did it? Alone?"

"I might be getting old, but you don't have to look so amazed."

"Without waking me up?" Ramses said.

Sobek grinned. "Magic. Of course, you being dead to the world helped a bit." His grin disappeared. "It's time I got back to the house, and you out to the fields. We've fallen behind again. If the harvest continues at this pace, we're going to be in serious trouble. You need to light a fire under the men."

Ramses nodded. "I know. But how? They won't listen. Not to me."

"Make them," Sobek said. "Hebony and I are depending on you."

CHAPTER 30

The Place of Truth churned with excitement. All around Neferet, examination fever gripped the villagers. Craftsmen talked about the new apprentice as if he'd already been found; mothers bickered over whose daughter was most in need of a husband; girls giggled at the prospect of so many boys crowding their front gates. And every person had been appointed a duty to prepare.

Whenever Neferet ran into Tui, the old painter gave Neferet a secret salute: he'd swirl his hand to acknowledge that she'd set this whirlwind in motion. She'd smile back, but fear would still grip her stomach. She'd remember her dream, see the monster with his dripping jaws just waiting for them all to fail.

The world seemed oblivious to her worries.

At dinner last night, even her father had seemed happier. For the first time in ages he'd actually laughed out loud, recalling a story of the day. His laughter was infectious. She'd gone to bed giggling.

It will be fine, she reassured herself now.

It was mid-morning. Neferet sat in the front room of Layla's house, crowded in with a dozen girls. They were assembled on the floor with a giant rectangle of fabric stretched between them. When complete, the fabric would form the final wall section for the judge's tent. The girls' fingers moved quickly, hemming its edges.

Sunshine blazed through the narrow window vents, slashing their faces and shoulders with light.

Neferet worked one corner of the linen in silence. As the

others sewed, their conversation buzzed with excitement.

"Have you decided what you're wearing?" a girl named Kiki asked Layla in a breathless tone. From the looks on the other girls' faces, it was obvious they'd all been dying to ask her the same question.

"Maybe," Layla answered with a smirk.

"Is it true you're having a new wig made?" asked another. "A short one?"

"You'll see," Layla replied in a singsong voice.

Neferet rolled her eyes. As usual, none of the girls could make a single fashion decision without knowing what Layla was wearing first.

Layla caught Neferet's eye-roll and made an exaggerated sad face. "Look at poor Neferet," she said, "Doesn't she look funny sitting here sewing with us? I hardly recognize her without her dirty face!"

All the girls tittered. Neferet stabbed her needle through the coarse fabric.

"Know why her face gets so filthy?" Layla said. "Because even after studying herbs for five years, she still has to stick her nose in the dirt to figure out which is which."

The girls laughed out loud.

Layla smiled. "It's pathetic. The only reason the physician chose her is because her father's Chief Scribe. He forced her to."

Neferet stopped sewing. "That's a lie."

Layla laughed. "I bet Merit throws away everything you bring her. I bet they all turn out to be useless weeds."

Neferet took another stitch. She had to ignore her. She couldn't let Layla goad her into an argument.

"I used to feel sorry for you," Layla said. "All alone, with no mother."

Neferet's hands began to tremble. "Shut up, Layla."

The others held the banner's hem, watching.

"Listen to you, shut up, Layla. You sound like you're five."

Neferet set her jaw. Even when they'd been friends, Layla had been cruel. She'd known just how to hurt her. But this time she wouldn't let her. It didn't matter what the backbiter said. Neferet pulled on her needle; it was stuck.

"Maybe it's a good thing your mother died."

The banner slid from Neferet's fingers. "Oh really."

"Yes. Don't you think girls?"

No one spoke.

"And why is that?" Neferet said.

"Why? I think it's pretty obvious. So she didn't have to see what a pathetic excuse for a daughter you are."

Neferet lunged.

But she only made it halfway. Before she could get her hands around Layla's throat, she found the sheet rising underfoot. From all four sides, the girls pulled it tight. They yanked upward as if pulling a carpet from the floor.

And Neferet flew into the air.

She flew so high, she hit the ceiling with a thump. In a shower of dust, she tumbled back down. The fabric held her, but only for a moment. Then, with a great ripping sound, it tore down the middle. She landed on her back, arms and legs askew.

Stunned, she stayed there, breathing hard.

The front door opened. "Neferet?"

Every head turned. It was Merit, the physician. Cheeks flushed as girls rushed to help Neferet.

Layla reached her first. "You poor thing, you're so clumsy."

"I'm fine." Neferet pulled her arm free.

When Merit spoke, it sounded as if she'd been running. "I don't know what you girls are doing. Right now I don't care. Neferet, the herbs for Tui? Can you find more?"

"I know where some are growing, I saw them the other day."

"Thank the gods. Quick, I have a sentry outside to take you."

"Has something happened?" Layla asked.

Merit shot her a withering glance. "It's none of your business. But the men brought Tui from the Valley of the Kings on a stretcher."

"Can I help?" Layla said.

"Only Neferet can help him now." She put her arm around

Neferet and bundled her out the door.

Outside, Neferet expected to see Jabari waiting. Instead, a man with heavy jowls and eyes smudged with dark circles met her with a curt nod. Inwardly, she groaned. It was Denger, Jabari's younger brother, who usually kept guard at the gates.

"I just have to grab my basket," she said.

Not for the first time she wondered how two brothers could be so different. Unlike Jabari, something about Denger made her uncomfortable. But that was silly. He was a guard. He was sworn to protect her.

Together they hurried out into the baking desert.

Soon, the village shrank in the distance.

CHAPTER 31

Neferet walked in silence, mentally ticking off the landmarks she used to navigate the desert: a flat, star-shaped rock, a scrubby outcrop whose roots must have found water far below, the mountain's pointy afternoon shadow.

"Where are these herbs?" Denger demanded, wiping sweat from his brow. "The physician ordered me to bring you back in an hour."

"Almost there, just over this hillock. See, down there."

"Go ahead. I'll wait."

With her basket over one arm, she slid down the hot sandy slope to the shaded oasis of scrubby plants. Above, the guard looked east, shielding his eyes from the sun. He stiffened.

"What is it?" Neferet called up to him.

"There's a donkey with no rider," he said. He sounded torn, as if wondering whether to stay with her or go investigate.

"Go ahead."

He shot her a wary glance. Clearly, he expected her to run off.

"I'll be here."

"Better be," Denger said. "I don't want to get in trouble because of a silly girl like you." He headed off.

Neferet crouched amongst the foliage. She worked rapidly, plucking the best specimens as Merit had trained her to do.

Denger had no reason to worry. She wasn't going anywhere, not without a full basket. And then she'd head home, as fast as she could. Hearing Tui had to be carried home had been a shock. She thought about his bright smile and his funny hand signal. Tears sprang up and she brushed them away.

"Hello," a voice said.

Neferet jolted upright. A tall boy stood inches from her toes. Oily strands of hair framed his high cheekbones. His eyes took in her own, and she knew the fear a rabbit felt with a jackal at its heels. Stepping back, she pressed her fists into her sides to hide their shaking.

"How dare you come up on me like that?" she demanded.

"Don't run!" He lunged and snared her by the wrist. "I want to talk to you. I saw you come out of the Place of Truth."

"Let go of my arm, you're hurting me," she said.

He loosened his grip but didn't let go. "Do you know anything about this examination? Or are you a servant?"

Neferet kicked at his shins; he dodged sideways. She tried to wrestle free, but he had a wiry strength and he pulled her down hard beside him so that they both landed on the scorched earth. His fingers pressed into her arm. His face was inches from hers. His eyes were dark and intense. For a minute she was terrified he was going to try and kiss her. Instead, he yanked her into a sitting position.

"Well, are you a servant or not?" he demanded.

"Of course I'm not," she spat. "We don't have servants in our village—it isn't Thebes. We do our own work."

"So you are someone then." He grinned. "In that case, I didn't mean to push you down."

"Let go of my arm!"

The boy's grin widened. "Don't look like that. I said I was sorry didn't I? Anyway, I need your help."

Neferet laughed. "That's your problem."

A flare of anger shone behind the veil of his dark eyes. "What, are you too good to help a stranger?"

She scowled. "What help do you need?"

"I hear you're expecting hundreds of applicants for this examination your Chief Scribe is holding. All I want is a chance to present him with my work first. Today."

"He'd never see you."

"He would if he saw my work. And he'd realize there's no need for this silly examination."

"What, are you worried about failing?"

"Don't be daft." His eyes fastened on to hers; they were dark and amused. "Let me finish talking, girl."

Neferet glanced uphill. Where was that sentry when she needed him?

"I merely want to make sure I get my chance, that's all. I know how these things work—the Chief Scribe will stop when he comes to the first one that pleases him, and the 'exam' will be over."

Neferet snorted. "If that's what you think, then come early. I can't help you."

"Don't you think it would be better if we started out as friends?" He reached into his tunic and pulled out a scroll of papyrus. "Take this."

Neferet turned away. She could hear him unrolling it.

"Look, girl. See that I'm no fool."

She tried not to look, but he grabbed her chin and forced her face around. Whatever he'd drawn, she was determined to hate it.

To her disgust, instead, she felt a grudging awe.

His drawing was gruesome, but powerful. He'd sketched out in gory detail the myth of Seth and Osiris: jealous Seth stood over what remained of his brother Osiris after having hacked him to pieces.

Neferet gulped. What if this horrible boy was chosen instead of Ramses?

Her untrained eye was uncertain—could this boy be better?

"You have no idea how gifted I am, but your Chief Scribe will. I'm exceptional." He rolled up the papyrus. "Take it. I'll come to the village gates tomorrow to wait for your message. My name's Akil. What's yours?"

"None of your business. And don't bother."

Akil's pupils constricted. "You don't know who you're dealing with."

"Yes, I do. A stuck-up fool."

He laughed. "Oh yes. I am stuck-up. You know why? Because that apprenticeship is mine."

"I think not."

A gleam came into his face. "Do you believe in curses?"

She laughed, but her throat was dry.

"You know, one can learn many useful arts in the alleys of Thebes. And I'm not talking about drawing."

The sun beat hot upon her head.

"Tell me this. Did an apprentice run away from here? Is that why there's room, so to speak?" He watched her face and smiled. "I thought so. And now a craftsman is sick. Isn't that right? Isn't that why you're picking these?"

"That's none of your business!"

"It's more than my business." He tore a handful of plants from Neferet's basket and crushed them until green juices ran down his wrist. "It's my doing."

Sweat trickled down her ribs. "That's impossible."

"Oh, you'll believe me when your craftsman starts to recover. I'll lift the curse as soon as the Chief Scribe agrees to see my drawings."

"Where are you, girl?" Denger shouted, "Are you done? Neferet!"

"Here!" she cried. "Hurry! Over here!"

"Neferet." Akil said her name as if, like a sorcerer, he'd gained power over her by knowing it. "I'll be back tomorrow. Don't forget."

"You can come every day. I won't help you."

Akil squeezed her arm. "I like you, Neferet. So for your sake, please just do as I say." A searing pain shot from his fingers. It felt like he'd lit her on fire.

She fell back, gasping, as he tossed his papyrus into her basket. Rubbing her wrist, she watched him lope away at a run. When Denger reached the top of the hill, Akil was just a shadow in the distance.

"What's going on?" the sentry asked.

"Nothing, forget it."

"Girls," he spat. "Then hurry up." Sour-faced, he turned his back and assumed a post toward the village.

Her legs shook. Could Akil really have that kind of power? Her wrist throbbed but showed no real injury beyond a slight redness. Before she climbed the hill, she took the boy's papyrus from her basket; the container seemed soiled by its presence. After quickly tearing his drawing to shreds, she buried them under a clump of dirt.

For once, she felt glad the guard was with her. All the way home, she sensed eyes watching. Akil would be back; that she knew.

She only prayed fate would not carry him through the village gates and into her life.

CHAPTER 32

"Wake up!" Ramses told the farmhand sleeping behind a pile of cuttings. "It's not lunch."

The man buried his face in his elbow. "Call me when it is," came his muffled voice.

The day was hot. Stifling. Dust hung in the air, rising to the sky in a soft brown haze. In the distance, the mountains hugged the horizon like the clouds of an approaching sandstorm.

"Fine," Ramses said. "But just so you know, Sobek's on his way."

The farmhand leapt up. "Well why didn't you say so?" With scythe in hand, he elbowed past Ramses and marched off to attack the wheat.

Ramses grinned. He might not have Sobek's muscle, but according to the reaction of the last five workers, the threat worked almost as well. Still, it would only work so long—he needed to steal Sobek from the kitchen and get him out here.

He edged around the field and made for the house. The baked earth soon gave way to the soft, wet ground that bordered the pond. Geese rustled inside the barn. The acacia tree drooped over the house's southern wall; it cast lacy shadows across the paving stones.

"Ramses!" Sepi called from his window.

Ramses drew up short, his eyes peeled for Aunt Zalika. "Shhh!"

"Come here, come meet my tutor!"

"Not so loud!" Ramses whispered.

"Who are you talking to, young man?" asked a deep voice

inside.

Sepi turned. "My cousin, you need to meet him. He's an artist."

"Is he now? Tell him to come in."

"I can't come in there," Ramses whispered. "Your parents will kill me!"

"They're at the tailor. Mother says Father's old clothes are embarrassing. They won't be back until dinner."

"Now you tell me? I'll be right there. I just need a minute."

"Hurry."

Nervous energy surged through him at the thought of meeting Weris. Mind buzzing, he slammed into the kitchen. Hebony knelt over a bucket of laundry, scrubbing at it with a clump of cleaning natron. Beside her, Bastet cleaned her whiskers with a regal twitch of her paw.

Hebony jolted upright. "Oh, I wasn't expecting you!" she said in a funny voice.

"Didn't mean to scare you."

"Not at all!" She dazzled him with one of the biggest smiles he'd ever seen.

"Um, is Sobek here?"

"He's in the cellar."

"Great, thanks—"

"Stop, I'll get him! Wait here." She turned and ran off shouting, "Sobek!"

Ramses stared after her, baffled. Not that Hebony didn't get excited. But this was odd. It sounded like she was dancing down the cellar steps. When she reappeared with Sobek they were whispering, and Sobek wore a lopsided smile.

"What's going on?" Ramses said.

"You tell him." Hebony said.

"No you."

Ramses cut in. "You're killing me. Come on!"

"It's your story," Sobek said to her.

"Oh all right . . . but you're so much better at telling stories. Anyway, here goes. Well, this morning, I snuck away to Thebes, and . . ." She glanced at Sobek and giggled. "I don't think I can tell it, I'm too excited."

"You went to Thebes," Ramses said. "And then what?"

Sobek snorted with laughter. "Forget the story. Just show him."

"That's an excellent idea. Are your hands clean?" Hebony asked Ramses, but didn't wait to hear. She grabbed a blade, crouched and shoved the pile of laundry clear. Then she did something extraordinary—using the blade, she started to pry up one of the large floor tiles. "Keep an eye on the door, husband."

"I've got you covered."

Ramses was at her side in a flash. "What in the name of upper Egypt?" Although the tile fit seamlessly into the floor, this one had edges much smoother than the rest.

"Let me help." Ramses took hold of the blade and pried the stone high enough to get his fingers underneath. The flat stone scraped as it slid across the others. A hole as deep as a man's forearm appeared. In it lay two bundles wrapped in coarse linen. One was tubular, the other round and lumpy.

Hebony lifted out the tubular one. "It's the only one I could get."

"The only . . ." And then he knew. Papyrus. But it couldn't be. She'd snuck into Thebes to get him papyrus? His mouth was dry. "But I thought you said—"

"Forget what I said." Her gaze flicked to his bandages. "You deserve the same chance as every boy in Egypt."

"Open it," Sobek said. "Let's have a look!"

"There's only one sheet," she warned.

"That's plenty! I only need one. Show me, I don't want to mess it up."

Her slender fingers shook as they unwrapped the bundle. Together they bent close. The pristine sheet couldn't have been worth more if it were made of solid gold.

Ramses' heart hammered. "It's a miracle."

"There's also a brush, a cake of ink, and one of those

burnishing stones they use to smooth down the papyrus. At least, that's what I'm told it's for. You know how to use these things, right?"

"Sepi's used it before, he can show me . . ." He broke off, looking at his two friends, suddenly overwhelmed. "I never would've been able to get this. Never. Thank you."

"Just seeing that smile makes it all worthwhile," she said.

"Tell Ramses how you got it," Sobek urged.

"Was it hard?" Ramses asked.

"Hard? The whole of Egypt wants this apprenticeship. They've stripped the papyrus vendors bare. And you're asking me if it was hard? I almost gave up. But then a miracle happened. A little girl appeared and offered to help me."

"Who wouldn't want to help my lovely wife?" Sobek said.

Hebony blushed, laughing. "Well, she was the funniest thing, tiny and dirty faced, but wearing a feather in her braids. You know, the way some people do to honor the goddess Maat."

Maat? Ramses shivered, feeling the amulet at his waist. Just a coincidence.

"What did the girl say to you?" he asked.

"Not much!" Hebony replied, laughing. "We'd barely exchanged two words when she grabbed my hand and took off running.

CHAPTER 33

Hebony told Ramses about how the girl led her across the noisy boat landing. Ramses could just picture the crowded water-steps. The city's streets overflowed with people going this way and that, and vendors selling everything one could imagine.

Apparently the girl dragged her down alleys, through maze after maze of streets.

"By the time she pulled me through a crumbling temple door," Hebony said, "I was completely lost. She ordered me to kneel before a blind old beggar. I did as she told me. The man touched my cheek, and asked my name. Then he blessed me and put these two packages into my hands."

"He was happy to find a buyer," Ramses said.

"Yes, that's what I thought. But then he refused my six pieces of deben."

"You're sure it wasn't a misunderstanding?" Sobek asked.

Hebony frowned, as if going it over again in her mind. "I don't know. Anyway, I left the coins on the ground. I wanted to pay the girl but she'd disappeared." Hebony laughed. "I would've paid well to get back out. It took forever!"

A gust of wind sent the door slamming open. All three of them glanced outside. Hebony quickly resealed the supplies beneath the stone.

"The workers," Ramses said. "I left them alone in the field!"

"Is everything all right out there?" Sobek said.

"Yes—except I need a favor." Ramses explained the situation. The farm manager grinned and cracked his knuckles. "I'd be happy to."

"Could I catch up?" Ramses said. "Sepi invited me to meet his tutor."

At the mention of Weris, Hebony wrinkled her nose.

"What's wrong?" he asked her.

She gestured at the enormous pile of laundry. "See that? The man has changed his clothes five times since yesterday. Five times! And he wants fresh bed linens every evening. My skin's going to dissolve if he keeps this up."

"Maybe he doesn't know the trouble he's making. Maybe he has a lot of servants back home?"

"Not even Pharaoh, may he live forever, has that many servants," Sobek joked. He was grinning as if the prospect of an errand to visit the field crew was the best thing that had happened in days. "See you out there."

Hot sunlight burst into the room and disappeared again as the door banged shut.

"I'm off, too," Ramses said.

A moment later, he stood alone in the dark, silent hall.

The air outside Sepi's door was stifling. For a moment, he wished he could forget meeting the famous tutor. His chest felt tight; he took a deep breath.

It was stupid to be nervous. Right now, he was the luckiest boy in Egypt. He was about to meet a highly skilled artist who knew exactly how to win the apprenticeship.

Quietly, he nudged open the door. Inside, the curtains were half drawn. Sepi sat at the desk. In one hand he held a brush, in the other, a pottery shard. He was trying hard to paint something on it. The tip of his tongue jutted from the corner of his mouth and his pale cheeks were flushed and damp.

Weris sat at his elbow, murmuring encouragement in a low, cultured voice.

"Let the brush become an extension of your mind. You're not writing a letter here! Let the image flow. There you go, you have it." He looked like he could be one of Pharaoh's own advisors. As if to confirm his scholarly rank, a jeweled neckpiece patterned with papyrus reeds glittered across his broad shoulders.

Meeting Weris, having this chance to learn from a master, was more important than anything Ramses could imagine.

Ramses was suddenly aware of how grimy his legs and arms must look. He glanced down at his kilt. Even in the shadows, he could see that the fabric was the color of dirt. Of course, that's what came of working hard. But he wanted Weris to think of him as an artist, not a farmer. This was no way to make a first impression; Weris would never take him seriously, let alone trust him to hold a paintbrush.

He should come back later. When he was clean.

He decided to bolt.

Just as he pulled the door closed, the tutor snapped around. "Hello?"

He squinted at Ramses, whose face was now the only thing visible. The man's irises were of the palest gold. "What are you doing, hiding there behind the door? Come in."

"I'll come back when you're not busy."

"Busy? We've been waiting for you."

"Yes. Get in here," Sepi said.

The tutor laughed. "Don't be shy." He waved a shard of pottery. "Have a go! You never know what hidden talents you might have."

The offer was too tempting. "All right." He pushed the door open and stepped forward to grab the shard.

At the sight of him, however, Weris recoiled. "What in the name of . . ." He wrenched the shard away. "Stop right there." He shot Sepi a look. "What is this? You think you can pull a joke on me? You think this is funny? Inviting a lice-infested slave into my presence? I'm not one of your little local tutors."

"There's no joke, I told you, he's—"

"I'm shocked. I'll have none of this. Out," he told Ramses.

"I'm not the one who can draw," Sepi said.

"Then I suggest you pay attention to your lessons instead of playing silly games. Your mother will be unhappy to hear of this."

Sepi put down his brush. "No. Don't tell her." The brush rolled across the table, making a trail of black ink.

"How much did you pay your whipping boy here to play this little joke on me?"

"Whipping boy?" Sepi said. His face turned a livid shade of red. Gripping the table, he rose to his feet.

Ramses felt his own pulse building at his temples. "Don't bother, Sepi." He made for the door.

"Wait for your dismissal," Weris said.

Ramses slowed. "Excuse me?"

"You heard me. Wait for your dismissal."

Months of frustration churned to the surface. His father's strong back had built this house. His father's strong hands had created this bedroom. He no longer cared who this snobby, overdressed tutor was. Blind with rage, Ramses prepared to lunge.

CHAPTER 34

"Stop," Sepi shouted. "Both of you!"

Ramses had made it halfway across the room. Weris might be twice his size and muscular, but it would be worth it to try and get a punch in, just to flatten those conceited, flaring nostrils. Weris hadn't moved. Instead, he eyed Ramses as if daring him to try.

"Stop!" Sepi hissed at Ramses.

Ramses paused. He seethed all over.

A breezed fluttered the window-shade.

Sepi turned to Weris. "My mother is paying you well. So I'll ask you once more. Give my friend a chance."

"It's a waste of time," Weris said.

Stillness settled in the room.

"I bet he'll amaze you," Sepi said.

A fat beetle bumbled past the sill and dawdled through the air. It landed heavily on the table. Weris smacked it dead.

"Fine." He gestured at the pottery shards and rolled his eyes. "Well, go on. Amaze me."

"Why should I?" Ramses said. "Sepi, I'm leaving."

"One drawing," Sepi said. "That's all I'm asking. Please?"

"Why?" Ramses met his cousin's pleading eyes. He let his breath out through his nose. "All right. You want me to draw something, I'll draw something."

A bucket held the pile of pottery shards. Curved ones and flat ones; worn ones with rough water-stains, and smooth ones with clean surfaces. He plucked out the largest, smoothest piece he could find.

Snatching Sepi's brush from the floor, he dipped it in the ink. He was too angry to care that he'd never used ink before, or that his bandaged hands were stiff as old bread. In a rage, he drew a long slash across the shard. And paused.

The ink had an intense quality that reminded him of how the charcoal had looked on the plaster wall. This was even cleaner, even more precise.

Unlike the charcoal, which lay on the surface of the wall, the thirsty shard absorbed the ink. The ink and pottery bonded themselves together. It was beautiful to watch, so much that for a moment he simply stared.

His second brush-stroke was softer, drier. He dipped the brush-tip into the pool of ink, swirling it around until it was heavy with liquid. Then he drew a third stroke, amazed at how he could create lines of such varying thicknesses. The same line could start thin, grow thick with brush pressure, and end thin once again.

Soon, three black figures came alive under his fingers. Warriors with bows and spears. They charged across the pottery surface, moving like shadows, growing clearer as faces came into crisp focus. He bent forward, pulled into the rush of their attack.

A hiss of breath at his side tore him from his work.

Weris stood over him wearing a greedy expression. "Your cousin was right." His teeth flashed in a broad smile. "You have amazed me." He took the shard and looked closer. "Incredible."

Taken aback, Ramses felt suddenly off balance. Despite himself, his pride swelled at the tutor's words of praise.

"What did I tell you?" Sepi said.

Weris tucked the shard away in the fold of his garment. "I see some potential—with training of course. Come, you can train with Sepi. I have enough payment for both of you. And this." He lifted a thick sheaf of papyrus from a trunk. "I hear it's scarce in these parts."

Ramses' jaw dropped. Suddenly his single sheet seemed paltry. With that great pile, he could make mistakes and never have to worry. "You'd give me that without payment? And train me?"

"How could I let such talents go to waste?" Weris said in a smooth voice. "I like everyone to be happy."

But everyone wouldn't be happy. Not Aunt Zalika. She'd be furious.

"I can't," Ramses said.

"Can't?" Weris said. "I don't accept can't."

"You will when my aunt finds you training me."

Weris flicked his words away with an irritated wave. "Come to my room after dinner. She'll never know. We'll work by lamplight. It'll be our secret. Just between the three of us. Agreed?"

Bastet leapt onto the windowsill. Her shadow fell across Weris's golden collar, dimming its gleam.

"You'd do that? Help me like that? Why?" On impulse, Ramses felt for Neferet's amulet of Maat, hidden at his waist. It felt strangely hot.

"We'd be helping each other—if you get into the Place of Truth of course."

"How?"

"Let's not bore one another with details. I take it you're interested?"

"Do it, Ramses," Sepi said. "Think what he can teach you— look at this." Sepi reached for a shard of pottery. "Look how good Weris is." He held it up for Ramses.

"Give me that." Weris wrenched the shard away.

But not before Ramses had seen it.

He gasped. The drawings were terrible, childish. Weris was no master painter. He might be good enough to fool Sepi, and his aunt and uncle, but Ramses' own skills were far beyond the tutor's clumsy attempts.

"Those are nothing," Weris snapped. "A few scratchings to clean off my brush. Well? What shall it be?"

Ramses swallowed. Did it matter if Weris was a farce? He had papyrus, and he'd offered to share. With only one sheet to his name, he'd be crazy to refuse.

He would accept. Of course he'd accept!

Weris drew close, his pale-gold eyes fixed on him. Before the word yes could escape Ramses' lips, the amulet turned hot as fire his hand. He snatched his fingers away and took a step back.

He had his sheet. One that Hebony and Sobek had sacrificed their savings to get.

"No," Ramses said. "No. I can't accept."

The tutor's voice went up a notch. "You turn me away?"

"I'm sorry, but thank you."

Weris crushed Ramses' shard to pieces. "Don't be ridiculous. You will come to my room this evening. Understood?"

Ramses looked to see Sepi mirror his own shock. Was that a threat?

"I said, is that understood?"

"I won't," Ramses said.

Weris's expression sent shockwaves down his spine. It didn't make sense. The man's grimace was beyond poisonous. It was downright deadly.

"I'm sorry, but I can't," Ramses said. Shoulders stiff, he walked out the door.

In the hall, he stopped to look at his hand. It still blazed from holding Neferet's amulet. He peeled back the bandages. His mouth widened in shock. The cuts looked as bad as ever; but he wasn't interested in the cuts.

Instead, it was the shadowy image of Maat, goddess of justice and truth that made him gasp.

She'd burned her likeness into the ragged flesh of his outstretched palm.

CHAPTER 35

Neferet had begun to dread meeting the daily delivery caravan at the gates. Still, she steeled herself against the fear she'd see Akil again and got ready to go. She put her basket over her arm and stepped out into a bright, clear morning.

She wasn't expecting much: grain, some vegetables, natron since she'd used the last bit to scrub her face this morning.

Instead of the usual trickle of villagers, today it seemed everyone was headed there. The bright chatter of women and children filled the narrow streets, echoing from the walls. Everyone had been madly ordering things for the coming event: wigs, hair-beads, scented oils, fabric for new outfits.

As she came around the corner to Kiki's house, the door swung open.

Neferet paused, hanging back.

Layla came out first, tossing her glossy bangs out of her eyes. Kiki and a half dozen other girls followed, all talking and giggling. As usual, Layla skipped along while the rest of the girls vied for a place beside her.

Until last year, it had always been Neferet and Layla in the lead. Arms linked, and laughing. It was amazing how they could reduce each other to giggles back then. It was hard to imagine she and Layla had been inseparable; even harder to believe they'd shared every secret, every wish.

That was before Paneb complicated their lives. Before Layla bought him presents and baked him sweets and batted her eyelashes at him. Before Layla thought Neferet was in love with

Paneb too—which she wasn't.

And as the days passed since he'd left, she'd begun to wish she'd never even been his friend at all. He was gone, but he'd left behind an ugly stain—a stain that marked every person in the village.

A woman jostled against her, breaking her thoughts.

"Sorry, dear," the woman said with a broad smile. "What a crowd!"

Neferet smiled back. "Have you ordered something special?"

"No, just two jars of beer, some chisels for my husband. But I like to watch you girls and all the excitement. Run and catch up, don't mind me."

Feeling awkward, Neferet pushed closer to Layla.

"I can't believe hundreds of boys are going to be coming here. Here, right outside!" Kiki said.

"Don't screech," Layla said. "Boys want girls to be mysterious, elusive. Not excited and loud."

"Ooh, I just love being elusive."

A girl snorted. "Yeah. Do you even know what elusive means?"

"Anyway," Kiki said to Layla, quickly changing the subject. "Don't you wish they let the delivery people inside?"

"Don't be ridiculous," Layla snapped. "I'd never want a bunch of filthy strangers coming to my door. Sometimes I think you forget we're special."

"I don't! But I hate lugging everything back home myself," Kiki whined.

"What are you getting anyway?" a girl asked Kiki. "I thought you just bought those gold hair beads you're wearing for the big day. How much did you pay for them?"

"Yeah," said another. "I thought you were saving them?"

Layla had worn ones just like them last week, but already she'd moved on to a new style: a sleek, simple bob with long bangs.

Kiki's cheeks colored. "Don't be silly, I'm not wearing these old things on the big day." She turned back to Layla. "Really though, don't you think it'd be nice if they at least let the donkeys in? To help bring stuff home?"

"I think it would be nice if everyone hurried up," Layla replied. "I want to see if my package is here!"

Then, as if sensing Neferet's eyes on her, Layla glanced back.

Neferet took a chance, inhaled a big breath and caught up.

"Hey, do you remember the first time we ordered something?" she said. "We both got those little sheep's wool wigs?"

Layla's brow flickered. She kept walking.

"And I was mad because mine wasn't curled enough, so I tried to curl it myself?"

The corner of Layla's mouth twitched with the beginning of a smile. Their eyes met, and for a brief moment Neferet saw her old friend looking back.

"And my mother had a fit because the whole thing went up in smoke?" Layla grinned. But the moment quickly vanished. She tossed her head. "Come on," she cried to the others. "Let's run!"

The girls took off squealing and giggling and pushing through the crowd. Neferet followed, slowly trailing in their wake.

At the village gate, Jabari wore a crisp uniform normally saved for special occasions; official armbands encased his biceps. He signaled them to a stop. When he had everyone's attention he said, "File out calmly please. We have an important visitor."

"An important visitor?" Layla demanded. "Who?"

"The mayor of Thebes. Now file out and get your things. Do not disturb his caravan. Do not approach his litter."

Neferet let the others go first and sidled up beside Jabari. "Why is the mayor of Thebes here?" she whispered.

Quietly, he said, "I heard he brought some apprentice-hopeful. Some favorite boy."

"The mayor has a favorite boy?" Neferet's heart quickened. "Did you see him? Was it my friend from . . ."

"Shhh." Jabari gave her a warning nudge.

Neferet followed the guard's gaze to see her father approaching. He was deep in conversation with an elder craftsman and didn't see her. They walked with swift, business-like strides. Her father looked buoyant. Clearly he was excited about meeting the mayor's special boy.

Was it possible it was Ramses? Somehow, she had to get near the mayor's litter. She ducked outside before her father saw her.

The smell of donkeys assaulted her and the sun's heat seared her nostrils as she glanced at the chaotic scene. A crowd filled the flat, baked plain in front of the village. To the right stood a long line of donkeys, all weighted down with packages. Their owners shouted and haggled for tips, while the villagers went from man to man in search of their orders.

On the left, the mayor's train stood silent and regal. Guards stood, stone faced and upright. Banners fluttered down the line, flashing with the Mayor's crimson and yellow colors. In the middle were two grand litters, the drawn curtains also decorated in crimson and yellow.

The donkey train jostled and shifted sideways toward the mayor's train, spreading ever wider as packages were lifted down and examined.

Neferet saw her chance.

CHAPTER 36

Quickly, Neferet made her way into the midst of the donkeys. She passed the girls, all crowded around a deliveryman with a mess of baskets. Everywhere, people tried sort out what belonged to whom. She'd never seen such confusion. Who would notice if she snuck over to the mayor's train?

A breeze lifted the edges of the curtains. If she could just get behind the litters, close enough to see. But when she reached the middle of the crowd, she groaned. A big gap separated the two groups.

Suddenly, Layla was at her elbow.

"Quick, come on," Layla whispered.

Neferet spun around. "Layla?"

She was leading a donkey. "Take its bridle!"

"Why? What do you mean?"

Layla's eyes sparkled with their old excitement. "Don't you want to see who it is? In the mayor's train? Isn't that what you're trying to do?"

"Maybe."

"Well then stop questioning me and hurry, just lead the donkey back there, you can hide behind him."

"Are you crazy?"

"No one will even notice! They're all busy looking for their packages."

Neferet took a step back. "No. I'm not falling for some trick."

Layla's sparkle faded. She dropped her gaze to the ground. "Look, I know I've been acting stupid." The donkey pushed his nose into her hand. She bit her lip and rubbed its fur. "I just . . . back there, what you said about the wigs . . ."

Neferet had no idea what to say. "Layla . . ."

"I should've believed you when you said you and Paneb were just friends." She met Neferet's stare, and very softly, she said, "I'm sorry."

Tears sprang into Neferet's eyes.

"I miss you." Layla gave Neferet a gentle shove. "Even if you are a brat."

They stood there grinning at each other and it was as if all the horrible months had disappeared. Layla shoved the bridle into Neferet's hand.

"Now come on!" Layla said. "Go! Before someone sees!"

The donkey blinked its soft eyes as if urging her to hurry. Neferet ducked down and began to lead it across the empty space. Straight toward the mayor's train.

Layla was right. No one seemed to notice.

She ducked, pressing close to the animal's shoulder. Two huge clay jugs of water still weighted the animal down, one strapped to each side. The nearest jug jostled up and down as the donkey walked, pushing against her arm. With each step, it seemed to sag lower and lower. Someone should've fastened the strap tighter.

But right now, that didn't matter. She was nearly close enough!

She moved faster, coming near to the back of the litter. If Ramses was inside, maybe she could get his attention. Maybe he'd stick his head out. Just a little closer—

Snap! The sound of breaking leather cracked the air.

The strap holding the water jugs flew free. The heavy cargo hinged downward. The donkey ripped the bridle from her hands as it reared onto its hind legs, eyes white with shock. Braying and kicking, the donkey plunged back down.

Neferet stumbled as the animal thrust against her and drove her to the ground.

A hoof missed her face by inches. She tasted sand as she

scrambled underfoot.

Then crash! Both jugs hit the dirt. The nearest smashed into a rock. The resounding explosion of clay was deafening. Water and shards flew everywhere. Fragments bit into her exposed skin. She threw her arms over her face. Liquid surged over her, drenching her dress and hair.

The donkey skittered away.

Silence fell. Slowly, she lowered her hands.

The whole crowd stood frozen, wide-eyed. But the only person Neferet saw clearly was Layla—Layla's lips forming the words, "Oh my!"

Neferet leapt to her feet. "You could have killed me!" she screamed.

Layla glanced sideways at the others, with a baffled, innocent expression. "Is she talking to me?"

"You could have killed me!" Neferet screamed again. Mud trickled down her cheeks. "You hate me that much?"

Layla bit her lip, frowning as if to say Neferet was crazy.

"Answer me!" Neferet screamed. "You hate me that much?"

At this, a man thrust aside the curtains of his litter. The mayor. His mouth turned down as he examined her with disdain.

"Our deepest apologies, sire," Layla said. "We're not all that uncivilized."

Neferet clenched her fists. "I trusted you."

Layla's tinkling laugh rang out. With a shout, Neferet launched at her. She didn't care if the whole village saw. Every guard. Even the mayor himself. She'd show Layla once and for all. She'd grind her face into the dirt, make her apologize, make her never try to—

Strong arms caught her from behind.

"Go home," her father growled. His eyes were dark and full of fury. "Now."

She swallowed, shaken from her fog. She sensed the mayor staring, saw his disgust mirrored in the face of every villager. She felt like a wild animal, instead of the highborn daughter of the Head Scribe himself.

"Father," she said, stepping closer to him. "I can explain! I'm so sorry! I just—"

"I said go home."

She nodded. How could she have humiliated him like this?

Clutching her soaked, muddy dress, she started toward the village gates. The girls clutched their packages, smirking and whispering.

Neferet walked a little faster.

A group of women shook their heads. Then a deliveryman snorted with laughter. The whole crowd joined in.

She broke into a run. At the entrance to the village, Jabari gave her a puzzled expression. She ignored him and ran down the shadowed streets, and kept sprinting.

In the silence of her room, she threw herself down.

Pulling a sheet over her head, her breath caught in her throat.

She didn't belong here. She didn't belong anywhere.

She was totally and completely alone.

CHAPTER 37

Ramses had hardly seen Weris in the last ten days. To his surprise, the tutor's strange behavior turned out to be empty threats. Instead, it was Aunt Zalika who hounded Ramses' every move. By some sixth sense, she seemed to know about his sheet of papyrus, and was determined to keep him from getting near it.

"I know you're up to something," she kept saying. And then he'd catch her tearing his cell apart.

Her hounding worked.

He had nowhere to hide.

The papyrus still lay untouched in the hole under the kitchen tile.

Gritting his teeth, he trudged into the barn. He needed to find some way to use it without her seeing! Cool shadows swallowed him and he made his way by instinct until his eyes adjusted to the light.

The dirt floor felt rough and pebbly. There had to be more harvest baskets in here somewhere. He tossed aside a crate and cursed. The exam was in two days! The papyrus was useless if he didn't draw something.

Shoving aside a storage bin, he heard an angry hiss. A huge goose rose up, flapping her wings in anger, feathers flying.

"Sorry Missy!" Ramses said. "I didn't know you were back there."

The goose honked at him. Behind her lay a downy nesting spot against the wall. For a moment he thought of hiding back there to create his entry. And laughed.

There had to be a place to go. Somewhere away from here. Somewhere she'd never think of.

"You are too kind, my dear lady," came a voice from outside, "But truly, I need no assistance."

It was Weris.

Curious, Ramses edged closer to the door. Dust hung suspended in the rectangular shaft of sunshine. According to Sepi, Weris had been away for three days—only coming back at night to sleep. Three whole days! What kind of tutor did that?

"Thebes is a big city, it's easy to get lost," Aunt Zalika said. "I grew up there. Let me show you around."

Tufts of goat hair from animals wandering in and out covered the doorframe, tickling Ramses' cheek as he peeked outside.

Aunt Zalika wore the most ridiculous pair of sandals he'd ever seen. They had high soles that looked like they were made of cork. Her eyelids were all fluttery, colored with green malachite, and a thin line of kohl extended all the way to her ears. Her perfume drifted toward him, so strong it overpowered the smell of the barn.

And not in a good way.

"The city streets can be confusing," she continued. "Maybe that's why you've had so much trouble finding what you need. Let me join you."

"You are too kind, my dear lady." Weris bowed to her. "But I fear your beauty would overpower me, and I'd be unable to concentrate on my duties."

At this, Aunt Zalika giggled. Ramses wanted to gag.

"Please let me come," she said in a funny little voice.

"Madam, it is a crime to leave your wonderful presence these many afternoons. But today shall be the last. I believe I've found what I'm looking for. After that, nothing shall prevent me from being your most dedicated servant."

"You bring such civility to our household," she said.

"Good-day, my lady." Weris bowed low over her outstretched fingers. "Until tonight."

She blushed all the way down to the beaded collar of her

dress.

Weris sauntered down the road in the direction of the river ferry that would take him across the Nile to Thebes. Sighing a little, she watched him stride off. Her flushed face looked so silly, Ramses almost choked from trying not to laugh.

That afternoon, Ramses managed to sneak into Sepi's room.

"Why's he going to Thebes?" Ramses said. "Why does he keep leaving?"

"He says we need more supplies."

"More supplies? He has piles of papyrus. He's supposed to be teaching you."

"I guess he needs something we don't have," Sepi said.

Ramses snorted. "Like what?"

"I don't know, but you're right, it's ridiculous," Sepi said. "Especially since we know he's a complete farce."

"That's for sure."

"What do you think he's up to?"

"I have no idea."

Puzzled, Ramses returned to the fields.

When he bent to examine the wheat, he had a churning sense of discomfort. The grain was nearly past its prime. Sobek's prediction was coming true. Without the farm manager's powerful muscles, they weren't cutting nearly fast enough. Even with Ramses' growing ability to control the team.

Wind sent dust into his eyes. He blinked, momentarily blinded.

"Where's your master, boy?" asked a raspy voice.

Ramses whipped around, scythe in hand.

"Watch yourself!" the man growled, eying the curved blade. He wore a plain kilt and leather sandals. His cheeks hung in generous jowls.

Ramses had seen him somewhere. Before he could think where, two more men closed in. Lowering the blade, his fingers tightened around the shaft.

Suddenly, he remembered: this was one of the sentries

who'd come looking for Neferet. His mouth went dry. Was he in trouble for meeting Neferet? Worse, had he gotten her in trouble?

"Don't stand there gaping like an idiot," the sentry said. "Where's your master? Or do I have to beat it out of you?"

"Sorry," Ramses said. "You surprised me, that's all."

The sentry's two companions were larger than Sobek; both had scarred faces and the thick arms of fighters. Ramses gulped, deciding he had no choice but to do what they asked.

"This way," he said, and led them toward the house.

Uncle Hay stood pottering around near the barn. At the sight of the men, he looked as frightened as Ramses felt.

"Greetings, gentlemen," he said with a shaky smile. "What can I do for you?"

"My name's Denger. These two good fellows are my cousins," the guard replied. "They're new to the area. Rumor has it you need field workers—"

"Rumor?" Uncle Hay said. "There's no rumor! We have plenty of workers. We're full up, we . . ." his voice trailed off as the hulking cousins took a menacing step.

"That's not what I heard," Denger said. "I heard your crew's having trouble. And as you can see, my cousins are the strongest you'll find."

"Well, of course. Oh yes, I see that!" Removing his black wig, Uncle Hay wrung it between his blotchy, trembling hands. "I suppose we could use a little help."

"Good, good."

"I mean, I'll have to talk to my wife about their pay." At this, Denger's leer returned, and Uncle Hay let out a nervous laugh.

Ramses stared, baffled. What was going on here?

At that moment, Weris appeared. "Ah, hello there!" He shot Denger a glance. The two men shared a brief nod.

They knew each other?

"Weris," Uncle Hay cried. He grabbed the tutor's sturdy shoulder like a drowning man. "Er, I had some important things to ask you, yes, very important, back to the house with us, lots to talk about." He gave the three men a friendly wave. "Must be going! Good-bye."

Uncle Hay departed in such a hurry that he stirred up a cloud of dust.

Weris shot Ramses a grin. Then he strode after Uncle Hay.

"I trust you'll take care of my cousins?" Denger said. He slapped Ramses hard on the back and laughed. "I'm off. Later, boys."

Ramses stood between the two massive men. Rubbing his neck, he glanced from one grimace to the other. He forced a smile, but neither man smiled back.

"I, uh, we better get to work?"

They followed on his heels. He stopped when he reached where he'd been cutting, and picked up his scythe.

The men crossed their arms, waiting. The shorter one's nose looked flat, like it had been broken so often it had given up and collapsed. On the other, a knife scar ran from his eyebrow to his chin. His eyelid drooped, but lucky for him his eye still worked. What a pair.

Flatnose and Scar-Eye.

Fine. If they were here to work, they'd work. "Hui!" he called to the man in charge of the blades. "Sharpen two scythes."

Great, Ramses thought, when Hui handed over the razor sharp implements. Flatnose and Scar-Eye now looked even scarier. As if that were possible.

Working up his courage, he said, "You can cut that section."

The cousins glanced where he'd pointed.

Neither moved.

"Yeah . . . okay, you know what? Forget I asked." He turned away.

A blade sang through the air. Back prickling in terror, he whirled around. To his amazement, the cousins were mowing down the crop at an impressive pace.

Maybe they were here to work. Maybe it was a coincidence Weris knew the guard from the Place of Truth.

Yes, and maybe crocodiles could fly.

CHAPTER 38

In the Place of Truth, several hours had passed and still Neferet's father hadn't returned home. Frightened at what he'd say, she scrubbed the kitchen floor as if she could scrub away the memory of Layla's laughter and the whole horrible scene. Water splashed as she ground the bristles into the tiles.

Her cheeks colored. She'd trusted her.

How could she have fallen for such a liar's tricks?

The front door slammed and her fingers tightened on the brush. Her father banged into the front room. A moment later, he darkened the kitchen entryway. He paused, arms crossed, and looked down at her.

She swallowed. "Hello."

"There you are," he finally said.

"I'm really sorry! Father, I've been trying so hard, honest—"

"You and Layla are becoming a serious problem."

"I don't know what to do! But I know, it was my fault for trying to get close to the train. I just wanted to see who was in there . . . to see if it was . . ." Her voice trailed off. She stared at the dirty wash water. Why explain? She'd shamed him in front of the mayor. In front of the whole village—when he needed her support.

He cleared his throat. "I saw Layla unbuckle that strap."

Her head jerked up. "You did?"

"But that doesn't excuse you. You need to end this argument with Layla."

"She hates me!"

"Then change her mind. Now sit. I need to talk to you."

She pulled out his three-legged stool, the one with the carved panther feet, and poured him a cup of water. The last few drops drained into the cup. The empty jug reminded her of her abandoned deliveries. She'd have to track them down later. "What's going on?"

"I met your friend today."

"My friend?" So it was Ramses in the mayor's train. "I knew it. I just knew it!"

He took a sip from his mug, and his eyes danced beyond its rim. "Apparently he's been coming for days. Asking for you by name."

"Oh father! And you like him?"

"His work, yes. But I can't say his character impressed me."

Her heart made an uncomfortable flutter. "Why not?"

"Frankly, he struck me as rude. But there's no question about his skills. Would you like to see the sample he brought us?"

She nodded. He reached into the folds of his tunic and pulled out a scroll wrapped in goatskin. But as he began to unroll it, the hairs on her neck prickled.

"I owe you an apology. I really am impressed," her father said, opening it wider. "I think you're right. We've found our apprentice."

"Let's see." Neferet moved a basket of dried beans that still needed sorting for stones, and glanced over his shoulder.

A gruesome picture met her: it was Seth murdering Osiris and cutting him into bloody pieces. She'd shredded one just like it out in the desert.

Akil. It belonged to Akil.

"No," she whispered in horror.

"What is it?" her father said.

"That's not Ramses' drawing! A horrible boy named Akil drew it! Oh father, you can't let him into our village. You can't!"

His brow darkened. "Akil? Of course it's Akil's. Who's this Ramses?"

"My friend!"

"Wait, another friend? How many friends are going to come

158

calling for you?"

"It's not like that! I should've told you before."

"You'd better tell me, now."

She nodded. Music drifted from somewhere outside. Someone was playing a reed flute. A girl started singing in high, clear tones. Layla. Her mother joined in. They sounded happy. There was no denying Layla had a pretty voice. But even a pretty voice could be grating if a person was mean enough.

"I was picking herbs. Akil snuck up on me, he threatened me. He threatened the whole village. He said he'd cursed us with black magic, and I didn't want to believe it but . . ."

"And you never told me about this? When was it?"

"That day Tui was carried back from your work-camp in the Valley of the Kings."

Neferet's father listened as she told him everything that had happened. When she finished, he picked up Akil's drawing and studied it again. "Ramses approached you and you weren't offended. Yet when this boy did, you threw away his drawing."

"Because he's evil!"

"Neferet, he's just a boy. And he's very skilled. I'm disappointed in you."

"Akil cast a spell over Tui, and Tui's getting sicker!"

"No. Tui's been sick for years. This boy was just trying to scare you into doing what he wanted. He's ambitious."

Neferet stared at him. Beyond the high kitchen window, Layla's song reached a crescendo. The flute struck up once again, piping the playful tune. Bright laughter accompanied the last few notes, which rose quickly and then faded away.

"I admit," her father added, "it won't be easy sharing our home with him."

She jolted upright. "Sharing our home?"

"At first, yes. He'll be my responsibility."

"No . . ." she said. "He can't!" Akil, living here? She remembered how her arm burned with eerie heat where he'd touched her.

"Neferet, I need your cooperation."

"But are you still holding the exam?"

"Unfortunately, yes. I've given Egypt my word."

She grabbed the basket of dried beans and started sorting it for stones. "Ramses will change your mind," she said.

"Don't hold your breath hoping your friend is better than Akil."

"You haven't even seen one of his pictures."

Her father stood to refill his cup. She glared at his back, wanting to rage at him, to make him see he was wrong. And how could he pass Akil's magic off so lightly? The boy was evil—she felt it in every bone. She wanted to grab Akil's papyrus and tear it up like the last. Yet that wouldn't make him go away. Not anymore.

The whole village knew about Akil's skills now. They honored him.

Already her father had called him their new apprentice.

CHAPTER 39

Ramses discovered to his surprise that he and the two hulking cousins made a great team. Together, they fell into an easy rhythm; blades swished back and forth; arms and hands moved to and fro. Flatnose grunted as he cut, Ramses hummed a tune. It felt as if they'd worked together for months. No, years.

Three persons wide, they moved forward, clearing in neat, perfect blocks. The stands gave way to rustling bundles of harvest underfoot. And all around them, the fresh scent of cuttings filled the clear, bright air.

Suddenly, the gong rang out.

The three of them faltered, and then stopped.

Ramses' awkwardness instantly returned. He cleared his throat. "Looks like the day's over."

Flatnose wiped his blade on the ground, and then fingered its edge.

"No need to stick around, you can go home."

Scar-Eye made no move to leave. Instead, he ran his blade down his forearm, shaving off swatch of hair. Flatnose crossed his arms, legs planted. What by the gods did they want?

"Or you can stay in the workers' camp," Ramses said. "Past the south field. But I have to go."

The cousins trailed on his heels.

When the pond came into view, he spotted Hebony wading in the shallows. Whether at the sight of her, or by some unknown signal, the cousins drifted off.

Hebony had her skirts in one hand and a net in the other.

Although the pond was well stocked with fish, she didn't seem to be having much luck. She splashed left and right, plunging the net into the water. She pulled it out, dripping and empty. Muttering curses, she plunged the net in again.

She glanced up and saw Ramses. "Either I'm getting old or these fish have been practicing! I can't catch a single one."

Mud squished between his toes and water swirled around his calves as he wove through the lily-pads. "Let me try."

When he reached her, she grabbed his arm and whispered, "Ramses, why haven't you used the papyrus I got you? It's still under the tile."

"I know."

"But the exam's day after tomorrow!"

"I know." He gulped. Day after tomorrow.

"You can't leave it to the last minute. You need to get ready or else you might not be able to—"

A long shadow fell across them. Ramses turned to see Uncle Hay cross beneath a cluster of overhanging palms.

"Hand over that net," Ramses said.

"Oh, wait, I got this one!" Hebony cried as a glint of silver darted along the surface. She lunged and slipped. Ramses caught her just before she went under.

"On second thought," she said, "I'll get the bucket."

Ramses cracked his knuckles. "Watch this."

By the time he'd filled the bucket with leaping Nile trout, he was drenched from head to toe; his sides ached from laughing, and her voice was hoarse with cheering.

They parted ways.

Still grinning, he decided Hebony was right. He had to make his entry before it was too late. Tonight, he'd take a chance and just do it. In his cell. He'd close the door, bar it tight, light his lamp and draw. What other choice did he have?

But as he neared his cell, his grin faded. The door stood open, swinging on its hinges. Outside, overturned on the ground, lay his wooden chest.

He hurried closer. Fanning out from his door, muddy rushes

had been strewn every which way. It took a moment to realize he was staring at his bedding—dirty and trampled. The lid to his wooden chest had been cracked down the middle. He flipped the chest upright. Inside, his jar of carefully hoarded lamp oil had smashed, smearing over everything. His spare kilt shone with splotches of grease.

Panicked, he threw it aside and ran to his cell to find his clay lamp.

Gone.

Outside, ground into the dirt, were fragments of pottery. He squatted down, and carefully gathered up a shard. It was a curved handle. His fingers trembled as they closed around the only remaining piece of his precious light.

"You can't hide from me," Aunt Zalika said harshly.

He jerked around.

"Now clean this up," she said. "I have guests coming for dinner, I don't want it looking like I have a dirty weasel living out here."

Fortunately, she turned and left. Because he was about to do something that would have made him sorry.

Guests were coming to dinner? Out of nowhere, a plan sprang into his mind. He knew exactly what to do. He knew exactly where he could go. He threw everything into his room and slammed the door.

The air felt hot and tense as he ran to find Sobek. His friend sat outside cleaning the fish. His knife glittered with silver scales as he scraped them into a bucket.

"I need your help," Ramses said, breathless.

Sobek threw down the knife. "As long as it doesn't involve cleaning fish for Zalika's guests."

"She's watching me. Can you take you-know-what from the kitchen and hide it somewhere else?"

Sobek nodded. "My room. She'd never go in there. But I wouldn't go so far as to risk working in there."

"No. I have a place."

"You picked a good night, we're going to have a big crowd."

Sobek wiped his hands and stood. "I'll keep the wine overflowing. In our room, Hebony has a box for storing linen. It's long and narrow—"

Laughter and marching footsteps rang out. Two canopied litters, carried by servants, rounded the far end of the courtyard.

Ramses took the bucket of half-cleaned fish from Sobek's feet. "I'll finish this."

Sobek left, looking ridiculously thrilled to hand over the slimy knife. Ramses positioned himself behind a sprawling cluster of potted herbs. From there, he could see Aunt Zalika greeting guests at the front door. Weris stood at her elbow, dressed in a fine gold-bordered kilt. They kept sharing smiles and giggles in a way that turned Ramses' stomach.

One woman tried to engage Weris in a conversation.

Aunt Zalika gave the woman a little shove. "Go inside. There's wine in the dining room."

The woman frowned but obeyed.

Uncle Hay's laughter blasted from the house; he sounded like a braying donkey. Aunt Zalika flinched; Weris shot her a sympathetic glance. Then his pale gold eyes spotted Ramses through the foliage.

Ramses ducked back.

After a tense hour, the party was well under way. It was time to escape. He found his two packages waiting in Hebony's linen chest. Holding them tight, he crept away from the blazing candles and wine-induced laughter.

A jeweled canopy of stars winked in the dark.

He set out the road.

He hoped he could remember the way.

CHAPTER 40

On the horizon, the moon rose slender as an eyelash, casting only a faint light. Pebbles scattered as he hurried along. Ramses squinted and made out a crossroads directly ahead.

A small shrine to Hathor appeared out of the darkness. Fruits and flowers lay piled at the goddess's feet, along with a stew pot, strings of beads, the burnt remains of incense cones, and even a small rake.

The sight made him break out in a sweat. Hathor wouldn't demand an offering for passing her shrine, but the gods he planned to visit were a different manner. He groaned inwardly for not thinking ahead more clearly. He could have taken a cone of incense from the dining room. Aunt Zalika had laid out so much, she wouldn't have missed it.

Instead, all he'd brought were things for himself. His drawing tools. No one in their right mind visited the gods without a gift. There would be price to pay. There was always a price to pay. If he'd been smart, he could have chosen exactly what that price would be. But now, because of his selfish stupidity, the price would be of the gods' choosing.

Well, he would pay it. Whatever they demanded.

Empty handed, he kept going.

He sensed it before he saw it—a place nearly forgotten. But now here it was, looking just as he remembered from his naming day all those years ago. Broad and powerful in the distance, the temple crouched long and low against the earth.

The sacred lake still separated them. The waters glistened

faintly, black as a pool of ink. He skirted the edge, cautious to keep from falling in as he peered into its depths. His silhouette reflected up at him; the calm surface looked like an entryway into the afterlife itself.

Somewhere in the distance, a hyena laughed.

Hackles rose on his back. He steeled his jaw and kept walking.

At the far side, the temple's stone ramp rose steeply to two pylons.

His chest tightened. He was four again, sketching in the dirt as he waited for his parents, waited for the endlessly boring naming ceremony to end, waited to go home. He saw the old priest—the Wab Sekhmet—approach and stare at his drawings; saw temple students, their faces strangely curious and then horrified; felt his mother catch his hand and hurry him away.

He blinked. The temple was deserted.

It was late. Of course it was deserted. The doors to the inner sanctuary would long since have been sealed with clay.

At the ramp, he began to climb.

Although he was barefoot, the slightest shuffle sounded loud. Somewhere above, a lamp burned softly. It was exactly what he'd hoped to find. Light, and a private place to draw. No one would find him here at this hour. As he reached the top, however, a problem quickly became apparent.

Yes, there was light. Yes, it was private. But the light was too far from the entrance to be of any real use.

The temple had no door. Instead, two towering pillars guarded the sacred hall. Elaborate spells, carved into their surface, warned intruders against entering. All of Egypt knew that only priests were allowed to cross the threshold. No citizen was ever allowed inside a temple. Any prayers or wishes had to be made outside.

Ramses peered at the hieroglyphs. His reading skills were limited. He was glad. He didn't want to know the unthinkable punishments and curses the gods could impose for entering without permission.

The lamp burned steadily in the distance. He stared longingly at it, across the vast space. He'd come so far. If this were for any other reason than the exam, he might chance trying to draw in the poorly lit shadow near the door. But he needed to see. The piece he submitted had to be his best. All he could hope to achieve if he were squinting in the dark was a huge mess. He felt sure of it. Time was running out.

He glanced left and right. His fingers felt for his amulet of Maat.

Entering was like begging the gods to curse him.

But he was already cursed.

"Goddess protect me," he whispered.

Holding his breath, he stepped over the threshold.

A breeze whispered over him.

Tension, thick and palpable, spanned the length of the rectangular atrium. On tiptoe, he made for the burning light. Heavy incense drifted to his nostrils; the strong fragrance made him dizzy. He shook his head, trying to clear it. The sickly sweet fumes cramped his stomach and sent painful tingles shooting through his limbs. It started turning his legs numb and he stumbled.

The lamp flared, illuminating the figure on the far shrine.

Maat.

It was as if his carved amulet had leapt from his pocket to stand upon the altar. The two figures were identical in every way. They looked so similar, he could almost believe they were one and the same, that she had simply jumped up there and grown in size to suit her whim.

Sweet incense wafted over him. Thick and heavy, he coughed, feeling his throat close. The sweet smell filled his lungs, filled his mind, until his head began to swim.

Suddenly, Maat turned her face and looked straight into his eyes.

He fell to his knees. Head down, he abandoned his papyrus and began to move back on all fours. The smoke swirled ever thicker. He coughed, choking, unable to breath. He grabbed at his throat, and the world went black.

Ramses awoke, disoriented. It took a moment to recognize his surroundings. He was sprawled out on the temple floor, lying there as if it were his own house. He scrambled to his feet and glanced around.

What if he'd been caught?

How could he have been so stupid to fall under the spell of drugged incense?

The air was clear now, the incense gone. Maat stood on her shrine, serene and regal, her eyes fixed on a point in the distance.

Shaken, he went to pick up his spilled bundles. The cake of ink rolled across the tiles. He chased after it, cringing at the noise. If he was smart, he'd leave—now. He glanced around.

He had no time to be smart.

The light still burned steadily ahead. He edged closer to the altar and placed his packages on the ground. The vendor who'd sold Hebony the supplies had included everything. He poured a few drops of water from a small, stoppered bottle into the mixing dish, and began crushing the black substance into a paste.

A scraping noise made him stop. A trickle of sweat slid down his ribs.

Just a rat. It had to be. Who'd be awake at this hour? Focus!

Cursing, he tried to steady his hand as he dipped the brush into the ink.

A fleck splattered the ground, just missing the perfect sheet of papyrus. Idiot! This wasn't sand that could be brushed away. One blob and it was over. Indeed, there'd be no fixing an eye too low, a body too long, or a hand with uneven fingers. With only one sheet to his name, he couldn't afford to make a single mistake.

He grit his teeth.

Focus.

He was not that boy, crouching in the dirt to draw. Not

anymore.

Maat's lamp shone brighter. He bent and touched the brush to the smooth, pale surface. A black line sank into the sheet's fibers. His arms relaxed as he curved the brush across the page. The second line came without thinking. He dipped into the ink and kept going.

A world came alive on his page, noisy and full of life.

It drew him in, deeper and deeper.

CHAPTER 41

Ramses had no way of knowing how long he'd spent inside his creation. He tore himself up and away, shaking his head as if emerging from the temple's sacred lake. A glance outside showed the wheel of stars glittering in the black sky.

Thank the gods. Still, it was time to go.

He now wished, more than anything, he'd brought an offering. Halfway to the ramp, he realized he had.

The precious brush. The ink. The mixing dish that was just the right size. He placed them all at Maat's feet. Then he touched his forehead to the floor.

"Thank you," he whispered.

He left, carrying only his papyrus.

Holding it close to his chest, he thought of the unearthly drawing. It was unlike anything he'd ever done. It vibrated with power. It was as if the gods had guided his hand. He'd given up all attempts at control. Instead, he just let it flow through him. He knew, with almost frightening certainty, that he held his ticket to the Place of Truth.

The lane to the farm smelled of humid dirt and fresh wheat cuttings. Tall grasses walled the soft roadway. He ran along, light on his feet.

The howl of laughter met his ears. Out of the darkness, two litters appeared.

Ramses threw himself in the ditch, seconds before the litter-bearers passed. They sang as they walked, the litters swinging drunkenly on their shoulders. Inside the fluttering curtains, a woman giggled and a man shouted something profane.

As soon as they'd passed, he shot down the lane, desperate to avoid a second close-call.

Myrtle shrubs bordered the courtyard. Parting the branches revealed a riotous scene. Guests lounged on cushions, noisily gulping goblets of wine and stuffing their shiny, red faces with handfuls of dates and nuts. A woman belched. Uncle Hay brayed with laughter, and others joined in. Aunt Zalika sat beside Weris, jabbering away in a high-pitched slur. The tutor turned to two ladies and said something that made them shriek.

It was obvious Aunt Zalika wouldn't be searching his room tonight, or getting up early either. Rather than risk meeting a drunken guest in the kitchen, he made for his cell. He'd return the drawing to its hiding place in the morning.

The heat woke him. He lurched upright in a sweat and peered out into the blazing dawn. He'd overslept, but there was still plenty of time.

The world was silent, deserted.

Papyrus in hand, he made for the shadow of the barn. The sun was rising quickly. Perhaps it was later than he thought. At its far end, he looked both ways and began what seemed like a long-distance dash across the broad, open space. His heart pounded as he leaped over torn cushions and crushed sweets, wove between spilled cups and lumps of oily, burnt perfume cones. The scroll felt like a giant thing, impossible to hide.

Almost there!

Somewhere, someone started whistling. He ran for the acacia and plastered himself to the wall. A man sauntered past. Just a farm worker.

Ramses exhaled and stepped forward.

A hand caught him by the neck.

"What have we here?" It was Kontar, the neighbor to the north. "What are you stealing, boy?"

"Let go," Ramses said, trying to break free.

"Looks like quite a party. Good pickings for a little scavenger, huh?" Kontar's hands were like iron pincers. "Show me what you've got there."

"Nothing!"

"You're pretty fierce for nothing." He twisted Ramses' arm until the bones threatened to snap, and wrenched the page away.

"It's mine!"

"Let's see what's so precious." Kontar wrenched it open.

The sight of him pressing his sweaty, dirty thumbprints into the pale, perfect surface made Ramses roar. He lunged for the scroll, but the man thrust him away.

Kontar suddenly gasped. Awe swept over his leathery features. "Where did you get this?"

"I'm telling you, it's mine!"

"That's ridiculous."

"Don't you remember my drawings on the shed? Can't you see they're the same hand? It's mine, I'm telling you. Where else could it be from?"

"I don't know! Why do I feel I should believe you?"

From inside the house came the click-clack of heels. Terror shot from Ramses' spine to his ankles. Aunt Zalika!

"Give it to me. Quick!"

The front door opened.

"Please!"

"Kontar?" Aunt Zalika's eyes swam as she took in the two of them. Her wig was off center, her makeup slapped on in thick uneven lines. "You're here early."

"No. It's seven. But never mind that now! Have you seen what this boy can do?"

She seemed to snap into focus. "What are you talking about?"

"Nothing," Ramses said.

"Don't be worried, son." Kontar's voice was father-like. He waved Ramses' drawing at her. "Come look, my lady. You have an artist here."

Her bleary eyes widened. She made a choking sound and

ran forward.

"You might have to give him up to the Place of Truth," Kontar said with a laugh. "What do you think of that?" He looked down at the page again, head softly shaking.

"Let go," she hissed, grabbing one edge of the fragile sheet.

CHAPTER 42

Flies droned amongst the riot of spilled cups. A torn red ribbon skittered on the wind. Aunt Zalika's hennaed fingers wrenched at Ramses' drawing. Oblivious, Kontar wouldn't let go. He looked as if he were falling, tumbling down into the scene on the page.

Out there in broad daylight, the black ink looked even bolder. The figures seemed to be moving—no, more than that—to be threatening to leap up fully formed, eyes ablaze, mouth's shouting, and pull all three of them into their reality.

Aunt Zalika tried to jerk the delicate sheet away. She gave it a vicious twist.

"Let go, Kontar," Ramses cried. But he was too late.

A loud, slow rip tore his world apart.

No. This couldn't be real. This couldn't be happening.

Kontar gasped, staggering back, pupils huge and unfocused. Half of the drawing fluttered in his hand. "Wh—what have you done?"

"I told you to give it to me!" she said.

"Are you crazy?" Kontar replied. "Do you have any idea of the value of—I could've sold that in the market for a fortune. I probably still could. If you don't want it, give me that half!"

"Don't be ridiculous. The boy stole it from my son's tutor."

"It's mine," Ramses said, his voice sounding far away. "You know it is."

Aunt Zalika flushed. "Shut your mouth, liar."

"Zalika, maybe you shouldn't be so hasty," Kontar said.

Ramses turned to him. "Help me, that's my only entry, I

made it for the Place of Truth, I . . ."

"Enough!" she screeched. In one lightning move, she snatched Kontar's half and made for the outdoor oven.

"Stop!" Ramses sprinted after her.

She yanked the oven open, grabbed the poker and shoved the papyrus deep into the smoldering coals.

"No!" There was still time, if he could just—

Swinging the hot poker at Ramses, she caught him in the chest. He fell back, the burnt smell of singed skin filling his nostrils. In the oven, coals sparked to life. He lunged again, trying to dodge the blazing poker. A flame licked the drawing's edge. The papyrus curled upward, bending and twisting. Orange fire sprang up and raced across it. A spasm racked his throat. A moment later, it burst into flames.

"You see?" Aunt Zalika's face spread in a slow smile. "I win." Her smile widened. "I always win."

Kontar raked a hand over his head. "Well . . ."

"Now, come inside, Kontar, it's much cooler in there."

"Actually—No. Some other time." He left, muttering.

All around, the farm was coming to life. Chickens rustled in the barn. Sobek and Hebony's marketing baskets were missing from the kitchen stoop; they must have left some time ago. From inside the house came the sound of Uncle Hay singing a drinking song, his warbling voice off-key.

Weris emerged from the front entrance hall. From the grin on his face, he looked as if he'd watched the whole thing.

"Good morning, my lady," the tutor said.

Aunt Zalika colored, turning. "Oh! I didn't mean to wake you."

At this, Uncle Hay hit a particularly bad note. Weris scowled, glancing toward the window, and Aunt Zalika quickly straightened her wig.

The tutor assumed a sickly sweet smile. "If I'm not mistaken, you seem distressed my lady. Might I be of service?"

"It's nothing I'd dream of bothering you with."

He bowed to her. "Well, it was a beautiful party, and you

175

were the most beautiful hostess."

She giggled. "But of course you were the shining star of the night." Her face was motherly when she turned to Ramses. "Well, come along. We'll see if we can't resolve this."

For the first time, he considered running. The only way she resolved anything was with a beating, and this time, she might just kill him.

A voice growled, "Boy!"

Everyone turned to see Flatnose and Scar-Eye lumbering toward Ramses, each holding their glittering, sharpened scythes.

"You! Boy!" Flatnose said again. He sounded like an angry, confused rhinoceros. It was the first time Ramses had heard him speak, and the effect was frightening,

Aunt Zalika tottered back. "Who are you?"

Flatnose ignored her. "We waited. In the field. You didn't come." He stated the obvious as if it were the strangest thing in the world.

"Um, sorry?" Ramses inched into their protective shadow. Still, it felt like jumping out of the cobra's path and into the lion's den.

"You come now," Flatnose said.

"Excuse me," Aunt Zalika sputtered. "But I'm speaking to the boy!"

Flatnose aimed his scythe at Ramses' chest. "You come now. Everyone waits."

Scar-Eye nodded, his blade dangling in his meaty fist.

"This is outrageous!" Aunt Zalika said.

Weris stepped in. "A lady mustn't let such things rattle her beautiful composure."

Her cheeks colored. "But I . . ."

He took her arm. "The exam is tomorrow. There's much to do. Shall we go inside?"

"Oh. I suppose. Yes, that's a good idea."

He shepherded her away. Ramses watched them go.

Last night, he'd entered Maat's temple without punishment.

But only because she'd been saving a fate much crueler. Today, she'd destroyed him completely.

Ramses had nothing now. No entry. No papyrus. No brush or ink to his name.

The gods had had the last laugh.

He was a slave and nothing more.

CHAPTER 43

There had once been a time when the fields had seemed a wonderful place. Full of changing colors, bright with the cycle of seasons. But that had been a lifetime ago. Now Ramses moved like the living dead. No longer leading, he cut in Flatnose and Scar-Eye's wake, mind empty to everything.

"Always working, aren't you my friend," Weris said.

Ramses turned slowly.

The tutor looked as if he'd just stepped out from giving a lesson in a royal classroom in Memphis. It was hard to believe he was a complete farce.

"What do you want?"

"No polite greeting then?" Weris held a dripping cup in one hand. "Right to the point, I see."

"Are you going to tell me what you want?"

He offered the cup. "Water?"

"I don't drink jackal spit."

The tutor made a show of letting the comment pass. "So, how do you like my friends?"

"Is that what they are?"

"Look around. In case you've forgotten, I gave you a big hand here. So don't go sounding ungrateful."

"Just tell me what you want."

Without warning, Weris's fist shot out and slammed Ramses in the jaw. The ground rose up fast. Razored stems broke his fall.

He spit a mouthful of wheat chaff at Weris's foot. "A coward's shot."

Weris leaned back with a bark of laughter. "I like your spirit, boy! Too bad you don't have the sense to match it."

Flatnose stopped what he was doing—helping Scar-Eye shove wheat ears into a large net sack—and glanced over.

"I'm fine," Weris told him.

He grunted and went back to helping Scar-Eye. Scar-Eye had his foot on the bag and was tromping it down. Grabbing the drawstring, Flatnose yanked it tight. Ramses wiped the grit and sweat from his face and stood.

"Now. Are you ready to accept my offer?" Weris asked.

"What offer?"

"Don't play dumb with me. Look at you, all crushed and forlorn because you were stupid enough to lose your papyrus."

"What, so you came to give me some? Is that it?"

"Unfortunately, I'm not in the business of giving gifts. On the other hand, you do have talent."

Ramses scowled, cursing himself for wanting to hear more. He should walk away.

"And I'm not talking business now. You have a real gift. I've seen what you can do with a paintbrush. I don't know where that magic comes from—but I do know you don't belong on this farm. And that's the truth."

Ramses shrugged. "Thanks."

"So how about it? We do each other a favor. I give you some papyrus, and you help me out?"

"How? I don't have anything you want."

"A piece of information, that's all—would you be willing to do that?"

Flatnose and Scar-Eye had set to work cramming ears into a second bag. Chaff rose skyward in a cloud of gold.

"What information?"

"Nothing complicated. Nothing that won't be common knowledge to an apprentice."

"What? A technique or something?"

"Actually, I'm interested in learning a little about the Great Place."

"The Great Place? You mean the Valley of the Kings?" Suspicion furrowed Ramses' forehead. "Why?"

"Don't look so upset now. A minute ago you looked ready to sell your soul for my papyrus. It's just curiosity on my part. Nothing more."

"Curiosity?" Ramses glanced toward the horizon, where the red mountains shrouded the Valley of the Kings in mystery. He was just able to make out the pyramid shaped peak where Meretseger, the snake-goddess, kept her terrifying watch over the craftsmen's work. It struck him that weeks had passed since he'd seen the deadly, turquoise-eyed cobra.

"There's only one thing you'd want to know about the Great Place," he said.

Weris remained silent.

"The hidden entrance to the tomb they're building for Pharaoh Tutankhamen."

"Well now. I think anyone would find that interesting. Don't you?"

Ramses stared at him. "You're insane."

"Insane enough to know how good Pharaoh's treasures will look in a boat headed north—instead of rotting with the bones of a dead man."

"The bones of a dead man?" Ramses took a few steps back. "Are you an idiot? Do you have any idea what happens to tomb-robbers? For the rest of your life, you'll start decaying in disgusting ways, your flesh will drop off. And you won't be able to stop it. And when you want to die, because it's so horrible, you won't be able to. You'll just go on living. A walking plague. You're not going to care about treasures when you're cursed for eternity."

Weris shrugged. "We'll deal with that issue when we come to it."

Ramses stared. "You'll what? . . . Oh, I get it. You'll make me and your 'friends' do your dirty work. So we'll be the ones who are cursed. Is that it? Is that what you think?" He thought of Maat tearing out the man's heart. "That's not how it works.

Already it's too late for you, just talking like this. Don't you understand?"

"A farm boy lecturing me about the gods?" Weris laughed. "Relax. You're my inside-boy. You won't be doing the 'dirty work'."

"I won't be doing any work. I'm not helping you."

"Ah, Denger," Weris said. "There you are, just on time. I think our boy here needs a little convincing."

The sentry from the Place of Truth stepped into view.

CHAPTER 44

Ramses watched Denger cover the last few steps.

So this is how a person looked when he was betraying the people he'd sworn to protect. Like just another person. A son, a brother, a traitor no one really knew. What could make him turn his back on them?

"He needs convincing, does he?" Denger squeezed his dagger's hilt. "Well, that should be easy."

"Really? What, are you going kill me?" Ramses laughed. "Go ahead. Like that's going to help your cause."

"Why such nasty talk?" Weris said with dismay. "There are riches to be made." He spread his hands wide to encompass the fields and wrinkled his nose. "Look at you, slaving away on some old farm that stinks of cow manure and Nile fish."

"This farm is my home," Ramses said. "And it's where I belong."

"There's a whole life ahead of you. A real life to be made. Not like this, but in there, in that village. As a craftsman. You could be one of them—and not just any one. You could be the best."

Ramses stared at the dirt.

"I'm right. You know I'm right. Think of it. Your drawings would live on forever, long after you're gone, carrying Pharaoh through all eternity."

"Eternity? Who's lying now? What do you care about eternity? I belong here. That's it. That's all."

"That's ridiculous," Weris said. "As your Aunt and Uncle's slave?"

"I'm carrying on my parents' work."

"On a farm that's been stolen from you? I'm sure your parents would really appreciate that."

Ramses opened his mouth, but nothing came out.

"Don't be a fool! Look at your hands." He turned up Ramses' palms. The slashes from Aunt Zalika's whip were still there; red, angry welts, caked with dirt. "Is this what your parents wanted? Is this what your gift was meant for?"

Ramses wrenched his hands away. "Leave me alone."

Smoke rose from cooking fires in the workers' camp; a smell of burnt vegetables choked his nostrils. Two men started yelling. Their angry voices carried across the field.

Weris said. "I guess I was wrong. Stay here, if that's what you want."

Ramses nodded, but he felt sick. That wasn't what he wanted. What he wanted was to take Weris's papyrus; to risk everything in the hope of finding a place where he belonged.

"I guess there's no point in carrying on, is there?" Weris said.

"No, there isn't," Ramses replied in a low voice.

Weris turned away.

Denger scowled. "I can make the boy draw. Just watch me."

"No. I'm packing my supplies. I'm leaving this wretched place. Now. This afternoon."

"But the plan," said Denger, his face reddening.

Weris took the sentry's arm. Whatever he said sounded frustrated but resigned. After a moment, Denger stomped away. Weris sighed. "Don't look so glum," he said to Ramses. "I'm sure there'll be other opportunities. Don't you think?"

Of course there wouldn't, and they both knew it.

Ramses felt ill, off balance. Like a chance had come and he'd failed.

Weris's harsh laugh stopped him cold. The tutor wore a grin so twisted, Ramses wanted to tear it from his face.

"I played you like a game of Senet. You made up your mind, didn't you? You do want to help me."

Ramses said nothing.

"I'll leave everything you in your room. Take your time.

Make it good."

Maybe he should do it. What would stop him from reporting Weris and Denger once he got in? He'd be a craftsman, and they'd be arrested.

"You need to hide your thoughts better than that, boy," Weris said.

"You have no idea what I'm thinking."

"If it's of double-crossing me, I do. You're a little too transparent for your own good. You wouldn't win. Not against the honor of a trusted guard like Denger. Especially since his brother is head sentry." The tutor smiled. "And then there's your cousin."

"What are you talking about?"

"I have so many ways to play you, don't you see? You lost a long time ago." He rubbed Ramses' head. "Come now, behave yourself. Do what's right for all of us."

Ramses smacked his hand away.

Weris laughed. "Sepi's not very healthy, is he? He's a nice boy. And a good friend to you. It would be a shame if he died in his sleep."

With that, Weris sauntered off.

Ramses sagged against a thick palm tree. Late afternoon light filtered through clumps of dates overhead. At the sound of the end of day gong, Flatnose and Scar-Eye stopped working and glanced his way.

"Leave me alone," Ramses shouted at them. "Just leave me alone!" He smashed his fist into the tree.

Of course he'd protect Sepi. He'd do anything to keep Sepi safe—even if it meant becoming a traitor to Egypt.

A sick realization hit: Weris's plan was the only way in now, and deep down he was glad he'd been forced to accept it; glad the decision had been made so easy; glad Weris had the means to blackmail him. Even if the means was Ramses' own best friend.

The truth was disgusting.

His face a cold mask, he straightened and headed home.

CHAPTER 45

There you are, Ramses," cried Hebony, her eyes shining. "Hurry, come and sit down." He was surprised when she dragged him around back, toward the garden.

"Where are we going?"

"Just come on."

Next to a tumble of blue cornflowers and gently waving spikes of larkspur lay a large, clean reed mat. Cushions were piled high around the mat's edges. Bastet dozed on one, curled into a ball of fur. In the center lay a feast fit for a festival.

"Who's this for?"

"Guess."

"Aunt Zalika?"

"You."

He smiled. "You're funny. Come on, I don't feel much like joking." Rich, spicy smells wafted from clay dishes. Honey-scented loaves studded with dates and sesame seeds were mounded high in a basket. "Where's Aunt Zalika? What's going on?"

"I told you, it's for you." She glanced past him. "Sobek, there you are, tell him."

"Whatever it is, she's right. She's always right." Sobek laughed as he came down the grassy path with an overflowing jug of ale. "So help me here and find some cups."

Still not quite believing, Ramses climbed over the cushions and grabbed the cups. "I don't understand. What about the others? We have to bring them dinner! Aunt Zalika's going to—"

"Whoa, there," Sobek said, grinning. "It's all arranged. Your friend Weris—"

"Wait, Weris? He's not my friend."

"All right, Snappy. Not friends then, but I know how you admire him. And he's a better man than I thought."

"What did he do?"

"Nothing suspicious! What's got into you tonight?" Sobek laughed. "He just got Zalika to hire some serving girls so we could take the night off."

"And musicians too," Hebony said. "Listen, they're tuning the harps. I love harps!" She flopped onto the pile of cushions, laughing. "Watch out, I told Weris I could get used to this."

Ramses bit his lip.

He now knew that there were ways of getting anything you wanted.

You just had to be willing to sell your soul in return.

He knelt, not wanting her to read the blackness in his heart. The slippery reed carpet brought back memories of a picnic along the river with his parents. He squinted, remembering their faces, trying to remember how he'd felt. But it had been too long ago now. He pulled Bastet into his lap; the cat stretched her claws, turned once, curled in the crook of his knee, and fell asleep.

"Let's eat," Sobek said. "I don't know about you, but I'm starved."

Ramses own stomach was clenched like a fist. "Me too," he lied.

"Can you believe it?" Hebony said, lifting the lid on a stew pot. It held roast meat with onions and vegetables, all baked and caramelized and crisp around the edges. She spooned some onto Ramses' plate. "Tomorrow's the big day!"

"It is." That's for sure.

"Now, no need to be nervous," she said. "You'll do fine." She reached out and squeezed his shoulder.

He nodded. For a moment, he almost confessed everything. He looked at his two friends.

This was the last night they'd spend together. The last time Sobek and Hebony would ever want to see his face. If they knew the evil thing he was about to do, he'd be dead to them already. He couldn't tell them. Not now. Tonight he'd hold tight to the people he cared about. Just for these few hours. He'd pretend everything was perfect, everything was what he'd dreamed it would be.

"Everything ready for tomorrow?" Sobek said.

He thought of Weris's papyrus. "Almost."

Inside, the musicians started in on a pretty tune.

"Good." Sobek swallowed a sip of beer, wiped his mouth on his muscled forearm, and grinned. "Then you won't mind us adding a few things to help our apprentice-in-training?"

"You've given me too much already. And I don't have anything for you!"

"You're more than enough," Hebony said with a gentle cuff to his head. She got up and retrieved a big sackcloth bundle, nestled amongst the far cushions. "Anyway, it's just a small gift. For luck. We're so proud of you."

Proud? He wanted to laugh. Or maybe cry.

Hebony scooted next to him. "Open it," she urged. Already she was pulling on the ties, helping him pull the contents out.

Fabric, white and soft and smelling of the herbs Hebony stored with her clothing, spilled into his hands. He started to unfold it, and a pair of magnificent sandals fell into his lap. The braided reed soles were tough and of the highest-quality.

"They're amazing," he said, running his hands over them.

"There's more," she urged.

He unfolded the fabric all the way. "A brand new kilt, and a tunic too? Look at this linen, it's so soft. But it must have cost a fortune."

Hebony flushed. "You'll look like a noble young man."

"I'll never forget this," he mumbled.

Sobek clapped him on the back. His grey eyes were solemn.

Proud. "Now let's get this celebration underway!"

"Can I join you?" someone asked.

They all turned to see Sepi coming down the grassy path.

Ramses leapt up to meet his friend. "Yes, are you kidding? Come on. But what about your mother?"

"I told her I needed to rest up for tomorrow. Like she'd ever come here to check?"

"Good point."

"Find a seat," Sobek said, filling a cup and handing it to Sepi.

Hebony fluffed up a pile of cushions, and waved him over.

The festive mood soon swept them all up. Ramses listened to Hebony's long-winded stories, Sepi told some of his own, and the two of them laughed with Hebony at Sobek's jokes. Music floated through the garden. The sky turned to purple and then to black. Sitting under the river of stars, Ramses felt safe and protected. He wished he could stay with them forever.

Only when he approached his dark cell did he face the truth.

The door was slightly ajar. Despite the darkness, he could just make out the thick roll of papyrus that lay on his wooden chest.

CHAPTER 46

Ramses left his door open and knelt down in front of the chest. The fine paper smelled clean and fibrous, the best money could buy.

He put his elbows on the trunk and massaged his forehead. The lid was still cracked from when Aunt Zalika tossed it outside onto the pavement. He pressed his face into his hands.

This is not what he wanted. He just wanted his old life back.

Footsteps sounded outside his door.

"Ah, there you are. Ready to work?" Weris said.

Ramses nodded. "Yes. But not here. My aunt will find me."

Weris glanced around. "What a hovel. I can't believe she makes you sleep out here." He scoffed. "Come on. You can draw in my room."

As he strode after the tutor, thinking of his aunt made him grit his teeth. Even if Weris hadn't threatened to take Sepi's life, he'd never change his mind. Not now.

Inside, a lone serving girl sang a soft, melancholy song as she cleaned up the mess in the dining room. The air smelled foreign, of stale incense and sweat. In the hall, the shrine looked sorely neglected: at the household god's feet lay the curled rind of a dried up lemon, along with a crumbly bit of old bread.

Weris ushered him into his room. After lighting several lamps, he crushed and prepared the ink himself. He laid the papyrus out on a small desk, and made Ramses comfortable in a low chair. Then he retired to a corner.

The house had long since fallen silent when Ramses handed over the finished drawing. "Well?" he asked.

The tutor took it and studied it a moment. A slow smile lit his golden eyes. "Boy, I think this might just work."

"I'm going to bed."

"Very good." Weris placed the drawing in a wooden chest. "My two friends from your field crew will get you in the morning. In case you need an escort."

"An escort? If you don't trust me, why don't you just use my drawing yourself? Or are you too much of a coward?"

"Not at all. I would, if I could."

"Then do it."

Weris smiled. "I wouldn't last a day. It's pretty evident I can't draw. Once they realized it, I'd be over."

"That's for sure."

"Look. I could care less about drawing. Just do your job so I can do mine."

Ramses scowled. "I said I was going to, didn't I?"

"Well wipe off that pathetic grimace. You're going to be a craftsman. That's the second wish I've granted you. That and your silly harvest, which you seemed so concerned about. Or have you forgotten?"

A dozen replies blazed through Ramses' mind. In the end all he said was, "I haven't forgotten anything."

Outside the door, the gurgle of Uncle Hay's snores rattled the hall. Ramses hand ached strangely, probably from holding the paintbrush. He tiptoed past his aunt and uncle's door, pressing it to his leg.

In front of the family god's altar with its pathetic offerings, he paused.

Crouching down, he swept the old rind and dried-up bread into his arms. As he did, his aching palm started to burn so hot, it felt like it was on fire. He gasped and wrenched open his fingers, letting everything fall to the ground.

A splash of moonlight washed through the window, over his burning flesh.

He bent close and stared in disbelief.

The raised mark of Maat that had burned itself into his

skin had long since faded away—until now. Somehow, it had returned. And this time, it was slightly different. Her feather no longer rested behind her ear.

It had fallen free.

It was halfway to her feet.

Ramses swore. He left the foul offerings where they lay, trampling them underfoot as he exited the house and headed for the blackness of his cell.

There he curled up, unseeing, as each hour drew him closer to the start of the exam.

Let Flatnose and Scar-Eye come for him.

It was time for this to be over.

CHAPTER 47

Neferet tried to focus on cutting bandages in the physician's whitewashed workroom. Like a curse, Akil's disturbing drawing flashed in her mind. It kept appearing, and she couldn't make it stop.

Shaken, she put down her knife.

Maybe it was a curse. Dark magic.

If only she'd never gone to Tui with her idea for this stupid exam! Everything would've turned out differently, starting with the day she'd met Ramses. She would've gone home, told her father about Ramses' drawing of Ptah, and her father would've insisted on finding him. Without the exam, Akil would've never come there at all.

She wound the bandages, shoved them into a basket and put them away on a shelf. It was time to get home and arrange the house for tonight. In a few hours, the men would be meeting to plan out tomorrow.

When she reached her front steps, her chest ached. She wouldn't cry. She bit her lip at the thought of Akil living in her home. Him with his leer, waiting to whisper news of some curse he'd cast on whatever craftsman stood in his way.

The sound of laughter tore her from her reverie.

Someone was in her house.

Recognizing Layla's snicker, Neferet's hand froze on the knob. She cupped her ear to door to listen.

"Are you done yet?" Layla said.

"Almost," came Kiki's whine.

"Hurry up!" Layla said.

"I'm trying." There was a clunk of pottery slamming down.

"Good enough. Miss Dirt-face is getting a little too full of herself, don't you think? I can hardly wait to see what happens when she tries to use those—"

Neferet shoved open the door. "What are you doing in my house?"

Layla whirled. Her lips curled in a smile. "What does it look like? As you can see, we're helping." She waved at the table.

"Yes. Helping you," Kiki said, arranging fresh sycamore figs on a platter.

This was the last thing she needed right now. What had they done? Neferet crossed her arms, her stomach tumbling with worry. "You can't wait to see what happens when I try to use what?"

Layla rolled her eyes. "What are you going on about? You can't just walk in on a conversation and expect to know something."

Kiki giggled.

"I don't even know why I'm bothering to help you," Layla said

"I don't want you to," Neferet replied, before she could stop herself. She grit her teeth. If her father caught them fighting again—"Hold on, what by the gods . . ."

Her laundry, which she'd spent all yesterday washing, had been kicked over. A sandal-print stained the middle of one of her father's white tunics. "Were you up in my room?"

"Don't be silly," Kiki squeaked.

Neferet started going over everything she had up there—clothing, some herbs she'd gathered and still needed to bring to Merit's. Nothing Layla could possibly be interested in. "What were you doing in my room?"

"You're annoying. Why would I—" Layla broke off and glanced over Neferet's shoulder into the street.

"What are you girls doing?" a man growled. It was Wosret, Layla's father. As always, the stone sculptor's face was dark and brooding.

"Hello." Neferet tried to put on a bright face.

He sneered back, making no secret what he thought of girls. Everyone knew he cursed the fact he'd had a daughter instead of a son to follow in his footsteps.

"Where's Nakht?" he demanded.

"Not home yet. But I'll tell him you—"

"Forget it. Layla, what are you doing here?"

Layla's voice sounded constricted. "Coming, I was just—"

"Just what? Gibbering, like a chicken?"

Layla's throat moved in a swallow.

"Get home and do something useful, for once."

"I am useful," Layla said, so low Neferet barely heard her.

"Is that another wig?"

Layla touched the wig's gold-beaded strands. "This?" she said in a pinched voice. "Of course not! I borrowed it from Kiki. Right Kiki?"

"From m-me?" Kiki stuttered. "Oh—yes! Of course. I wear that one all the time. So much, I'm really very tired of it. It's getting a bit old, I think, because—"

"That's enough," Layla said. "You see, father?"

Wosret ground his jaw, the muscles bulging as he glared at his daughter. "Get home, now," he said, and stomped away.

Layla waited until he was out of earshot. Then she tossed her wig's shiny, beaded braids over her shoulder. "Bring the dishes back clean, dirt-face." she said.

Twilight settled over the village. Laying on a carpet on the roof of her whitewashed house, Neferet listened glumly to the men gathered in her front room below. Over the general buzz of voices came her father's deep one, resounding through the vents.

"Everyone, please find a seat."

Stools and cushions rustled as the craftsmen found their places. The men grumbled, they sounded unhappy.

"Now. I'm sure you've all heard—the officials in Thebes have advised us to expect at least two thousand contest entrants

194

tomorrow."

At this, Neferet gasped. Two thousand? Even if Ramses came, could he compete against that many? She pulled her blanket around her shoulders and shivered.

"That's a nightmare," came Wosret's voice. "And there's no point to it now."

"I agree. Let's accept Akil and be done with it," said another.

"We've given our word," her father said. "The exam continues as announced."

Neferet let out a sigh of relief.

"Fine, but with that many, how long will this take? Weeks!" Wosret growled.

"It's taken too much time already," a second man said.

"We need to get back to work," said a third.

Wosret cut in. "We need to get back to Pharaoh's tomb, not dally around here meeting two thousand hopefuls."

Neferet's father called for silence. "Quiet, quiet please everyone. The contest will not be extended."

"Then how do you expect to perform this miracle?" Wosret demanded.

"Simple," her father replied. "Painter or not, everyone in this room has an eye for craftsmanship."

A general agreement followed.

"So here's how we'll handle it."

Neferet whisked a fly from her ankle with an impatient gesture and strained closer to the vent.

"There are fourteen of us here tonight. Our sentries will direct the two thousand entrants into fourteen lines. We'll each man a station at the head of a line. You'll have approximately one hundred and forty boys each."

"After the entrant presents you his papyrus, examine it and decide if he's skilled enough for further consideration. If the answer is no, direct him to a sentry who will guide him out of the examination area. If the answer is yes, keep the scroll, make a note of the entrant's name, and send him to the waiting tent. At the end of the day, we'll all meet to review the scrolls we've kept."

Everyone started talking at once, all of them sounding relieved. Excited even.

"Now how about another round of beer?" came the voice of old Tui. "I've seen far too many serious faces lately."

Her father's gruff laughter was followed by the sound of footsteps in the kitchen. The floor cellar creaked open. "Someone give me a hand with these jars," he called. "If you want beer, you'll have to work for it!"

Cups rattled, the large containers were hammered open. The noisy mood spilled into the night. What if Ramses didn't come? She pictured his friendly laugh and bright, honest smile; compared it to Akil's frightening one. Neferet reached for the amulet at her throat. Her fingers closed around empty space.

She rolled over and covered her head with the linen sheet.

CHAPTER 48

Dusty blades of morning sunshine pierced the gaps in Ramses' door. He lay like a mummy, his breathing so soft an intruder would think him dead.

Any minute, Flatnose and Scar-Eye would come looking for him. By all the gods how he wished they'd hurry. How he wished they'd get here so this monstrous day would be over. He rolled away from the light.

Fists pounded on his door. "Ramses!" a man shouted. "Help! Are you in there?" The door swung open under the barrage. Hui, a field worker, stood pale-faced and panting.

"What's going on?"

"I need bandages!"

"Bandages?" Ramses shook off his sleepy fog. The fright in Hui's eyes sent him leaping to his feet. "Hebony's room. She has a supply chest." He pushed past the man.

Hui ran after him, breathing hard. "Four hippos attacked a fishing boat. Sobek helped fight them off, but—"

"Sobek?" He grabbed Hui's wrist. "Is he—"

"Hurt? No. But he pulled two fishermen out of the river."

"Then who is?"

They'd reached Hebony's door. "You know those two new farmhands?" Hui said. "I think they're cousins or somewhat."

Ramses hand slipped on Hebony's door handle. Flatnose and Scar-Eye. He steadied himself and pushed it open. "What happened?"

"It was unbelievable. This huge hippo charged at Sobek, and we all stood there, like a pack of idiots. Except that guy with the flat nose—he ran into the water shouting, and drew the hippo off. I thought he was going to get away, but the hippo trapped him in the shallows. Crushed him. The other cousin got in there and the hippo laid its jaws into him too. Sobek finally drove it away . . ." Hui paled. "It was horrible. One has broken legs, the other's bleeding to death."

That's why Flatnose and Scar-Eye hadn't come for him? Because they were saving Sobek's life? He remembered working alongside them, the three of them cutting as a team. They hadn't had to work. He realized that now. So why had they?

He found the bandages and ran, fabric flapping as he crossed the fields.

Sobek saw him first. His face went from surprise to relief to anger. "What are you doing here? Why aren't you at the Place of Truth?" He grabbed the bandages hurried toward a heap of figures on the riverbank.

"Are the cousins—"

"They're my responsibility. You need to go!"

"I need to help you."

Sobek wheeled on him. "You need to go. Hear me? Now!"

Ramses watched his friend's retreating back. Sobek was wrong: he didn't need to do anything—not any longer—not with the cousins too hurt to force him.

Disappointment washed over him; disgust quickly followed. He'd been freed. He should be happy.

Sobek glanced back at him. "Don't just stand there, go!"

Ramses' legs shook as he walked away.

Back in his cell, he closed the door. He'd be all right. He'd have to be. Days would pass, then weeks and months. Sobek and Hebony would forget, he'd repay them for the papyrus eventually, and Hebony could barter his new outfit in the market. The gods didn't want him. The old priest had been right—he was cursed.

And it was time to stop struggling.

Shadows shifted across his room as the sun disk marched across the sky. The day moved swiftly onward, dying a little with each hour. He wanted to run outside, run to the Place of Truth before it was too late.

Instead, he forced himself to remain still.

Finally, stiff with agony, he slipped into a half-sleep.

He was standing in a dark room, lit only by a small lamp. Drawings covered an entire wall. He took a breath of cool, dry air and glanced around. A drawing on one wall was half completed. He moved to it, and bent forward to study it. In the way of dreams, the lamp appeared in his hand and he brought it close to the wall.

It was a half-drawn figure of Ptah. But there were lines that didn't belong. Was it a kind of grid? He tilted his head sideways. Yes, the gridlines crossed at different points of the body—one under the feet, another at the knees, a third at the waist and so on. A thrill ran through him; here was a technique, a simple but brilliant technique to create the perfectly proportioned figure! If he were to use this, every time he drew a figure, they'd all be equal! They'd be—

Hebony's voice came to him. "Look at the hour! Do you think Ramses is back?"

Two sets of footsteps paused in front of his door. Please don't come in! Please don't find me here!

"He can't be. He would've come to find us," Sobek said.

"Oh, I hope they want him!"

"So do I—there's nothing for him here now."

"It's just not fair, he's their nephew! And he's a good boy."

Sobek lowered his voice. "It's worse than you think."

"What do you mean?"

Ramses crept to the door and leaned against the rotted wood.

"Zalika is selling the farm."

A coldness filled his chest. She couldn't. She wouldn't dare. This land, this home, it wasn't hers! It had never been hers!

"Selling . . ." Hebony gasped. "Why?"

"Zalika's terrified he'll find a way to claim his inheritance. If she sells the farm, Ramses will have nothing to claim."

"Oh Sobek . . ."

"I heard that tutor, Weris, got her started. They're going to take the money and go into business together in Memphis."

"It'll take ages to find a buyer," Hebony said, her voice hopeful. "And we can all stay here, even if the owner changes."

"Kontar's made an offer."

"But she hasn't accepted, has she?"

"He's already talking about getting rid of the wheat and grazing cattle instead. Getting rid of the living quarters too."

"The house?" Hebony whispered. "Our wonderful home?"

"He has a house. It's just land to him."

"Where will we go? What about Ramses?" she asked.

"That's why he needs to the apprenticeship. I couldn't tell him, I didn't want him to know, but Zalika's planning on selling him. As a slave."

The cell's stench felt suddenly overwhelming. Ramses wanted to retch.

"May the gods protect him," she said softly, starting to cry.

Their voices faded as they walked away.

She couldn't destroy his parent's house, everything they'd worked for. And Sobek and Hebony's lives too?

If the price of freedom meant joining Weris, so be it. What did he care about Pharaoh's sacred tomb? The gods hadn't protected him any more than his aunt had. They'd forsaken him, and he'd do the same. Let his soul be destroyed forever—while he was alive, he still had the power to act.

He slipped on his new sandals, and hurried to fasten his kilt.

The acacia tree threw sharp shadows as he ran for Weris's room. He yanked his papyrus from its hiding place, then climbed back out over the sill. His eyes went to his cell. The door hung open on its hinges. The gaping threshold loomed like a hole of eternal darkness.

With a growl, he sprinted away from the house.

Never again would he return to that room.

Never again would he live trapped like a slave in his own home.

CHAPTER 49

Gulping, Ramses glanced up at the sun god's progress. Ra was dangerously close to the horizon. What time did the exam end? Would he even make it?

He tore across an unfamiliar field of barley. A mass of acacia rose up. It cracked and slashed under the force of his arms and legs. He burst out the other side and kept running. His new sandals grated against flesh, the thong grinding between his toes. He ran faster. Soon, beyond the humid sprawl of farms, the hills of the desert rose skyward.

A line of dusty date palms marked the border between the two worlds. The trees threw cold, dark slashes across the earth; the day was rapidly headed for dusk.

He had to hurry. But which way? There were no clear roads like there were to Thebes—the Place of Truth wasn't a place you just visited. He'd been stupid to think he'd just go there without directions! Why hadn't he thought to ask someone when he'd had the chance? His hands started to sweat around his papyrus.

He could wander the desert for days before he found it. The exam would be long over. The sacred village could be anywhere.

"Where are you going?" a small voice said.

Ramses spun around.

A child, a small girl, sat at the base of one of the date palms.

"The Place of Truth, do you know where it is?" He almost laughed; of course she wouldn't! Why would she, a little girl like that?

She wrinkled her dirty nose at him. "Why do want to know?"

"Because . . . just, do you know where it is?"

She shrugged and said in a singsong voice, "Why do you want to go there?"

"Please! Do you know the way or not?"

She pointed east. "That's the way the deliverymen go. They have pretty donkeys. Sometimes they let me pet them."

He followed her gesture and made out a raised dirt causeway, snaking away toward the sands. "Thank you!"

His feet churned across the earth, leaving a wake of pockmarked tracks. Only when he reached the causeway did he realize she'd been wearing a white feather in her dirty hair.

He thought of the amulet of Maat, and then of Neferet. How could he face her, knowing he was a traitor? The thought made him sick. He forced it from his mind.

All around, the world stood out in brilliant focus; a flock of white birds swooped low over the earth; the silhouette of a tamarisk tree stood out in bold black lines. The distance between sun and earth was shrinking, rapidly. He urged his legs onward, alternating his papyrus from one sweaty palm to the other to try and save it from smearing.

Soon the last holdout of dusty farms gave way to lifeless desert. The causeway grew hard and stony. It flattened out into a simple road, curving up and right, weaving its way into the mountains. The gulch deepened; cliffs closed in on either side.

After what seemed like forever, a small valley opened ahead. Then he saw it. Cupped in the bowl of hillsides, at the far end, lay the Place of Truth. Two big tents sprouted in front of its earth colored walls. Colorful banners waved in the soft breeze.

He shouted with joy. The girl had been right!

With a burst, he renewed his speed. There was no hesitating now. Closer, he could see pole stanchions to which ribbons had been tied, as if to form long lines. All the lines headed toward the tents. Yet the lines were empty. Most of the ribbons hung broken and fluttering in the wind.

He tore down the road, heading for the nearest one. People

trickled toward him: parents with crestfallen faces, boys clutching scrolls of papyrus. Ramses drifted through them in a blur. He saw only the door.

Then he was there, face-to-face with a sentry.

Trying to catch his breath, he gasped, "I'm here for the exam."

"Too late," the sentry said. "Exam's over."

"It's . . . over?" Ramses stood there, stunned. "But, it can't be over." How could it be over? Not now! Not after everything.

"Go home. I said it's over, all right?"

"Please . . . I'm begging you!"

"You're too late. The finalists have been chosen."

"Finalists. So they haven't decided yet?" He grabbed hold of the tent flap. "Let me give them my scroll, please—"

"Stand back, you arrogant whelp," the man growled, hand going to his dagger.

"What is it?" called a gruff voice from inside.

"Just a late one," the sentry called back.

"A late one, huh?" The flap was thrust aside and a face appeared.

Ramses heart turned to lead. It was Denger, the corrupt guard, and Weris's inside man. Suddenly he knew with every bone in his body that he'd been wrong to come here. He couldn't do it. He had to get away.

Denger's bloodshot eyes met Ramses', and the guard grinned.

"Well, well." He darted forward. "About time you got here. Give me your papyrus. Quick."

Ramses ducked as Denger's arm shot out. The guard growled, reaching for him. Ramses lurched sideways. He slammed into a gang of boys. They swore at him and pushed him away. He sprinted through the crowd. He had to get out of there!

"Stop him!" Denger bellowed.

"Hey you!" one of the boys shouted and lunged at Ramses. His hand closed around Ramses' elbow, but he tore free.

"Get him!" the boy shouted.

Ramses' legs moved like lightning. He surged forward, gaining ground. An old woman shot out her cane, sending him sprawling to his knees. Over his shoulder, he spotted Denger closing in. The sentry rammed through the crowd and mowed down the ground between them. Ramses scrambled to his feet.

Just before he turned to run, he saw four familiar figures emerge from the examination tent: Aunt Zalika, Weris, Uncle Hay and Sepi. Aunt Zalika marched in the lead, her proud chin jutting forward like a battering ram.

It was too late to hide. Their eyes met, and she screamed. Ramses took off.

"Thief! That's stolen papyrus," Aunt Zalika shrieked. "He's getting away!"

Sepi's voice came as a faint shout. "Mother, leave him alone! Leave Ramses alone!"

"Get him!" Weris shouted.

The sound of Denger's grinding footsteps spurred Ramses on. Picking up speed, he tore around the high wall of the village and headed for the Peak of the West. Maybe he could find shelter there, hide until they gave up the chase. Onward he ran, beyond the village, across the hard, sun-beaten sand. The rocky earth hissed with the coming of dusk, cooling in the evening air.

Shadows from the mountain reached for him. He followed their darkness, climbing onto higher ground. Under his feet, dusty pebbles scattered and slid against his sandals.

Yet even as he ran, his heart screamed for him to go back. The day wasn't over. Not yet. It couldn't end like this!

Choking with dust, heart threatening to burst from his ribs, he strained to listen for Denger. He heard only his own footsteps, scrabbling against the dry, stony earth. Finally, he risked a glance back.

The hill was deserted.

He'd made it. They were gone. They'd given up.

Then he understood why.

They had no reason to follow him. Somewhere along the

way he'd dropped his precious papyrus. He'd left it lying in the dirt, abandoned and forgotten, waiting for them to find it. His entry, his last hope, was gone.

On the horizon, the sun hovered briefly like a tiny spark. Then the gods snuffed it out. Darkness fell like a cold hand, crushing his hopes into the earth. A sob racked his chest. In the dryness of the desert, the tears never came.

In the valley below, bells began to ring. Their clanging rose to the sky.

The exam was over.

They'd chosen their apprentice.

CHAPTER 50

Crouched in the back of the judge's tent, Neferet's fingers slid from her legs. They left bruises where she'd pressed them into her thighs, harder and harder as the day had progressed. Outside, the bells continued to ring.

It wasn't possible. It couldn't be possible.

It was over.

How could Ramses not have come?

She'd been so sure he would in the end. Like an idiot, she'd given her trust to hope instead of doing something. It was too late. Her head felt strangely light.

Her father, along with the twelve elder craftsmen, talked in low voices, all looking hot, weary and irritable. No one noticed her in the deepening gloom.

"Quite the day. Two thousand applicants," Neferet's father said, rubbing his eyes. "How many are still in the holding tent?"

"Four," said Paimu, the painter.

"Akil's the only one with any talent," grumbled Wosret. "We could've done away with this wretched event."

Akil—always Akil. She felt sick. His prophesy in the desert had come true.

"Let's take a look at what we've got, Wosret," her father said. "Bring in their entries. We haven't made the final decision quite yet."

The rapidly cooling air dried the sweat from her forehead. So there was still hope. Nightfall stifled the chaos outside, fading it to silence. She pictured Layla and her mother searching for her back in the village, along with the other girls in their fancy wigs and face-paints, and felt a brief moment of satisfaction that she'd managed to escape. No doubt they'd forget her soon enough once they started gossiping about the boys who'd come today.

Four scrolls were brought in. The thirteen men gathered around a small table. One by one, the entries were passed, discussed, carefully examined.

When the debate slowed, her father said, "I think we're ready. Unless anyone wants more time?" In the absence of a reply, he chose a scroll, and displayed it around. "I'm told this one's father is a woodcarver. He's skilled with the brush, as you can see."

"It's really not bad," Tui said. Others agreed.

"Any votes?" her father said. He waited. She crossed her fingers.

Despite their enthusiasm, not one craftsman raised his hand.

Good things were said about the second artist; the boy's name was called to a vote. Once again, all hands stayed at the craftsmen's sides. Her father named the third boy. Neferet got to her feet, willing the men to vote.

He waited only seconds before moving on. "Last, as a formality, do we have votes for Akil?"

Thirteen hands went up, and she cried, "No, you can't!"

Faces turned in dismay, frowned when they saw her there, and with more than a few gusty sighs, turned back to the discussion. Well she could care less about their disapproval. And she didn't give a beetle's snout for formalities now. It wasn't supposed to end like this. This wasn't supposed to happen. They had no idea what they were doing. If they knew Akil like she did, they'd never let him through the gates.

Let alone share with him the secrets of Pharaoh's tomb!

"Stop this!" she said.

Her father's lips turned white. "Neferet! Get out. Immediately." To the others he said, "It's unanimous. Akil's our new apprentice."

"Good." Wosret nodded. "Give the verdict so we can go."

She tasted tears of rage as a sentry tried to pull her toward the door. "Don't make me carry you," he growled.

"Try it and you'll be sorry," she hissed.

But before they could leave, the flap opened and Denger—Jabari's younger brother—slammed into the sentry holding Neferet's arm.

"Watch yourself!" the sentry said.

Denger gave him a black look. "Out of my way. I'm here to see the Chief Scribe."

"What is it?" Neferet's father demanded.

"Sir? It's urgent." Denger waved a scroll. It looked dusty and creased, as if someone had dropped it and others had trampled on it. "I found this on the ground."

"Another papyrus?" Neferet's father sounded as if he'd seen enough for a lifetime. "Some applicant must have thrown it away. You should have arrested him for desecration. Anyway, it's too late. We've made our decision."

"With all due respect, sir, you might want to look," Denger said.

At his tone, Neferet's heart quickened. "Did you see who dropped it?" she cried.

"I did." Denger's face was sweating beneath his leather helmet as if he'd been running, and his eyes were bloodshot. He smiled. "It was your friend, Miss. The boy you met by the river."

For a moment, she paused. Had Denger been there by the Nile? But what did it matter? Her heart leapt. Ramses had come! She dashed forward. "Let me see!"

"Neferet!" her father barked.

She skidded to a halt.

"I'll take it." Her father reached for the scroll. He unraveled it halfway. For a moment he stared down in silence. His eyes widened. Then, with a gasp, he unrolled it completely.

"What is it?" Paimu said, hurrying to his elbow. His jaw dropped.

The other craftsmen pushed in close. Shocked murmurs

went up. Neferet shoved her way between them. She squeezed through to her father's side.

For once he didn't scold her. He simply held the page for her to see.

A magnificent image almost leapt from the papyrus. Meretseger—cobra goddess, sacred protector of the tombs—looked out at her. Either a breeze was moving the page, or the goddess's chest was rising and falling of its own accord. The illusion was so real, so complete, she jerked back in a moment of panic.

"Is it alive?" she whispered.

As if in response, Meretseger's eyes flashed. The men stumbled backward.

"What trick is this?" Wosret whispered.

The figure of the cobra shimmered, bulging up from the page. Brighter and brighter she glowed, until her light reflected in every man's staring eyes. Meretseger was rising, a frightful goddess made of gold.

Men paled. Some fell to their knees and covered their faces.

Neferet stood stock still, unable to move, unable to fall to the floor. Ramses' drawing filled her vision. Meretseger had awakened, called to life by Ramses' hand. But had he gained her patronage—or her wrath?

Over the noise, she heard a voice. It hissed into her ear: "Death shall come on swift wings to him who disturbs the peace of the Pharaoh!"

Broken from her trance she spun around. There was no one there.

CHAPTER 51

Neferet searched for a sign that others had heard the voice, too. A few feet away, Denger swallowed visibly, his face ashen. She realized that even if she shouted, no one would hear over the throbbing hum that shook the air.

Suddenly, it broke off.

The silence felt deafening.

The drawing of Meretseger hadn't moved from her father's calloused hands. She was shocked he hadn't thrown it down, impressed in a way she'd never imagined. His fingers rolled it shut, then closed protectively around the scroll.

"We must find this boy," he said.

It was as if a spell had been broken. Everyone started talking at once.

"Call Jabari," he told the sentry at the door. "Have him round up the men. I don't care if we have to search every farm, every alley in Thebes, from the desert to the Nile. I want this boy found."

"On my way, sir."

He ordered lamps lit, and then to Denger said, "You are to be commended, sentry."

Denger colored, smiling slightly, and stared at the dry, sandy floor.

From outside, shouts arose. "Let me go! Let go of me!" The tent flap was torn aside by a tall, lean boy with dark, oily hair. He hurtled over the threshold. Akil.

Two sentries followed, red-faced, and seized him by the arms. Akil cursed and kicked at them and wrestled free. The sentries darted after him, roaring with rage.

"Did I win?" Akil shouted. "I won, didn't I?"

"Stop right there," Neferet's father said.

Akil drew up short. "But the bells . . ."

"I'll tell you when—and if—to come!"

The sentries caught up, panting. One had a bloody gash on his cheek. "Sorry, sir. This boy's a slippery one." He grabbed Akil by his tunic. "You're coming with me."

Akil held his ground. "I demand to know what's going on. I deserve to know what's going on! We've waited long enough."

"You demand nothing. Not from me, or anyone else." Her father's eyes were hard. "Now find some patience. A decision has not yet been made."

"A decision? About what? You can't compare me to any of those idiot boys in there." Akil gestured rudely toward where he'd been waiting. "And you all know it. So what kind of decision are you talking about?"

"He's talking about someone who's not in there," Neferet said loudly.

All eyes turned to her. Paimu cursed under his breath and her father let out an angry snort. "Thank you Neferet, but that's no one's business but ours."

"Someone else?" Akil scoured the tent. "I don't see anyone else. Show him to me, show me his work. I'm better. I'll prove it!"

"You'll prove nothing," her father said. "What you'll do is wait."

Akil crossed his arms. "How long?" he demanded.

Tui cut in, his voice smiling but firm. "As it says in the sacred texts of the Ke'gemni, 'comfortable is the seat of the man of gentle speech—but knives are prepared against the one that forces a path, that he does not advance, save in due season.'"

A few men laughed.

"There's no point in keeping it secret now," her father said. "You'll wait until dawn. That's when we'll make our decision."

Neferet ran to her father. "Dawn, tomorrow morning? But

that's only hours away! That's not enough time to find Ramses, he could be anywhere, he—"

"Stop. I think you too need a study in the sacred texts!" Then to Akil, "You have your answer. You'll wait until Ra escapes the mouth of Nut. If the boy hasn't been found, the apprenticeship is yours."

Akil's mouth curled into a wide grin. "Then it's mine already. You'll never find him before dawn." He loped out the door, laughing. Something about his walk had an eerie familiarity to it; then she realized why it seemed so familiar: the boy from her dream, the last one. Akil was the jackal of death.

Jabari entered. "Denger?"

"Here." Jabari's brother stepped forward.

Most of the craftsmen had turned away by now to busy themselves with other things. Neferet, curious however, watched the two siblings in their formal uniforms.

"This is your mission. I want you to lead," Jabari said.

There was something almost awkward in the way Denger said, "You do?"

"You found the scroll, little brother." Jabari shot him a grin. "It's your triumph, not mine."

Denger stuttered out something that sounded like embarrassed surprise. He quickly recovered though and said, "I'll break the men into groups. Twos or threes, so we can cover more ground. Don't worry, I'll find Ramses—the boy." He motioned to Neferet. "Come outside so you can give a description of your friend."

A moment later, she stood before the gathered sentries. As loud as she could, she recounted Ramses' height, his cropped hair, his dark, almond shaped eyes.

"That's half the boys in Egypt," a man said.

"We need more than that," said another.

She glanced sideways at her father. In a breathless voice, she said, "He wears a turquoise amulet of Maat."

"A what?" someone called out.

Her father regarded her a moment, as if just realizing she

hadn't been wearing the treasure for weeks. He let out his breath, and then addressed the sentries. "An amulet. Of Maat. And not a trinket from some market stall—a precious one, carved of turquoise. If he has it, that's your proof."

At the second tent, Akil stood framed in the doorway. He made a strange sign in the air, and then a guard yanked the flap shut. She closed her mouth and swallowed, and fear slid down her spine.

The sentries slid off into the night. She wanted to run after them. She wanted to help. Her stomach tensed and her head swam.

Dawn would be here all too soon.

CHAPTER 52

In the darkness, Ramses curled into a crevice in the cliff. Hidden from the horrors below, he'd wait until dawn. Then he'd figure out what to do. He needed to numb his mind, force himself to sleep, to forget everything.

Why had he run? He could've let Denger take him inside. It's what he'd wanted, wasn't it? He wrenched himself up, his heart dull and heavy in his chest.

The world was black as kohl.

Cursing, he wiped his gritty forehead. It was over. It was time to stop thinking about it. It was time to move on. Time to get away from this place, to erase it from his memory. Time to never draw again.

Overhead, stars sparkled like candles floating on the river. It had to be around four in the morning. He rose and looked down from the Peak of the West, out across the desert to the fertile fields, now dark and hazy in the distance. From here the scene looked peaceful. The Nile winked, jet black and flashing.

Somewhere down there lay his farm.

He pictured it with its worn paving stone courtyard, the solid, whitewashed walls of the house, the smells of wheat and hay, of baking bread; his home, with Sobek and Hebony, and the steady, predictable rhythm of working the fields; his world, with his best friend Sepi who grinned and joked and heckled better than anyone. All of it seemed so precious. Like treasures he didn't realize he had until they were gone.

He tore his eyes away. How did he ever think he could be a craftsman in the Place of Truth? He deserved this punishment.

Rubbing his face, he cleared away his exhaustion.

The valley would not welcome him again. His only choice was to disappear, to go where Aunt Zalika would never find him. He'd head for the river, find work on a boat. Now, before the fishermen pulled up their anchors.

By dawn, he'd be gone forever.

Standing, he shook the stones from his sandals. The cool night air ripped away his sweat, making him shudder. The faster he got moving, the warmer he'd be.

He picked a route down the steep mountain, over boulders and across shale landslides. At its base, he didn't bother to find the raised causeway, he simply trekked across the rocky desert, headed for the lean date palms in the distance. The grassy scrub that marked the border of the farmlands felt cool and damp.

An irrigation ditch ran at right angles to the field. He crouched and drank to kill his hunger. But the water tasted gritty and he stopped after a few gulps. Cursing, he wiped his mouth and kept going. Dawn would be here all too soon. He needed to find those fishing boats.

Finally, a familiar swampy smell filled the air, along with a gentle lapping sound. Pushing through a thick stand of rushes, the Nile came into view. He looked right and left, and his heart leapt. For the first time in ages, luck was with him.

A boat was moored just a few hundred paces out, and a lamp moved on deck. Squinting, he made out the shape of a man, walking to the stern. The fisherman bent over the ropes. He was preparing to cast off.

Ramses shouted, "Hey! Wait!"

The fisherman raised the lamp and his grizzled head peered over the side.

"Do you need a boat-hand?" Ramses called.

"Depends who's asking."

"My name's Ramses, and I'm a hard worker." He started wading out.

The captain scowled at him. "You don't look like a fisherman."

"Maybe not, but I work hard."

This got a grunt. "We'll see about that. I'm headed north, leaving right now."

"So you'll hire me?"

"Better not be a sea-sick sort."

"I'm not," Ramses said.

"Humph. We'll see."

Ramses waded the last few yards and climbed on board, dripping.

Instantly, the smell of rotting fish hit him. He struggled not to gag. His sandals slipped on fish guts smeared across the deck. He grabbed the railing to steady himself, and when he pulled his hand away, scales and slime came with it. Anyone who bought fish from this man was risking an early death. The old captain watched him, his eyes narrowing, and started to laugh.

"What, you got a complaint already 'bout my boat?"

"No."

The captain glanced down at Ramses' unsteady feet, and swung his lamp toward them. "Why don't you give me those sandals, boy? I don't need no fancy boat-hand, dressing like he's some kinda prince or something."

The idea of going barefoot made him shudder. But he needed this job. "They won't fit you," he blurted.

"Humph." The sailor wiggled his gnarled feet; they looked like giant fish that had sprouted big scraggly toes. "Maybe you're right."

Ramses tried to hide his relief. Then the fisherman bent and wrenched the sandals off, sending Ramses slipping backward. He caught himself just before he sprawled flat-out onto the stinking deck.

"I'll barter them up river later. Now grab those ropes. We got a long way to go."

He nodded.

"That's a yes sir," the fisherman said.

"Yes, sir." Barefoot, he slid across the deck, his throat choking against the overpowering stench. He'd get used to it.

He'd have to.

Neferet's amulet bumped against his chest. His fingers went to it. It wouldn't be long before the fisherman discovered the only thing he had left of her. No doubt the man would search him for valuables as soon as he fell asleep. At the thought of Neferet's grin, a bleak emptiness closed in on him. He wondered if she even remembered him. One thing was certain, he'd lost the hope of seeing her again.

Maybe it was for the best. He couldn't have faced living in her village as a traitor, he knew that now. It struck him that his palm had stopped burning. Glancing down, he saw smooth skin. It was as if the amulet's mark had never existed.

The gods were finally happy. So this is what they had planned for him all along.

CHAPTER 53

Get a move on, boy," the fisherman barked.

Cursing, Ramses grabbed the mucky rope that held the anchor and started hauling it in. It rose, dripping, and clanged onto the deck. They were moving. Leaving. And he was glad to be gone.

"Halt!" a man called from the bank. "You there, halt that boat!"

Out of the darkness came the form of a helmeted man, wading into the water. A sentry. Ramses gulped. This had nothing to do with him. Denger wouldn't have organized sentries to find him, not now that it was all over.

Still, Ramses crouched lower, thankful to feel the boat moving into the current.

"I said, halt!" The guard plunged through the water after them.

"Didn't you hear the man?" the fisherman shouted. He threw himself at Ramses and sent the anchor splashing into the river. The boat jerked to a stop.

"Good!" the sentry shouted. "Now what's your boat-hand's name, fisherman?"

"Dunno! I just picked 'im up." He shot Ramses a furious look.

"We're looking for a boy of his description."

"I've done nothing wrong!" the fisherman whined. Then he grabbed Ramses by the collar. "What kind o' scoundrel are you, bring the law down on my boat?"

"I'm innocent. You have to help me."

"Why should I?" the fisherman growled.

Ramses realized the man was waiting for some kind of offer. "I have something valuable. Very valuable. You can have it. Please!"

"Something wrong?" the helmeted sentry called. He'd waded almost to the boat. "Send him down!"

"I'm just a slave," Ramses called to him. "I have work to do!"

"So do I," the sentry said. He turned, cupped his hands around his mouth and shouted, "Denger, I got one, down by the river."

Denger?

"Over here," the sentry called.

In horror, Ramses watched his enemy make his way onto the bank. It was crazy—why had Denger tracked him down? The exam was over; it was too late! Then, with sudden clarity, he understood. Ramses was a risk. He knew too much. Denger had come to kill him.

"Fisherman, hold your lamp to the boy's face," Denger said.

Ramses flinched as the flame lit him for the world to see.

Denger laughed. "Might be him. Send him down."

Might be? What game was Denger playing?

The fisherman gave him a shove. "You heard 'im. I don't want no trouble. Off my boat!"

"He's going to kill me."

The fisherman grabbed him by the neck and flung him into the water. The sentry caught hold of his tunic. Laughing, he pulled him to shore where Denger stood waiting.

Denger looked into Ramses' face. "Might be the one. I can't be sure."

"What about the amulet?" the sentry said.

"Look at the filthy beggar, if he had it, he sold it long ago. Am I right, boy?"

Ramses said nothing.

The sentry looked doubtful.

"The girl can verify it." Denger took Ramses' arm. To the sentry, he said, "Check the other boats. We're almost out of

219

time. I'll meet you back at the village."

"Understood," the sentry said.

"And good work." Denger hauled Ramses past the border of thick rushes.

They emerged in a dark field. Up ahead, like the back of a giant snake, a raised earth road curved toward the mountains. He recognized the causeway to the Place of Truth. Unknowingly, he'd walked right back to where he'd started the day before.

"I haven't told anyone anything," Ramses said. "I swear it!"

"Shut up." Grabbing him in a headlock, Denger pulled out a rope. Ramses kicked hard and slammed him in the gut. Muscled as a bull, the man just laughed. "Nice try."

He crushed him to the ground, snaked the rope around Ramses' neck and wrists, and bound his hands together. Then he lashed the other end to his own thick forearm and set off down the causeway, pulling Ramses like an obstinate donkey.

The rope jerked him forward, threatening to pull his arms from his sockets. Denger kept glancing at the horizon, where a brightening glow divided the earth and sky. In less than an hour, Ra would escape the mouth of Nut to peek over the earth.

If only they'd come a moment later, Ramses would've been gone.

"Let me go," he gasped, "I won't tell anyone."

"Shut up and move." Denger growled. "I thought you wanted to be a craftsman."

"A what?"

Denger glanced back. "The plan's still on. They saw your drawing."

"I don't believe you. Please, just let me go, don't kill me. I'd never tell anyone! I don't care about what you tried to do. I just want to leave, get on a boat, go away!"

"Yeah—not after I showed the Chief Scribe your drawing. Everyone's out looking for you."

"That doesn't make sense! The exam's over."

"If I wanted you dead, I'd have slit your throat already. You think I'd bother dragging you around? What do I look like, an idiot?"

"People are looking for me?" Something in Denger's eyes told Ramses he'd spoken the truth. They wanted him, really wanted him? A rush of excitement surged into him. Faster and faster until it threatened to propel him skyward.

"That's right boy, smile. You should've seen the men when they saw what you drew. We got 'em right where we want 'em." Denger said.

At this, Ramses' feet dragged in the dirt, his mind sobered. What did it matter if they wanted him? They didn't know about Denger's plan. And he couldn't be a part of it. Not anymore.

"I'm not doing it."

"Oho, yes you are."

"I'll tell him you found the wrong boy. The Chief Scribe doesn't know me."

"Maybe not." Denger leered at him. "But his daughter does." Denger tore open the neck of Ramses tunic. Grinning, he clamped his thick fingers around the amulet of Maat. "And how do you explain this?"

"I found it," Ramses lied, trying to pry Denger's fingers away.

"Nice piece." After snapping the amulet free, he shoved Maat headfirst into the folds of his tunic. "Don't try me," he growled, pulling out his sword. The curved blade glinted evil in the dusky light.

"You can't threaten me with death."

He pressed it to Ramses' throat, then slid the blade lightly across the skin. "It's not you I'm threatening." Ramses felt a warm trickle ooze down his neck.

"What are you talking about?"

"Just do what I say."

"Or what?"

"Or I'll kill your little girlfriend." Denger sneered, triumphant. "Now run."

CHAPTER 54

The desert air rang with the running crunch of their footfalls. Denger had tied the ropes well, and Ramses' wrists bled from trying to pull himself free. He watched Denger's sword jangle at his belt; twice he'd almost come close enough to grab it.

Lungs burning, he darted for a third try. It was inches away. Struggling against his bindings, he spread his fingers wide and reached for the hilt.

He had it! Careful now, just pry it out of the scabbard—

A pothole made him stumble and he lost his hold. Denger didn't notice. The sentry's leather sandals beat out a steady rhythm. His whole attention seemed focused on getting to the gates as fast as possible.

On either side, hills sloped up and away, disappearing into the pre-dawn gloom. Ramses knew this spot: it was the ravine to the Place of Truth. Denger had to be stopped, now, before it was too late.

Desperate, he bent forward, the blade inches away.

Come on, just a little more—

Denger skidded to a halt.

Ramses slammed into his back with an oof.

"Shut up, boy, someone's coming."

Ahead, a small figure hurtled down valley toward them. Her hair streamed over her shoulders, dark against the ghost-white fabric of her dress. It felt like a waking nightmare: if Denger got hold of Neferet, who knew what the sentry would do?

"Go back!" Ramses shouted.

Denger grabbed him in a chokehold. "Shut up or she's dead."

"Who's there?" Neferet's voice was high-pitched, full of what sounded like excited hope. She kept coming, closing the distance. Gazelle-like, she flew easily across the hard, rocky ground.

"Stop!" Ramses shouted, but his words were muffled by Denger's hand.

"Another word and I'll break her neck. Understood?"

Ramses nodded. Denger took his hand from Ramses mouth, but kept a tight hold on the rope. Close enough to see her clearly now, she looked how he imagined a daughter of Pharaoh might look. Regal. A simple gold clasp shone in her hair, and her sheath-like dress gleamed the purest white.

"Ramses, it is you! Denger found you!" she cried.

He glared at the ground.

"But what are the ropes for?" She laughed. "Denger, Ramses isn't a goat being taken to slaughter. Untie him, right now!"

"I will, Miss, when I hand him over to your father. Run along, we'll follow you."

"No. This is ridiculous. Untie him!"

"Miss, I'd like to, but he's trying to get away."

"Get away?" she said.

Ramses refused to look up. If she'd just listen to Denger and go home!

"It's not true, Ramses, is it? You really want to get away?"

Denger's fingers bit into Ramses' neck. "He's suffering from nerves. That's all."

"Go home, stupid girl," Ramses growled, forcing his voice to sound thick with loathing. He didn't care if she hated him, if it was the only way to make her leave. "I don't need some stuck-up idiot in a fancy dress sticking her nose in my business." He steeled his face into a cold mask and met her gaze.

The hurt in her eyes made him sick.

"Hear that?" Denger said, snorting with laughter. "Go home!"

"I don't care if he thinks I'm stupid. Untie him!"

"Let me do my job," the sentry said.

Neferet paused, but looked ready to explode. "Do your job? You think this is your job? You think this is what Jabari wanted you to—" Her voice broke off as her eyes went to Denger's hip pocket. "Is that my amulet? Why do you have my amulet?"

Despite Denger having shoved it deep into his tunic, the goddess figurine had almost worked its way free. Even stranger, the tiny figure had righted itself, so that it stared straight at them.

CHAPTER 55

"Answer me, Denger," Neferet said.

"I'm warning you, get out of my way," Denger replied.

"Tell me or I'll—"

"You'll what?" Denger snarled, his hand reaching for his sword.

"Run!" Ramses shouted; the ropes catapulted him back. "Run! He'll kill you!"

The sentry lunged, but she was too quick. She jumped out of the way and sprinted up the path. With a shout, Denger sprinted after her. Ramses dug in his heels, straining to hold back the heavily muscled sentry. Sand skidded under his bare feet, the ropes tore into his flesh. He fell to his knees and was dragged forward.

Neferet was fast, but her dress kept catching underfoot. Denger gained on her, his powerful strides dragging Ramses forward.

She glanced back, tripped and fell in a sprawl. With a cry, she jumped up.

But Denger was on her—he caught her hair in his fist.

"Should've listened to your father." Denger wrenched her head to look at him. "Too late for that now."

"Stop it!" Neferet screamed.

Somehow Ramses got his bound hands around a stone. He slammed it into Denger's head. The rock hit with a sickening thud. The guard didn't pause. His elbow shot straight back into Ramses' jaw. Pain exploded in his mouth. Denger's fist slammed into his head, again and again.

"Stop!" Neferet screamed, kicking him. "Stop it!"

Denger smashed her aside and kept pounding Ramses. Seeing stars, he fought to ward off the blows. He was almost unconscious when he realized Denger had stopped. The man's face swam into view overhead. Blood oozed over his left eye. Somewhere in his fogged mind, Ramses registered satisfaction. Denger was hurt. The stone had made a nasty gash. He wasn't invincible.

"Bad idea." Denger laughed.

"How could you?" she cried. "You're supposed to protect us."

Holding a kicking Neferet by her hair, he yanked his sword from its scabbard and pressed its into her back. "Walk," he growled. "Quickly."

"Jabari trusts you," she said. "Your brother trusts you!"

"Shut up."

"Did you see his face? How much he cares about you? Don't do this!"

"Shut up or I'll kill you right here."

Ramses head swam as he scanned the ground for another weapon, a stone, a stick, anything.

Denger yanked him up. "You too. Walk! Both of you!" Sword to Neferet's back, he angled her away from the path. The three of them headed left for the steep valley wall. They soon reached the slope's base.

"Up," Denger said.

They started to climb. It was hard work.

"Faster!" Denger said, glancing at the ever-brightening sky.

"Let her go," Ramses said, his words muffled by his swelling jaw. "I'll help you!"

"Shut up, climb."

"They're going to find out," Neferet said. "Jabari will find out, I swear it!"

"Shut your mouth!" Denger said, jabbing her back. A red spot oozed through the fabric of her dress.

Dawn was approaching; the hills looked gray as ash. Ramses' throbbing skull pounded in time with his anger. He spat the blood from his mouth, his mind furiously searching for a way to take Denger down.

Life just got worse and worse. He'd tried to be happy on his farm. He'd tried to enter the Place of Truth. He'd tried to leave and go away forever. He'd tried everything to make the gods happy. The old priest was right. He was cursed.

All he'd wanted was a place where he belonged. Behind them, the houses of the craftsmen's whitewashed village were growing visible. He imagined the sound of chisels ringing in the clear air, the smell of paints filling his nostrils.

He had been so close. So close.

They'd reached a dizzying land-bridge that connected this hill with the next. The narrow ridge could only be traversed in single file.

"Move," Denger said.

"Why should I?" Neferet spat. "Why don't you just kill me now?"

"And hide your body where?" Denger laughed. "Just a little further now."

"Your brother will never forgive you," she whispered.

"Keep him out of this." Denger thrust his blade harder; the stain on her back deepened.

Soon, the three of them were on the narrow ridge. Pebbles skittered over the edge and clattered far below. Ramses struggled to stay focused, but his head oozed blood. Glancing down at the breathless drop, he started to slip.

Denger glanced back, his face white. "Quit it you nasty—"

The rope tugged at the sentry; trying to keep balance, he let go of Neferet's hair. His arms swung as he fought to right himself. "I said, quit it!"

The drop gaped under Ramses' feet; the dizzy sight sucked his breath away. But then, with suddenly, with total clarity, he knew what he had to do. It was the only way to keep Neferet safe. It was the only way to end this.

He jumped.

And then he was airborne. He was free.

It was finally over.

He watched Denger teeter on the edge, eyes peeled wide in terror. The rope stretched tight between them. Denger tried to pull Ramses up with his left arm. His right arm, his sword arm, began to spin in circles. The blade flashed, arcing wider and wider.

"Too late," Ramses said, and thrashed out violently with both arms and legs.

For one breathtaking second, Denger hung over the valley, his feet still on the earth. And then he toppled. Neferet screamed.

The fall was exhilarating.

They plunged downward. Ramses' stomach lurched into his throat. Wind ripped in his ears. The air was crushed from his lungs.

The free-fall seemed to last forever.

CHAPTER 56

Shoulder first, Ramses hit the earth. He slammed, bounced and flipped upward. He hit a second time, his knees grinding into the ground. The hillside reared up at him and he thrust out his hands. Driving his fingers in, he scraped to a stop.

Denger slammed into his back. Knotted together by the rope, they rolled over and over, falling downward all over again. Ramses' hands were twisted, bound down against his legs. Pebbles flew high over Denger's back.

"Boulder," Ramses gasped, his eyes peeled wide in horror.

The boulder clipped his foot. He sailed past. But Denger took it full force. A sickening crunch sounded as the man hit the stone.

The rope wrenched them both to a halt.

Rocks and pebbles rained down in a violent shower of dust. Ramses lay, gasping under the onslaught. Finally, the world fell silent.

A few long moments passed. Then Denger made a low whine—eerie and frightening. Wincing in agony, Ramses forced himself to roll over. Still knotted by the ropes, he inched across the few feet that separated them.

The whites of Denger's eyes showed. He was half-slumped at an awkward angle, staring at his belly. Ramses followed his horrified gaze.

Buried in the man's stomach, all the way to the worn leather hilt, was the sentry's own sword. Worse, it wasn't a clean cut. The blade had gored him badly, exposing his guts.

Weakly, his sweaty hand grasped at Ramses. "Help . . . me!"

No matter how much Ramses had wanted to hurt Denger, hollow desperation stole over him—he didn't want this. He nodded quickly, avoiding the sentry's terror filled eyes. "You'll be okay," he lied.

"So much . . . blood."

"Don't move." Ramses brought his bound wrists to the exposed sword-edge. Swallowing his nausea, he carefully began to cut himself free.

"Please," Denger gasped. "Please . . ."

"I have to get help."

Ramses tore off his tunic. He tried to staunch the wound, but the blood was coming too fast. Scrabbling footsteps sounded on the hillside, and then Neferet was beside him.

"By the gods . . ." she gasped and put her hand over her mouth.

At the sound of her voice, Denger searched for her as if through a fog. "It wasn't me," he whispered. "Not me. It was Weris. I . . . didn't want to . . ."

"We'll get help—from the village—"

Denger's shoulders sank back against the earth. "Too late . . ."

"We're going to help you!"

"Tell Jabari, tell my brother I . . ." He swallowed and closed his eyes. A tear slid down his rough cheek.

They waited for him to speak, but his eyes didn't open.

Ramses met Neferet's horrified stare. "We need to get help. Now!"

And then they were running. Sprinting. Flying across the earth.

The Peak of the West glowed in shades of ruby. Up ahead, the walls of the Place of Truth came into view. A group of men stood gathered in front of the village gates. A boy stood between them, a lean boy around Ramses' age.

At first, Ramses thought they were watching him and Neferet.

But as he came closer, he saw they were looking the wrong way. The boy and the craftsmen weren't facing the road; for some strange reason, they were staring at the place where Ra was about to shine his rays across the earth.

The sky grew brighter and brighter, glowing with the coming light.

"Run!" Neferet shouted at him.

At her urgent tone, he found a reserve of strength he didn't know he had.

Suddenly, the boy at the gates thrust his fist in the air and whooped. "It's mine! I'm the new apprentice! The apprenticeship is mine!"

"Father!" Neferet screamed.

Everyone turned at once.

"I have him," she screamed. "I have Ramses!"

The boy who'd been shouting turned quickly. "Too late. It's daylight already!"

"Not quite," Neferet's father said.

At that moment, the first burst of golden sunlight shot across the horizon. It beamed over Neferet's father's shoulders, and illuminated Ramses' face. Ramses glanced down to see his bloody kilt shimmering as if it were made of precious metal. His whole body shone so bright that Neferet stumbled back with a little cry.

All of the craftsmen—gnarled men with paint-stained fingers, giant blacksmiths with hands like sledges—stared.

CHAPTER 57

"The sentry!" Ramses said quickly. "We need help! Now!"
Instantly, the spell was broken. The pain from the fall suddenly threatened to overpower him. He ground his jaw, determined to control it.

"It's Denger," Neferet said. "He's hurt, he . . ."

A man stepped forward. "My brother?" His face was ashen beneath his leather helmet. "Where? What happened?"

Ramses spoke through his swollen mouth. "Sir, he—"

"No!" Neferet cried, stopping him from saying more. "What I mean is, there was an accident." Her voice broke. "I'm sorry Jabari. He's in the valley."

Jabari spun on his heel and took off.

"I need to find the physician," Neferet said, her voice shaking.

"Go, find her, now!" her father said.

Without a word, she fled through the gates and disappeared. Ramses was left standing alone. In the commotion, he'd forgotten the boy who'd shouted at him earlier, but now the boy barged forward.

"You're accepting him?" the boy said. "Instead of me?"

"Hold your tongue, Akil," Neferet's father said.

"You don't even know if that drawing was his!"

"Do not presume to do my job."

The boy's face reddened. "I've been more than patient. I've stayed here all night."

"So have we, my friend." A huge man with the black, stained fingernails of an ironworker slung his arm around the boy's shoulders. Then he shot Ramses a dark look.

The Chief Scribe took a deep breath, rubbed his face and turned to Ramses. "We've all had a long night. And I'm sorry, but it's not over."

He called for water. Moments later, a jug was produced, along with a handful of clean rags. Skin had peeled away from Ramses arms and legs, replaced with ground in pebbles and dirt. He winced, cleaning it as best he could. The bleeding on his scalp had slowed to a trickle. Despite his wounds, he sensed the man's impatience.

"Again, I'm sorry to do this. But it can't wait," the Chief Scribe said.

Ramses was glad the man didn't seem curious about how he'd got this way. He was glad to keep the details to himself. He'd seen the way Neferet had protected the sentry she'd called Jabari from the truth.

"If you're ready?" the Chief Scribe said.

Ramses nodded.

"Good. Follow me." He motioned him into one of the tents.

All Ramses wanted was to rest. For just a little while. He wanted to put his aching head down and sleep. His ribs throbbed. From where he'd landed on his right shoulder, spasms of pain cramped his right arm to all the way to his wrist. It was his drawing arm.

He glanced down at it; it was swollen. He tried to form a fist. When he couldn't, he broke out in tiny pinpricks of sweat. A black foreboding swept over him.

"Sit down. There's something we need you to do."

Ramses flexed his hands, trying to bring the feeling back. His fingers had gone numb.

A craftsman approached, holding a sheaf of blank papyrus.

Ramses should've known this apprenticeship was far from decided.

They'd want him to prove himself.

He should've realized there would be a test in store.

CHAPTER 58

Haunted by the image of Denger's sword jutting from his belly, Neferet ran for the physician. But it was the memory of Jabari's face—his shock at hearing his little brother lay bleeding to death on the mountainside—that made her run faster.

Her breath came in ragged gasps, the air dry and sharp. She passed silent windows, hardly able to believe the villagers still slept on, peaceful and oblivious.

Merit, the physician, however, had an ear for emergencies. She opened her door as Neferet approached.

"What is it?" she demanded.

"There's been an accident."

"Yes?"

"It's Jabari's brother . . . He—he fell. On his sword."

"You mean tripped? As in cut himself? His leg, arm?"

" . . . It went through his belly."

At this, a shadow crossed Merit's face. "I see." She came to life, striding down the steps. "Where is he now?"

"On the mountain. But they're bringing him here."

"I want the linens sterilized, the needle and thread boiled." Neferet nodded.

"I'll meet him at the gates. Have a sleeping draught ready." She paused. "Take care you make it right."

"Of course!" Hadn't she always made it right?

"I'm telling you because there's something wrong with your herbs."

"There's—what?"

"Just do it. Understand?"

"Yes." She hurried inside and stopped dead at the sight of the workroom. All the herbs had been pulled from the shelves. Over a hundred drawstring bags, ranging from tiny to large, were spread across the huge wooden table that filled the center of the room. All of them open. It looked as if Merit had been in the middle of examining the contents of each one.

She had no time to think what it meant. Instead, she searched, frantic, for the bags she needed. She began pouring measures into the stone mortar.

Out of the last bag spilled a black, wrinkled berry.

The evil thing sent horror slithering down her spine.

A deadly belladonna berry? Here, in her own stores?

It couldn't be. She didn't believe it. It was something else. It had to be. Hands trembling, she picked it out of the mortar, pinched it and held it to her nose. The scent of its oils confirmed her worst fears.

Carefully she set it aside, trembling like a bird before a sandstorm. Never once, out gathering herbs, could she remember seeing a belladonna plant. Clearly she was worse than blind. Worse than incompetent.

She was downright dangerous.

A knock sounded at the door. It swung open and Layla stood there in a new, gold embroidered gown. She looked perfect, except for her kohl-lined eyes, which were bleary with sleep.

Layla took in Neferet's torn dress. "Well, look at you. Filthy, as always."

Neferet felt her cheeks color. "What do you want?"

"Where's Merit?"

"Do you need medical attention?" Neferet went to stoke the flame in the oven, then poured water into a pot and set it there to boil.

"Please. You can drop the act."

"Excuse me?"

"You know why I'm here." Layla laughed, making the strands of her gold-beaded wig jingle and chink. "Or maybe Merit didn't tell you? Apparently it's a matter of business. I think someone might be losing their job."

"Wait, Merit told you to come here because—" She stopped. Of course. The physician would never want to keep her on now. She could've poisoned someone!

Layla's eyes glinted with amusement.

"She'll be back soon," Neferet said numbly. She reached for Merit's needles, stabbed her finger and cursed.

"Perhaps I should do that for you," Layla said.

"Out of my way." She threw the needles into the boiling water.

Layla reached for the mortar and wrinkled her nose. "Eww! What is this foul brew?"

"Don't touch that!"

"I'll touch whatever I want. And do a better job than you." She plunged the pestle into the sleeping draught. The mixture exploded, splattering across the table.

"A guard is hurt. You want to help? Get the linens from the shelf."

"Don't you dare—"

"Then leave me alone! I have work to do!"

"You think you're so important. You think—"

"This isn't about me. Someone's dying!"

"Always so dramatic, aren't you." She pushed Neferet aside and reached for the linens. "I'm perfectly capable of getting them. And doing whatever else you think you know how to do. What next? Hmm? Shall I make some soothing tea to calm his nerves? Or think of a nice story to relax him so he can feel better?"

"By the gods," Neferet said, thinking of Jabari's brother. "You have no idea what's coming."

And just then, the door burst open.

Blood smeared, Jabari lurched inside, cradling his brother in his arms. Denger's sand-caked face flopped at an unnatural angle. His lips were blue and gaping. His eyes stared, dull and unblinking. A bloody mess of fabric tried to hold his midsection together. The sword jutted from it.

Surreal, and red, and wet.

Layla made a sickening gurgle. Neferet ignored her. Instead, her heart wrenched at the look on Jabari's face. To him, Denger wasn't a villain. He was his little brother, and he was dying.

"Put Denger on the couch," Merit barked. "Now."

The next hour became a blur. They worked to remove the blade, pulling it carefully from his ruptured belly. They tried to stitch the gore back together. They tried to stop the blood, the oozing blood that poured over everything.

Jabari watched as if he could will them to stop it. Will them to fix him. Will them to keep his brother's ka there.

But there was no fixing him. There was no keeping him.

Quietly and alone, Denger's soul fled to the Hall of Judgment.

"Maat protect him now," Jabari said quietly.

"Maat protect him," Neferet whispered, and turned quickly away.

CHAPTER 59

In the far corner, Layla leaned over a bowl, scrubbing blood from her hands. Her dress was filthy, her eyes smudged. She looked like she was going to throw up—again.

Neferet tried to stop feeling satisfied, but she couldn't help it. "Don't worry," she whispered, elbowing her way in to scrub her own hands. "I'm sure that dress will make a fancy rag."

Layla swallowed deeply, as if to stop from being sick. When she got hold of herself, she said, "You know what? You're even uglier when you're jealous."

Neferet's cheeks colored. "I just hope you're up for this."

"For what? Taking your place? Don't worry about that."

"Girls," Merit called from across the room.

"Yes, right here!" Layla called back in a sweet voice.

Merit said something to Jabari, who stood beside her. Grim-faced, he nodded, turned away and knelt beside the cot where his brother still lay. Gently, he placed a clean sheet over his brother's body.

Motioning to Neferet and Layla, Merit said, "We'll go to the other room."

Layla floated gracefully out of the room after her.

Neferet pulled her hands from the murky bowl, splashed them with fresh water and dried her hands on a cloth. She made for the door, but Jabari called to her.

"That cut, in the middle of your back?" he said.

Neferet tensed. "Yes?"

"I heard you tell Merit it was from falling."

She nodded quickly.

He looked at her long and hard. Then softly, he said, "Thank you."

Maybe Denger had been conscious when Jabari found him. Or maybe Jabari just guessed the truth. For it was plain, in his eyes, he knew. She wanted to tell him it wasn't like that; it wasn't what he was thinking. That his brother never tried to kill her, would never betray them all. But she couldn't. She had no words. She didn't know what to say to make it better.

"You'd better go," he said.

She touched his arm. "I'm sorry," she said softly.

"I know, little one," he replied. "I know."

"Neferet?" Merit called sharply.

Her tone sent a lump into Neferet's throat. She glanced at the table covered with all the opened herb bags. They'd shoved it up against the wall when Denger had been brought in. The mess was like an accusation—like one hundred angry fingers all pointed at her. Saying goodbye to Jabari, she turned and hurried from the room.

"There you are," Merit said.

Layla smirked.

"Please, sit down," Merit said.

Neferet sank onto a clean but tattered cushion. Villagers' voices drifted in through the shuttered window, chattering about the exam. She wondered if Ramses was still in the tent with her father and the other craftsmen.

Merit pushed the shutters open. "Let's have some light in here. The three of us need to speak frankly."

Squinting against the sudden brightness, Neferet stared at a crack in the floor. How many times had she sat there without a thought to the future beyond what lessons Merit had to teach?

"This isn't the morning I expected to have," Merit said. "And I'm sorry you had to witness something so brutal, Layla. But at the same time, I'm glad. Because you see just how serious our work is."

"Oh, of course, I thought it was . . ." Layla gulped, looking green. "Exciting."

"Exciting?" Merit said. "A man is dead."

"I just meant . . . I mean, I'm suited to it. To the work." She smoothed a braid from her sweaty cheek.

The physician looked weary; yet her piercing eyes had a birdlike quality. "That's certainly a pretty wig you're wearing."

It was the oddest thing Neferet had ever heard Merit say.

Layla colored. "Thank you."

"I noticed it the other day," Merit went on. "The gold beads in particular."

Layla looked pleased. "It's very well made. My mother says one should always look like a lady."

"Indeed. Lean forward for me, please?"

"Of course!" Layla let Merit examine the braids.

"This strand has come undone. Did you see you're missing some beads?"

"What?" She grabbed the offending braid and pulled it forward. "They promised me the ends were fastened in a new style that wouldn't come undone! Those beads are pure gold. They're—"

"Right here," Merit said.

Layla paused. "What?"

"I said, they're right here. The beads are right here."

"I don't understand. Right where?"

Merit took one of their herb bags from her pocket. "Right in here."

"What in the name of the gods are you talking about?" Layla asked, licking her lips.

"Why don't you tell me?"

"Tell you what? There's nothing to tell." Layla shifted on her cushion, reaching her trembling fingers for the pillow's frayed edges and digging in deep.

"Isn't there? Unfortunately I think there is. Or would you like me to tell it?"

Layla said nothing.

"Why did you do it?" Merit demanded.

Letting go of the cushion, Layla leaped to her feet. "Kiki has

240

gold hair beads too! They're not mine. They're hers!"

"No, they're not," Merit said in a patient voice, although Neferet sensed her straining to keep from yelling. "I spoke with Kiki's mother. Her hair beads are made of wood, and painted to look precious. Yours are the real thing. And so are these."

"What are you saying?" Neferet said.

"Nothing!" Layla cried.

"Sneaking into Neferet's house and tampering with our herbs can hardly be described as nothing," Merit said dryly.

"Wait, you snuck into—" Neferet put her hand to her mouth. "I knew it. The laundry on the stairs. You were in my room. You were up in my room!"

Layla grabbed the bag and crushed it. "You can't prove it. You can't prove anything. You're wrong. How dare you accuse me!"

"You could have killed someone!" Neferet said.

"Me?" Layla screeched. "You're the one who's irresponsible, always running off into the desert!"

After a long moment, Neferet said, "It was a belladonna berry. If I'd mixed it in a draught—for your mother, or your father say—they'd be dead."

"Everything's always so dramatic with you, isn't it. It's not always about you."

"I'm not talking about me!" Neferet said. She wanted to scream, but instead hot tears stung her eyes. "We were best friends. You risked all of us, our whole village. Because you hate me?"

White-faced, Layla glared at the door.

"What?" Neferet said. "For once you don't have anything to say?"

"No," Layla said. "I think you're pathetic. And your high and mighty job is pathetic. And you deserve to grub around in blood and dirt for the rest of your life."

Merit stood. "I hope you'll find something better than that to say to the village elders."

CHAPTER 60

Inside the examination tent, Ramses watched the Chief Scribe go to a table and open a wooden box. The man took out a leather-bound scroll and held it up for Ramses to see.

"Wrapped in this leather binding is the scroll we found last night. Reproduce its contents. That's all we require."

Ramses desperately tried to bring the feeling back to his hand; he flexed and un-flexed his fingers. He needed to buy himself more time. "Sir . . . could you give me a clue of what's on the page?"

"I cannot."

"What if that scroll's not even mine?"

The man replaced it in the box without answering.

"I need something to drink," Ramses said.

"I'll have it brought."

Someone gave Ramses a nudge. It was a craftsman with gray, bushy hair and friendly eyes all crinkled in a smile. He shoved a load of drawing supplies into Ramses' arms, and Ramses saw that the man's own arms were stained to the elbows with paint and ink. "Name's Tui. Just do your best."

A bead of sweat trickled down Ramses' temple. "Thanks," he said. His hand had begun to alternate between numbness and shooting pain. What if he couldn't draw? What if his fingers wouldn't work?

What if that scroll wasn't even his?

He wiped his hands on his legs. He wasn't even sure he could hold a brush without dropping it.

The craftsmen had gathered to watch; they pressed in on him. Trying to ignore them, Ramses picked up the dry cake of ink. They frowned as it slipped and rolled away; stared as he spilled the pot of mixing water.

He couldn't do it. He just could not do it. He threw down his brush.

Tui, the gray-haired craftsman, waved his gnarled arms at the others and shouted, "Move, you old busy-bodies! Give the boy some room!"

With snorts of disappointment, they shuffled to the far corner. There they stood in a huddle, muttering to one another.

Ramses closed his eyes and rubbed his palm. He focused on the last moments he'd spent drawing in Weris's room. He'd come so far. Maybe that scroll wrapped in leather was his, and maybe it wasn't. If it was his drawing of the cobra goddess, of Meretseger, he wasn't even sure if he could repeat it.

But the truth was, he had nothing more to lose.

The least he could do was try.

He said a quick prayer, sat back and willed the image to come to him. At first, it was hazy, like a soft edged cloud, drifting into his thoughts. Slowly it took on sharp, definite edges. The black lines grew thicker, larger, firmer. Then he saw her clearly in his mind. Every flicker of his brush, every stroke he'd made stood out in vivid detail.

Ramses eyes flew open.

On the papyrus, a faint outline shimmered, matched with the image in his mind. Breathless, he bent to trace it with his brush before it disappeared. His hand was sluggish. He willed it to move faster. He couldn't hold the illusion much longer.

Already it was beginning to fade.

Desperate, he clenched his teeth. The illusion was almost gone!

Quickly, quickly! The last piece, the ankh—the symbol of life—on Meretseger's scepter. He traced it in as the shimmering glow dissolved into the ink. The light abruptly vanished. Meretseger was complete. The lines were just lines, black and solid.

In a daze, he set down his brush. It felt as if he'd woken

from a trance.

The craftsmen still stood at the far end of the tent. He studied his drawing once more.

An imperfection sprang to his attention, and then another. Horrified, he started to scrunch it up. He'd have to start over. But could he do better? What if these were the same imperfections as on the original scroll?

What if the other one wasn't even his? There must have been thousands of applicants. Anyone could've dropped their papyrus.

He let go of it and smoothed it out once more.

"Sir?" he called, his voice low. He gulped, hoping they hadn't heard. He had to try again—this drawing was terrible!

"You called me?" It was too late. The Chief Scribe was walking swiftly toward him. "What do you need? More papyrus? Ink? A different brush?"

Ramses' held out the sheet, his hand shaking. "I'm done."

"Done? You can't be. You just sat down!"

The thought of another moment at this table tied his stomach in knots. "Really sir, I'm done."

At this, the Chief Scribe looked suddenly old and tired. Disappointed even, as if he knew now that it was impossible Ramses could be the one. "I see." He paused. With a sigh, he took the scroll. "We'll just be a moment then."

The big metalworker snorted. "Let's see this thing."

"Bring the other papyrus," the Chief Scribe said, gesturing at the box with the second scroll.

"Ha! Why bother?"

"Come, we'll examine them in the light," the Chief Scribe said.

Ramses wondered if they were leaving to save him the embarrassment of hearing their laughter. They headed for the tent flap. Instead of stepping outside, however, the Chief Scribe stood in the doorway. Several craftsmen shot frowns at Ramses.

He knew they were furious that he'd come to waste their time.

CHAPTER 61

After removing the leather wrappings, Neferet's father gave the first drawing to Tui. The old painter held it open for the men to see, while the Chief Scribe busied himself unrolling the drawing Ramses had just given him.

He tilted it to catch the sun.

Ramses held his breath.

"Impossible," the Chief Scribe growled.

At the tent entrance, the craftsmen's voices rose in commotion. Ramses' heart sank. He wished he were dead. The Chief Scribe broke away and approached, frowning.

"It wasn't mine, was it?" Ramses said softly.

"Oh yes, it's yours." He held the two pages side by side. "These are the same drawings." He paused. "The problem is, they're not just the same, they're exact in every way. Either we're witnessing a miracle, or you've drawn this picture so many times, you've memorized the strokes. Have you copied this from somewhere, trained yourself to replicate it? Is this some sort of trick, the only thing you can draw?"

A woman entered with the drink Ramses had requested. Impatient, the Chief Scribe waved her to set it down. She left quickly in a swish of skirts.

"No! I've only drawn it twice. Once on the first scroll, and then here, on the second. You told me to repeat it!"

"Repeat it? Yes but—" Neferet's father made a frustrated noise.

Tui approached. "What if what the boy says is the truth?"

"Tui . . ."

"We can't afford to pass this off so easily. This is the Place of Truth. We ourselves make the magic that carries Pharaoh to the underworld; magic that ensures his safety, that keeps him for all eternity. Can we risk letting this boy's talent, if it is indeed a talent, slip away?"

"What, then do you propose?"

"A simple test."

The Chief Scribe passed his hand over his face. Then he nodded. "You may go ahead."

To Ramses, Tui said, "When we create a royal tomb, one of the most important skills is uniformity. We strive to make our images the same—to put it simply, when I draw an image of Ptah, I want all the other images of Ptah to match. I don't want one to be tall and thin, and a second shorter and rounder. Do you follow me?"

"Yes, he has to look the same every time. Otherwise the story panels won't make sense if his appearance keeps changing," Ramses said.

"Exactly! Well put. However talking about making them match, and actually doing it are two different things. If you can replicate your images line for line—"

"Line for line—but I never said I . . ." Ramses stopped. It's not what he'd said. But it's what he'd led them to believe, and it was too late to take it back. He swallowed, guessing what was coming next.

"Make us a new set of images. A matching set. Demonstrate that what you did was no trick, no trained repetition of a single image, but an actual skill. Something you can do with any image."

Ramses' stomach churned. "What do you want me to draw?"

Tui thought a moment. "You met your opponent, Akil," he said. "He drew us the death of Osiris at the hands of his brother. Now as you know, Osiris had a son named Horus. Horus fought to take back the precious things that had been stolen from him and his family. Their honor. Draw that for us."

Ramses thought of Aunt Zalika and Uncle Hay. In some

small way, he understood how Horus felt, even if Ramses was only a boy, and Horus was a god.

Tui added, "Just to ensure your skills, you will draw the first one, and hand it to us. Then you will draw the second one, without the aid of the first."

Ramses gulped. Still, he took the materials.

In truth, it was easier said than done. Drawing a pair of identical images was nearly impossible. Yes, he'd done it with Meretseger, but could he do it again?

He thought of his father. His father had always said that success came to the man who planned carefully, and then followed through.

An idea came to him. Was it possible to lay such plans here and now? To do something that would ensure the drawings would be the same? Even if Tui took the first one away?

He remembered his dream of the grid.

He could see it in his mind's eye—the lines on the tomb wall. If he could make a grid like that, he could repeat the image nearly exactly, by placing the figure of Horus within the lines. There was only one problem—on the tomb wall, one could erase the gridlines at the end by painting over them. Yet he couldn't erase an ink grid from the papyrus. Then he had an idea.

Why erase them if he didn't need to?

Did he dare? What if they thought he was cheating?

"Are there any rules?" he blurted.

"Rules?" Tui said. "Only the one—that you give me the first drawing before you start on the second.

"Then I accept."

CHAPTER 62

Neferet headed for the gates.

Outside, the men were up in arms. They argued heatedly. She caught scraps of words, and Ramses' name was mentioned over and over. She swallowed, searching for her father, and saw him debating with Paimu. She headed his way, but then thought better. Instead, she pulled Tui apart from the crowd. He was the only man smiling.

"What's happened?" she said.

"Nothing, yet."

"Then why is there such an uproar?"

"Because I think your friend Ramses has beat us at our own game."

"What are you talking about?"

"Look for yourself." He pulled aside the flap.

Ramses sat at a table, so lost in concentration he didn't notice her standing there. He had several sheets of papyrus on the table, one of which had thick black lines crisscrossing left to right, top to bottom. It looked like a lot of squares. No, she corrected herself, a grid, that was the word for it.

"What's he doing?" she asked as he laid a second sheet over top of it.

Ramses bent forward and started to draw on the top sheet. Tui started to laugh. He laughed so hard, tears leaped to the corners of his eyes.

"Tui! What is he doing?"

"Don't you see? He gave us the first drawing, and he used the grid underneath as a form of measure! I asked him to draw matching images. He's using the grid once again to do the drawing a second time."

"But . . . you mean, I don't understand.

"The head goes in the top square, the shoulders in the second one and—

"But that's cheating!"

Tui wiped his eyes. "It's not. That's why everyone's in a huff. He asked me right at the start if there were any rules. I gave him only one. Hand me the first papyrus, and that is all. Don't you see? He's brilliant. Your friend is brilliant. He has more than a gift, he is smart. He doesn't rely on the whim of the gods. He puts a method to work, a reliable method that nothing can foil. A farmer. The boy is a farmer. And farmers are stubborn, determined people. Perhaps there are things we can learn from one another."

She watched Ramses; he was oblivious to the filthy state of his clothes, to the grime in his hair, to the purple bruises welling up on his cheeks. Instead, he had his head down, his whole attention focused. Clearly he could care less what others thought, not when there was work to be done. Maybe she could learn something from him, too.

He glanced up and handed her father his finished work.

Ramses looked worried, but when he saw her, and gave her a small smile that sent her stomach flipping. The craftsmen retired to a private corner of the tent to vote. She headed over. Ramses tore his eyes away from the group that would decide his future and focused on her.

"Are you all right?" he asked her.

"Yes."

"And Denger?" He let the question hang.

She sat down. On the ground, ink had splattered like black blood. "No. We tried."

"By the gods!" Ramses ran his fingers over his scalp; they raked his gashes and he winced as if having forgotten they were there. "I didn't know what else to do. It's all I could think of! He was going to kill you, he—"

"That's twice you've saved my life. I'm sorry for Jabari, but I can't tell you how glad I am we're alive right now."

At that moment, her father approached. "Ramses."

Ramses stood. "Sir?"

"We've made our decision." He waited for the men to gather around. "Several months ago, we lost an important member of our community. A very skilled, young apprentice painter. The likelihood of finding someone to fill his sandals seemed impossible." A gentle breeze ruffled the open flap. "Today, however, it seems fate has carried someone to our door who not only fits in, but exceeds our hopes in every way. A boy with a talent so rare, a gift so special, that one can only believe he is a favorite of the gods themselves."

The morning sun made the tent walls glow soft white.

"Ramses, you have more than met our expectations," he said. "You have surpassed them in every way."

Ramses looked as if he were hardly able to believe what her father was saying.

"Do you mean?" Ramses stopped, unable to voice his hopes.

"Yes. You're accepted."

Neferet jumped into the air and whooped. She couldn't help it.

"Welcome," her father said. He stepped forward and shook Ramses' hand.

A cheer went up and the other craftsmen crushed in to do the same. Tui and Paimu, the two old painters, slapped him on the back. From the way they looked, smiling from ear to ear, it was as if they had just won the exam themselves. In a way, Neferet thought, they had.

Tui suddenly glanced at her, and then shouted over the others. "There's someone else we need to acknowledge here," he cried. "The person who came up with the idea of this examination in the first place."

"Yes, Tui," they all shouted, laughing, "you were wise. We acknowledge you. Are you happy?"

"I am, but it's not me you need to acknowledge," he said.

Neferet was trying to shy away, but Tui caught her by the shoulder and pushed her forward. "A cheer for Neferet!"

The Chief Scribe stared at his daughter. "This examination was your idea?"

"Well—I, um . . . I would've told you but—"

Her father looked skyward. "By the beard of Ptah, I should have known." But he was smiling. Wider than Neferet had seen him smile in a very long time.

CHAPTER 63

The craftsmen swept Ramses from the tent. He glanced at Neferet, who ran along at his side. Up ahead stood the gates to the village. They'd been thrown wide open, waiting to welcome him in.

"Tell me I'm not dreaming," Ramses said to her.

"You're not," she said, grinning. "Believe me, you're really not. And neither am I."

Ramses took a breath. Then he stepped over the threshold, and into the sacred world of craftsmen. But he couldn't celebrate. Not yet. Not until he knew what had happened to his best friends back home.

All around him, villagers streamed down the streets to congratulate him. He grinned and laughed and shook their hands. Together, he, Neferet and the other craftsmen made their way down the alleys. Ramses was mesmerized. The neat, whitewashed houses, all in a row, were so different from his farm. The doors were labeled with names; the air was dry and clean. He caught glimpses of tiny workshops through open doorways. He breathed deeply, taking it all in.

When they reached a house with the Chief Scribe's name above the door, the group made their way up the steps and into the front room. The walls were painted white and cushions lay scattered across the floor, giving it a comfortable, welcoming, homey feel. A table had been mounded high with dishes of food—savory pastries, sweet dates, baskets of bread, platters of grilled meats, and sweating jugs of beer.

Toward the back a door stood ajar, and he spied what must

be the Chief Scribe's office. Shelves were piled with papyrus scrolls, there were baskets of ostraca shards, and pots crammed with brushes.

"That's where my father keeps records of all our supplies," Neferet said.

"And we'll be ordering a pile for you soon enough," Tui added.

"Really? I'll get my own supplies?" he said without thinking, and then laughed. Of course he would. His own brushes! And paints! It was that single thought, that simple realization, which made Ramses finally realize he'd found a place he truly belonged.

It was afternoon by the time Ramses had a chance to get the Chief Scribe alone.

"I don't know how else to say this. Except that I need your help."

"I'm listening."

"My aunt and uncle are going to sell my parents' farm. If I don't stop them, two of my closest friends will be turned out. They'll have nowhere to go, nothing."

"I don't understand. It's your parents' farm? Why do you need my help? You're the legal heir."

"Yes, well, not really."

"I'm listening."

As Ramses' explained, the Chief Scribe's frown deepened.

"I think I'd best come with you. I'd like to speak with your aunt and uncle in person."

Accompanied by a handful of sentries, they headed out. At the ruins of the old plough shed, the procession halted.

"Go, we'll find you as planned," the Chief Scribe said.

Ramses nodded.

Alone, he made his way across the familiar fields. Sheltering his gaze against the afternoon sun, he spotted the farm workers loading the last of the cut wheat into baskets. It all seemed so normal, as if nothing had happened. In the middle of them all, he caught sight of Sobek; he'd recognize those broad shoulders anywhere.

The farm manager turned. When their eyes met, Sobek's jaw dropped. He looked as if he were seeing a ghost; he hurried to meet him, grabbing him by both shoulders.

"We thought you were dead!"

"Not yet," Ramses said, grinning.

Relief flooded his friend's face. Still, he said, "Zalika's furious. It's not a good idea you show yourself. We need to get you—"

"Wait," Ramses said. "I have something to tell you."

"Not here, we need to get you out of sight. Quickly. Come with me."

"No, she's not going to make me run away."

Sobek paused. "There's something you're not telling me, isn't there?"

"Sobek, I'm the new apprentice."

His friend stared at him in confusion. "What? How is that possible, they said you were in trouble, guards were looking for you . . ."

"They were." Ramses explained everything. About how he'd lost his papyrus. About Weris and Denger being tomb-robbers—at which point, Sobek's eyes darkened. He told him about Neferet, and the test in the tent. And finally, how he'd walked down the streets of the Place of Truth to the Chief Scribe's own house.

Sobek let out a bellow of joy and gave him a crushing hug. "I knew you could do it. We all did." He swiped a tear from his leathery cheek, and laughed. "Wait until Hebony hears about our famous Ramses! In fact, why wait? Go tell her! I'm right behind you."

The men had dropped what they were doing and were heading over.

"Don't stop!" Sobek shouted. "Let's get this work done and over with, we have something to celebrate!"

Alone, Ramses skirted the pond. A fish broke the surface

and disappeared. It was strange to be here. He slowed when he reached the courtyard. The front door opened.

Aunt Zalika stepped out.

"Ramses," she gasped. She lunged and snatched his wrist. "Come back have you? What have you done? How dare you ruin my good name?" Her cheeks were puffed and red beneath her jeweled headdress. "Sentries came here last night, looking for you! And now here you are, crawling back for handouts. Well you'll get them all right. This time I won't stop until those fingers of yours are broken for good."

He was trying to pull away, when her expression changed. The glare drained from her kohl-lined eyes; she attempted a smile. The effect was a sickening grimace.

"But of course," she cooed, "we're so happy to have you home. Even if we get angry sometimes, you're like a son to us, you know that." She released his hand. Rigidly, she patted him on the head.

Ramses flinched.

"There will be no more punishments for Ramses," the Chief Scribe said in a voice deep with calm authority. He stood at the side of the house, together with Sobek.

"Punishment? Oh no, of course not!" Aunt Zalika's hands fluttered. "I'd never really hit the boy. I'd never do anything to harm our little darling." She tried to pat Ramses' arm.

Ramses sidestepped her.

The Chief Scribe frowned. "I've come to tell you that Ramses is master of this farm. You may have been its caretakers, but this house—and this land—has never been yours. If I had my way, you'd be facing the authorities. But your nephew wants to allow you to remain on the farm."

She puckered her mouth at Ramses. "I should hope so! After all we've done for him. I'm his aunt."

"Yes, you are," the Chief Scribe said, distaste plain in his voice. "You and your husband will move your things to Ramses' room. Sobek and Hebony will take over as head of the household, since Ramses has accepted our offer to join us as our new apprentice in the Place of Truth."

Aunt Zalika stared at Ramses. "New apprentice?" After a moment she shook head as if to clear it and said, "Well, why would we move to Ramses room? That's where our son Sepi sleeps!"

The Chief Scribe glanced at Ramses, confused.

"Not my old room," Ramses said. "The room where I've been sleeping since my parents died."

"You mean . . ." Aunt Zalika paled. "That goat pen? That dank hole? That's barely fit for a servant. Or, I mean . . ."

"Exactly," the Chief Scribe said. "And it will take many years to repay your debt to Ramses."

One of the guards stepped from the house. "The Weris fellow is gone."

Hebony was right on his heels. "Of course he's gone," she said, swiping flour from her cheek. "What's all this chaos, then, what's happened, what's he done?" She stopped dead at the sight of Ramses. "Ramses!" She glanced from face to face and then rushed to throw her arms around him. "You're okay."

"He's more than okay," Sobek said.

When she heard the news, she rejoiced, screaming, howling, and jumping up and down like a girl half her age.

"My sentiments exactly," the Chief Scribe said.

CHAPTER 64

Only one person remained who hadn't heard the news: Sepi. Ramses stomach churned with worry. How would his best friend feel about everything? But there was no point in waiting. He wiped his damp palms on his kilt and headed into the cool interior.

"Sepi?" Ramses said, shoving open the door to Sepi's room. He stopped dead.

Sepi was nowhere to be seen. Instead, the priest with the serpent tattoo sat at Sepi's desk. The sight sent terror whip-lashing down Ramses' spine.

It was as if he'd sprung up from the memory that had haunted his dreams all these years. The priest still wore the white, sacred robes, and his head was shaved, save for the sacred lock of hair tied in a ribbon at his neck.

"You," Ramses whispered.

"Come here, my child," the man said.

When Ramses had been three, the priest had towered over him; yet now the man seemed so much smaller. And his gaze didn't look ready to spit fire; instead the hazel eyes that studied Ramses' face looked wise and intense.

"You told me I was cursed!" Ramses said.

"I understand you have faced challenges, these long years."

"Am I cursed then? Was it true?"

"Perhaps you know better than I."

"Me? You want me to say? That's not enough! You made a prophesy about me. And now you say I'm the one who's supposed to know the truth?"

The room fell silent.

Finally the priest spoke. "All of our days are shared between darkness and light."

"Tell me the truth! Am I, or am I not?"

"I have tried many times to foresee your future. As a priest, it is my duty to guard this world from evil."

Ramses shifted uncomfortably.

"Your father was a man of strong will. He and your mother called what you do a gift. An accidental gift. And because of them, you chose to see it that way too. Their belief helped set you on a path. A path very much different than the one destined for you."

"Which was what? Why were you so afraid?"

"When I saw you, when I saw so much power had fallen into the hands of a boy—the markings of a dark power that . . ."

"Dark power? That's not true!"

"Only as long as you use them for good purpose. But you know what I speak of. You've felt the power in your creations. They are not mere drawings, Ramses. They have life. They become alive. And your power is growing stronger."

"What's that supposed to mean? What are you saying?"

"I don't know. But in the Place of Truth, your skills will be safe."

An ominous shiver pricked at his skin. "Safe from what?"

The man looked away. "I am only a priest. I can't live your life. One thing I know, you've found your way this far. I'm afraid some paths are beyond my ability to see."

Ramses wanted to get more out of him. He had a lot more questions.

"My blessings go with you," the priest said, holding up his hand to signal the conversation was over.

There was a sound in the hallway. Sepi appeared in the doorway, his eyes bright. "Is it true?" he said, stepping inside. "You're the new apprentice?"

Ramses nodded, searching his cousin's face. "Yes, but Sepi—"

Sepi shouted with a strength that surprised Ramses. "I knew this would happen! Last night sentries came looking for you. All night, I knew! Somehow, I could feel it! I knew you were the new apprentice."

"Sepi, there's something I have to tell you."

"What's wrong? You look worried."

"You're my best friend, and I'd never want to hurt you."

"How could you hurt me?"

"It's . . . about your parents. After what happened—the Chief Scribe wanted them to go to court."

Sepi said nothing.

"But I made an agreement with him."

Sepi listened as Ramses explained. When he was done, he said, "I'm sorry Sepi, I didn't know what else to do."

"You did the right thing," Sepi said.

Ramses met his cousin's gaze. "I did?"

"It's a lot better than worrying they're in some jail."

"So you don't hate me?"

"Of course not. You're my best friend. And my parents will live." He went to the window. The hot sunlight colored his pale skin.

Ramses joined him. From there he could see his old cell door.

"You know what?" Sepi said softly. "Maybe it will even be good for them." He faced Ramses, a twinkle in his gray eyes. "But don't you dare tell them I said that."

"It's time you finished packing," the old priest said.

Ramses glanced back at the man. What was he talking about? He had nothing to pack.

To his surprise, Sepi said, "I'm almost ready."

Almost ready? Sepi was going somewhere?

The priest stood. "Good. Then I'll leave you boys to say your goodbyes."

"You're packing? Why? What's going on?"

Sepi broke into a grin. "Don't look so worried. I'm fine. More than fine. I have my own good news."

"Tell me!"

Sepi sat on the bed. Ramses sank down beside him.

"Something happened yesterday at the Place of Truth," Sepi said. "I was standing there with my parents. In my hand was the scroll that should've been yours. And the reality struck me. I couldn't do it anymore, I couldn't take their expectations. All my life, I've never been myself, never thought about what I wanted. It was always about their dreams. Not until that night by the shed when you asked me what I wanted to do."

Bastet slid through the door and padded over to where the boys sat. Ramses reached down and picked her up.

"I might not have the hands of an artist," Sepi said, "Or the strength of a farmer. Or the shrewdness of a city official that would make my parents proud. But I have an important task to fulfill. It called me for years. I sent word to my old tutor, that's why the priest came. He arrived an hour ago and has agreed to take me on as his scribe. I'm to maintain the temple's written secrets, the very books of the gods."

Ramses stared at his friend. Then, grinning, he shook his head. "And you said I'd be leaving you behind—I think it's you who's going to forget us all!"

At this Sepi laughed. "No. And don't you forget that the temple is close to the Place of Truth. You'd better plan on visiting."

"Believe me, I will."

They talked a little more, and Ramses realized just how reluctant he was to leave. Would they really get to see one another again? If they did, it wouldn't be like this. Their lives would change, grow busy and demanding. They'd never have the easy knowledge that the other was right there.

All too soon, the priest returned for Sepi, and the Chief Scribe called to take Ramses to the village.

Outside, Hebony was tearful but smiling. She hugged him at least three times. Sobek's voice was gruff as he said his goodbyes. Ramses own throat felt tight, and before they could see that his eyes were damp, he bent to scratch Bastet behind the ears.

"I'm going to miss you," he told her. "But I'll be back, I promise."

CHAPTER 65

In the Place of Truth, Ramses sat with the Chief Scribe and Neferet on soft cushions around the dinner table. Neferet and Ramses were laughing about how they'd met.

"It's not often you make somebody's acquaintance by falling in a hole," Neferet said.

"Maybe people should do it more!" Ramses replied.

Neferet's father turned his eyes to the sky and shook his head, but Ramses knew the Chief Scribe was laughing too. And soon all three of them were telling stories like old friends. Even Neferet's father had some funny tales. So funny, in fact, the three of them were choking with laughter.

Above the tiny village, stars twinkled in the night sky.

Ramses glanced out the window. He couldn't help missing Hebony, Sobek, and Sepi. Still, he knew they were happy and he'd visit them often.

There was only one thing that would have made this wonderful night complete; But that thing was impossible. He wished his parents could know what had happened, so that they could rest easy in the afterlife. Maybe somehow, they did know. Someday he would tell them, when he found them on the path of eternity and flung himself into their waiting arms.

Neferet was looking at him across the table, a slice of bread halfway to her mouth. "Is everything all right?"

Ramses grinned. "I just can hardly believe I'm here."

"Make that two of us," Nakht said.

It really was hard to believe. He, a simple farm boy, was the new apprentice in the Place of Truth. The future stretched out like a fantastic painting, just waiting to be drawn. In three days, he'd meet Pharaoh and take part in a royal celebration. After that, Ramses would start work inside a secret, magnificent tomb. He'd be learning from masters to create images that would last forever, and adding some of his own.

Someday, if all went well, he'd be considered a master himself.

When the house grew quiet and the others had gone to sleep, Ramses knelt before the wooden chest he'd brought from home. Tui had let him keep one of the pair of drawings that had been his final test. Lifting the lid, Ramses removed the scroll and crept to the window.

By the light of the moon, he unrolled the precious sheet of papyrus.

On the page, Horus stood at the helm of a powerful chariot. Four war-horses with plumed headdresses charged under his command, their nostrils flaring and manes flying. Ramses thought he heard the sound of turning wheels, and the hammer of pounding of hooves. A breeze blew up from the page. Prickles ran along his arms. Suddenly, Horus turned.

His eyes were dark and penetrating as they met Ramses' gaze.

Horus smiled.

It was a terrifying sight. But this time, Ramses smiled back.

Author's Note

This story is a work of fiction. However, many of the locations described in this book are based on historical facts from the time 1323 B.C. The Place of Truth was a real village. Its remains still exist and can be visited and explored today.

The Place of Truth (Deir el Medina)

Archeologists unearthed a great deal of information about Egypt's people from this village because the tomb makers who lived there kept such detailed records of their daily lives. They recorded the art supplies they ordered, as well as their food, clothing, and many other things. They also recorded how such items were divided up between the inhabitants.

Tomb robbers were a very real threat during this time. Guards were placed around the Valley of the Kings, but without modern technology, it was hard to keep an eye on such a large area. Many tombs were looted and destroyed.

Egypt's people believed that the gods took on living forms in myriad ways: through animals, insects, reptiles, the sun, the moon and more. In this story, Ramses' interaction with the gods had supernatural elements, yet for ancient people the gods were very real and could be seen all around them in the natural world. It was a different time, perhaps a time when magic felt truly real.

Glossary

Amulet: A protective charm usually worn or carried by its owner.

Craftsmen: Archeologists discovered that the tombs in Egypt's Valley of the Kings were built by highly skilled craftsmen. These craftsmen lived in the village known as the Place of Truth.

Eye of Horus: Horus was a sun god, often represented as a falcon. His right eye was the sun and his left eye was the moon. The Egyptians believed the Eye of Horus held protective powers, and used it used in amulets and funeral drawings. The eye found on American money is derived from the Eye of Horus.

Kilt: Standard male attire, kilts were linen skirts that could be worn straight or pleated.

Kohl: Black eyeliner made from ground malachite and lead, and mixed with oil or fat. Stored in jars, the wearer used a small stick to apply it. A line was traced around the upper and lower lids, and extended toward the ear. Both men and women wore kohl, for it was believed to have both magical and healing powers.

Linen: Fabric made from the flax plant. In ancient Egypt, linen was preferred over wool or cotton as the material is extremely lightweight and breathable.

Maat: Goddess of order, justice, and truth. She wore an ostrich feather, which she used to weigh the heart of the deceased. Those with a heavy heart full of wrongdoings ceased to exist. Those with a light heart enjoyed a happy afterlife.

Memphis: Egypt's old kingdom capital. Nicknamed the White

City. Located near present day Cairo, much of this important city and its history were lost to the Nile floodwaters.

Meretseger: The cobra goddess believed to inhabit the Peak of the West, overlooking the Valley of the Kings. Protector of the pharaohs' tombs, her wrath was feared by the craftsmen in the Place of Truth. Those who angered her were struck blind, a horrible fate for a craftsman.

Nile Inundation:
Egypt's year consisted of three seasons rather than four:
   1. Inundation: June-September, when the Nile rose high on its banks. During this time, farmers had a chance to relax.
   2. Emergence: October-February, when the water drained and left rich topsoil behind. Farmers trapped the retreating water in pools and tilled the soil.
   3. Drought: February-June, farmers harvested their crops and repaired irrigation ditches for the coming Inundation.

Ostraca: A thin, smooth flake of limestone used for making notes, sketches and calculations.

Papyrus: Paper made from the papyrus reed, the bulrush that grows along the Nile banks. Paper makers sliced the pith into long strips and placed it crosswise in a double layer – one strip running down, the other running crosswise. Using a mallet, they pounded the paper and the sap made it stick together into a single sheet. Egypt exported papyrus until the 12th Century AD when rag and wood pulp paper began to replace it.

Pharaoh: King of Egypt

Place of Truth: The craftsmen's village located by the Valley of the Kings. Now called Deir el-Medina, its Arabic name, the remains can be visited today. The site is of great archeological importance, for its inhabitants left behind large amounts of written material documenting life in the village, and their work on the tombs.

Ptah: God of creation and patron of artists. In Egyptian mythology, he created the Moon, the Sun, and the Earth. Greeks in later times associated Ptah with the god Hephaestos.

Scarab beetle: A dung beetle.

Scythe/Sickle: A long, single-edged, curved blade with a bent handle, used for harvesting or reaping.

Shaving: Lower class men made hairstyling easy by shaving their heads. This also kept them cool and kept lice away. Razors were hard to come by. Generally shaving was performed by a traveling barber, who set up his stool on the street or in the shade of a tree.

Thebes: Located 400 miles south of Memphis on the Nile, Thebes was once the religious capital of Egypt. It is the site of modern day Luxor.

Tombs: Ancient Egyptians did not believe death was the end. Instead, they considered it the beginning of the afterlife. Wealthy people and pharaohs spent a good deal of time preparing their tombs. Early in a pharaoh's reign, he made plans with the craftsmen for his tomb, including its site and its decorations. He then traveled to check up on its progress. It was believed that the dead could take things with them into the next life. Therefore, the tombs were filled with all sorts of things, from food to cosmetics, clothing, jewelry and furniture, much as a person would pack for a long journey.

Wigs: Both women and men of upper class wore wigs. They were made of human hair or sometimes palm fibers and cut in many styles, often curled and perfumed as well. Wax kept the wig's style in place.

Writing:There were around seven hundred hieroglyphic symbols, as well as cursive equivalents.

Valley of the Kings: The burial site of pharaohs during the New Kingdom—including Tutankhamen. Once known simply as "the Great Place", the valley is located on the west bank of the Nile, across from ancient Thebes.

ABOUT THE AUTHOR

Scott Peters has always had a fascination for all things ancient Egyptian. Scott has created over 300 museum, science center and theme park installations for such places as the Smithsonian, the Washington Children's Museum, Walt Disney World and Paramount Pictures. Scott hosts a blog for kids, teachers, and fans of ancient Egypt here: www.egyptabout. com. Come visit!

Also by Scott Peters

The Zet Mystery Series
Mystery of the Egyptian Scroll
Mystery of the Egyptian Amulet
Mystery of the Egyptian Temple

Mummies: 101 Ancient Egypt Mummy Facts

THANKS TO:

Scott Lisetor, Peter, Judy, Jill and Sarah Wyshynski,
Sharon Brown, Amanda Budde-Sung,
Ellie Crowe, Adria Estribou and Beth Greenway Skinner

FURTHER THANKS TO THE FOLLOWING SOURCES:

Romer, J, 'Ancient Lives: The Story of the Pharaoh's Tombmakers', Weidenfeld & Nicolson, 1984

Booth, C, 'Ancient Egypt: Thebes and the Nile Valley In The Year 1200 BCE', Quid 2008

Casson, L, 'Everyday Life in Ancient Egypt, Revised and Expanded Edition', John Hopkins University Press, 2001

Brier, B, PHD, 'The Murder of Tutankhamen', G. P. Putnam's Sons, 1998

Morell, V, 'The Pyramid Builders', National Geographic Nov. 2001

Fletcher, J, 'The Egyptian Book of Living and Dying', Duncan Baird 2002

Oakes, L and Gahlin, L, 'Ancient Egypt, An illustrated reference to the myths, religions, pyramids and temples of the land of the pharaohs', Anness Publishing 2003

Muller and Thiem, 'Gold of the Pharaohs', Sterling, 2005

Klum, M, 'King Cobras, Revered and Feared', National Geographic Nov. 2001

Printed in Great Britain
by Amazon